HOW NOT TO FALL IN LOVE

HOW
NOT
TO
FALL
IN
LOVE

JACQUELINE FIRKINS

CLARION BOOKS
An Imprint of HarperCollins Publishers
BOSTON NEW YORK

Clarion Books is an imprint of HarperCollins Publishers.

How Not to Fall in Love

Copyright © 2021 by Jacqueline Firkins

clarionbooks.com

Library of Congress Cataloging-in-Publication Data is on file.

ISBN 978-0-358-46714-4

The text was set in Weiss Std.

Cover design by Kaitlin Yang

Interior design by Kaitlin Yang

Manufactured in the United States of America

1 2021

4500841004

First Edition

For dreamers of impossible dreams

ONE

I'M KNEELING IN FRONT OF FROSTY THE SNOW-
man's lesser-known and more flamboyant cousin, Fluffy the Sparkle Monster. Buried inside Fluffy is a very slim, very non-fluffy
bride-to-be. Her name is Karén, but she prefers to go by Kay-
Kay. Her long brown hair is poker straight. Her narrow features
are pinched into an expression of mild but palpable dissatisfac-
tion. She pats down the organza ruffles that spill out from her
waist. They bounce back into place as if determined to display
their full glory.

"It's huge." A reedy girl in double topknots shakes her head in
wonder. I think her name's Hallie. She's the bride's younger sister.
She's wearing a navy spandex mini-dress and a skintight bolero.
Every piece of clothing probably seems huge to her.

The bride's mother steps back, tapping a finger to her lips.

"Is it supposed to be so . . . white?" she asks.

The bride shoots her a glare. "What should it be? Scarlet?
Puce? Puke green?"

A trio of the bride's friends chimes in, all offering cheerful but
bland support on how Kay-Kay would look beautiful in anything.

The bride pouts, her mother scolds her, her sister offers a biting retort, a bridesmaid snaps back, and soon everyone is squabbling. I wait until the noise dims. Then I ask the bride to make a quarter turn to her left so I can continue pinning her hem. It's a glamorous task. No doubt I'm the envy of all my peers.

My mom enters from the back room, carrying a tray of fruit and cheese. Her sleek dark hair rises in a tidy twist, the perfect match for her equally sleek black suit. We all wear black at Beneath the Veil, not because it's timeless and chic, but because we're not supposed to be seen. All eyes should be on the bride. My mom smiles as she sets the tray down next to several flutes of sparkling cider. Her smile looks warm and genuine, honed from years of practice. I've tried to mimic it, but I don't have it in me. I can push out a bland compliment here and there, but the wedding industry irritates the crap out of me. It advertises a beautiful, blissful fairy tale. What happens in this shop is anything but.

I keep pinning the hem while my mom checks the fit of Kay-Kay's bodice. It has so many beads, I'm not sure how she finds the seams.

"I can give you another half an inch on the sides," she offers.

The bride whips toward her, sweeping a swath of ruffles across my face. "I don't need half an inch. Why do you think I need half an inch? I don't need any halves of any inches!" Her voice is practically manic. Her fingers tense and curl like claws.

My mom takes a step back, renewing her smile. "Of course. My error." She doesn't look my way, but she flashes me two fingers behind her back. We're not letting out the dress half an inch.

We're going for the full inch. That way the bride will not only fit, she'll think she lost more weight than she planned. The happier she is, the better her review will be, and the more likely my mom's business will stay afloat another year.

The bride tears up, blubbering about the cookie she shouldn't have eaten last night. One of her friends finds the tissue box we keep handy near the cluster of faux baroque sofas and chairs at the center of the store. The other girls coo and coddle, patting Kay-Kay's hair and rubbing her back.

"I'll lose the last ten," she sputters through her tears. "I can do it, right?"

Her friends all chime in on cue.

"Of course!"

"Absolutely!"

"You'll look perfect."

I grit my teeth around the end of a safety pin. If the bride loses ten pounds, she'll disappear. The groom will have to marry the dress. I hope they'll be very happy together.

My mom and I spend two hours with the bride. We could do the fitting in less than half that time, but we pad the appointments to allow for the preening and bickering. Sure enough, by the time I hang the dress on its padded hanger, Kay-Kay's friends and family have argued about the dress, the shoes, the hair, the venue, the food, the flowers, the table decorations, and everyone's all-time favorite: the guest list. No one has mentioned the word *love*. They haven't mentioned the groom, either. He appears to be less important than gluten-free crostini. Like usual. After working in this store from the time I was old enough to thread a sewing needle or tally a spreadsheet, it's hard to believe weddings have anything to do with love. Frankly, it's hard to believe in love at all.

Pippa enters the shop as we're finishing with Kay-Kay's bridal party. She greets everyone before scheduling the bride's final fitting and the bridesmaids' dress alterations. Thank god we're not building them all from scratch. And thank god for Pippa. She's not only brilliant with scheduling and handling the calls, she can smile through anything. And her smiles aren't even fake. She's happy by nature, infectiously so. She credits her unrelenting cheerfulness to her many freckles. Apparently when she was little, her mom told her freckles resulted from fairy giggles. With all that mirth and magic stamped onto Pippa's skin, how could she not be happy?

With a few artfully delivered compliments, my mom ushers Kay-Kay's group out, causing the jingle bells on the door to ring. That sound is my cue to relax. I sink onto the green velvet chaise at the center of the room, surrounded by tossed-aside veils, unboxed satin pumps, and several padded hangers with the store's scrolling gold-print logo. Pippa joins me, collecting scattered shoes and pairing them up in their boxes.

"How you holding up, Harper?" she asks me.

"Need coffee. And anti-bride spray."

She rolls her eyes, unimpressed with my snark, as usual.

"Let me guess," she says. "They wanted everything to be *perfect*."

"That word should have a trigger warning."

"Going to make it through three more fittings today?"

"As long as they're 'perfect.'" I fall sideways onto the chaise, wishing school was still in session so I wasn't working here basically all the time. "Saturdays are the worst. Especially in June. Is the entire state of Pennsylvania getting married this summer?"

"Get that attitude out of your system now," my mom scolds from the fitting room, where she's collecting undergarments. "I need you smiling by the time the Smith-Whartons arrive. Gloria's bringing all seven bridesmaids and—"

"Seven?!"

"—and her influencer account has over ten thousand followers. I can't ignore that kind of press. She'll spread the word if she's happy with everything."

"No bride is happy with everything." I drag myself off the chaise and help Pippa tidy up as my mom takes the wedding gown into the back room so she can start picking off beads. It's the only way to get to the seams she needs to alter. Once the seams are altered, we sew all the beads back on again.

I grudgingly gather the pins and measuring tools while Pippa boxes up shoes as though the task is actually fun. She has a bounce in her step and a smile on her face, as usual. Even her clothes are chipper. Unlike my mom and me, Pippa expresses a strong sense of personality through her wardrobe. Maintaining her personal style was a stipulation of her hire, and it works since she doesn't have to kneel at anyone's feet, trying not to detract attention from a bride-to-be. She's in the requisite black, but where my mom and I wear tailored basics, Pippa's in a cute fit-and-flare dress, a fuzzy cardigan, and a pair of thigh-highs with cats on her knees. With her bright blue pigtails, she looks like she popped out of a comic book. I look like a lazy funeral attendee.

"It's going to be a long summer if you're already miserable," she says.

"I can't help it." I grab a wedding magazine from the glass coffee table. A happy bride and groom run hand in hand along a beach. Four words cross the glossy surface: *love, family, community, happiness.* I hold it up to Pippa. "Look at this."

She blinks at the image through dense lash extensions.

"How is a magazine making you miserable?" she asks.

"It's not just a magazine. It's an entire industry using love as a marketing tool, encouraging couples to hemorrhage their income on an absurd me-party so they can capture their moment of curated bliss and repost it once a year on social media. *Look how happy we are! Look how in love we are! Don't you wish you were us?* Meanwhile they're fighting over where to spend the holidays or how to load the dishwasher. It's nauseating."

Pippa rolls her eyes again as she restocks shoeboxes in a wall of white and gold cabinets that look like they're from Disney's *Beauty and the Beast,* without the singing.

"Have you always been such a grouch about weddings?" she asks.

"No. Not always." I set aside the magazine and glance around the shop, taking in the accessory displays, the beautifully dressed mannequins that pose by the windows, and the long racks of sample gowns. Everything's light and airy, as though it fell from a snow fairy's wand. My irritation ebbs, replaced by an odd sense of nostalgia. "I used to love hanging out here. I'd twirl around in my mom's creations, imagining an endless row of Prince Charmings desperate for my affection."

Pippa stifles a laugh. Badly. "What happened?"

"Twirling's cute at age seven. At seventeen, it's self-indulgent. Also, no one gets through adolescence still believing in Prince Charming."

"You sure about that?" Pippa checks her phone. "Twelve ten. Bet he's over there." She scurries toward the big picture window at the front of the shop, tucking herself behind a mannequin dressed in an ivory charmeuse halter dress with a train that ripples like newly stirred cream. Pippa nudges aside the train as she waves me over.

I join her, though I avoid the duck-and-cover spy routine in favor of calmly adjusting the dress's neckline. Together, we peer out the window. Past a row of cherry trees and across a quiet street are a card shop, a chocolatier, and Blue Dog CrossFit.

"I was right," Pippa says, her voice low as though she's worried the other mannequins will hear her. "He's there."

I nod appreciatively. Yes. He. Is. *He* is Felix Royce, or "Flex" as Pippa likes to call him. He's sitting on a workout bench doing curls with a barbell. His soft caramel waves sweep over his broad forehead, pulled to the left by a stubborn cowlick. His lips press together as he strains to draw the barbell toward his chest. He's in a sleeveless shirt today, providing us an excellent view of his biceps. He's a track star, not a body builder, so he's not crazy ripped, but he's tall and strong, with chiseled features, deep-set gray eyes, and full lips more than one girl has sighed over. Admittedly, I might be one of those girls. Also admittedly, he'd fit very nicely in a Prince Charming costume.

He glances our way, halting mid-curl as the corners of his lips lift. I become deeply interested in a chiffon rosette that adorns the dress. Pippa shakes her head at me.

"I can't believe you haven't asked him out yet," she says.

"Of course I haven't asked him out. We go to the same school. If he said no, the humiliation would follow me all through senior year."

"And if he said yes?"

"Even worse. I'd have to date him." I force a smile but Pippa purses her lips, seeing right through my vain attempt to dodge her question with humor.

"Isn't it about time to revoke the No Dating manifesto?" she asks.

"Why? So one day I, too, can force my friends to wear mauve satin while my mom weeps over her hundred-dollar corsage and some dude jams cake into my face?"

"'Some dude'? Seriously, Harper? Forget all this." She flings out her arms to take in the whole room. "We're not talking about marriage. Just a date. See a movie together. Hold hands. Look longingly into each other's eyes."

"*Long* is a jacket measurement. Not a verb or an adverb."

Pippa marches back to the seating area and whisks a used napkin off an armchair.

"Fine," she says. "But I'm not stupid. You spend way too much time ogling that guy to claim you're not interested. You know damned well a date doesn't equate to a wedding. You're not anti-social, and I don't believe for a second that you read *Jane Eyre* three times for its biting religious criticism."

I open my mouth to tell her I read *Jane Eyre* three times because the wife shreds the wedding veil, but it's not true. Pippa's right, and we both know it. My transition from dreamy kid playing dress-up to hardened cynic didn't happen that long ago. And it isn't only a result of spending too many hours in the narcissist factory. As I wilt against the mannequin, I expect Pippa to pounce at my obvious defeat, but she doesn't. Instead, she drops the napkin onto the fruit tray, her eyes brimming with sympathy.

"Flex isn't Liam," she says.

"Liam wasn't Liam. Until he was." I flash through memories. Meeting at counselor orientation for sleepover math camp last summer. The instant spark of attraction. Six weeks in which we were inseparable. Marking tests side by side. Sharing massive sundaes in the cafeteria. Making out in our dorm rooms when our roommates weren't around, also in classrooms, restrooms, closets, parks, anywhere we could steal a moment alone. Working up the courage to say *I love you*. Two naked bodies colliding in the dark. And then . . .

I stop fussing with the dress. "I can't be another guy's summer fling."

"You'd seriously give up a summer making out with that incredible specimen of manhood" — she flaps a hand toward Felix

—"because you think the moment you get attached, he'd dump you?"

"Stranger things have happened." I sneak another look at Felix. He sets down his barbell and checks his phone. Whatever's on the screen draws out his smile. Something shifts inside my chest, as though his smile's settling into my heart like a book sliding onto a library shelf. He's so beautiful. He's also nice, the sort of guy who holds doors and says *bless you* and gets signatures on environmental petitions. But I just . . . can't.

Pippa shakes her head at me as though I'm a child and my bumbling missteps have grossly disappointed her. She has no right to act parental. She's only two years older than I am, and just as single. Since she moved to New Hope and started the job here a little over a year ago, she's dated a few guys she met through her community college art classes. Nothing lasted past a month or two. More proof that dating is pointless.

Before we can argue the matter further, my mom peeks into the room and asks if one of us will make a coffee run. Pippa volunteers, but as my mom takes in the shoeboxes that still scatter the floor, she suggests I go instead.

"If we let Harper finish here, she'll be packing those shoes for hours, making sure she doesn't add new creases to the tissue paper." She and Pippa exchange a sly smile at my expense. I shrug off the joke. My mom has a point. Pippa's far less obsessive than I am. She's also less likely to get my coffee order right. So I make the run.

As I head down the street, I do the very thing I keep promising myself I won't do again, always right before I do it. I peek at Liam's Instagram account. After a shot of his band and another of his dogs, I find a photo of him with his arm around his most recent girlfriend. He looks like he did last summer: hipster fauxhawk, worn-out concert tee, cuffed black jeans. Too bad his affection is less consistent than his personal style. And too bad we met when I was still a gullible fool, ready to believe that when a guy said he loved me, he didn't mean he'd only love me while I was convenient.

We'd never make it, he said on the last day of camp. *A few emails, maybe. Some dirty texts. Within weeks we'd be fighting about a flirty photo one of us saw on Insta or a text the other didn't respond to fast enough. We'd spoil a perfect summer fling with jealousy and insecurity. Is that really what ·you want?*

No, I told him. *I want you to love me back. Not just in words but for real.*

It didn't matter what I said. He returned to Allentown, I returned to New Hope, and what I thought was the start of a relationship became the end. Just. Like. That.

I'm so busy staring at my phone, my pace propelled by mounting resentment, I smack into a tree. As I stumble backwards, I realize I didn't hit a tree. I hit Felix Royce.

We leap away from each other, sputtering apologies and slipping quick *hey*s between the *sorry*s. I jam my offending phone into my back pocket. He hikes his gym bag up on his shoulder, looking as sheepish as I feel. The two of us shift and shuffle as though we're trying to outdo each other for sheer awkwardness. I open my mouth to say something, but I have no idea what, so I close my mouth and step past him, assuming the best plan of action is to pretend the last ten seconds never happened.

"You in a hurry?" he asks through a soft laugh.

"Urgent coffee run," I say through no laugh at all.

"Coffee's urgent?"

"You haven't seen my mom uncaffeinated." I try to slip my hands into my pockets, only to remember I have no side pockets because women's fashion is a farce.

Felix peers past me toward Beneath the Veil. A trio of pale blue awnings caps the windows. The outer ones are just big enough to display a pair of my mom's designs. The central window provides a view of the entire shop from the front desk all the way to the mirrored fitting area and wall of cabinets. Maybe Felix *has* seen my mom without her coffee. Maybe he's seen a lot of things, like a girl who spends a lot of time on her knees, groveling for divas. I don't know why I care if he's seen that, but I guess I do.

"I should, you know, the coffee," I stammer. "Sorry I bumped into you."

His forehead rumples with confusion. "You are?"

"The collision? Just now? You, me, zero space between us?"

"Zero space, huh?" He grins a little, offering me a quick peek at his perfect teeth. If I didn't know better, I'd say he was blushing, but the slight flush on his cheeks is more likely an effect of all the time he spends running outside.

Determined to give his cheeks no further thought, I wave and turn to go.

"Hey, Harper?" he calls after me. I stop and face him. He tugs on his earlobe. The habit's weird but cute. He does it all the time, like when he takes tests or sizes up his competition at a track meet. "Do you, I mean, would it be . . . ?" He jams his hands into his pockets, which he can do because he wears boy clothes. "Where's the nearest coffee shop anyway, you know, if I wanted to get some, too?"

I point down the road to the left. "Drip House is that way. Only a block. Bland but drinkable." I point to my right. "C Factor's that way. Better coffee. Worse service." I snake a hand farther to my right. "Down that alley, left at the end, right at the four-way stop, and you'll find Beans 'n' Leaves. Totally worth the walk."

"Unless the situation's urgent?"

"Right. That. Better get to it." I sense that he's teasing me, but I don't know what to do with that information, so I wave again and take off. Halfway to the coffee shop, I realize his question made no sense. He spends almost as much time on this block as I do. Even if he didn't live at the gym, this town is hardly a sprawling metropolis. It's so cute, they almost put the whole thing on a postage stamp last year. Anyone who's lived here longer than a month should be able to map every decorative streetlamp and ivy-covered balcony. So why did he ask where to find a coffee shop? And why does that little shelf in my chest feel another addition to its inventory slipping into place?

TWO

MY MOM STAYS LATE TO KEEP PUSHING THROUGH alterations at Beneath the Veil. She's taken on more custom work than usual this season, and it eats up time. She loves sewing, but she's not great at setting limits on her workday, or on mine. Tonight I head home on my own, trudging up our driveway shortly after 8:00 p.m. Since we live within a mile of downtown, the shop, and my school, I walk almost everywhere. I haven't bothered to get a driver's license, though I'll have to reconsider that before college. Thankfully driving lessons can wait. I don't know where I'd find the time this summer. A week in and I'm already tired. Brides two and three weren't much better than bride one. They're probably really nice people most of the time, but weddings bring out the worst in people.

I grab a single-serving lasagna from our well-stocked freezer. While my dinner heats up in the microwave, I fill the silence with a podcast about America's excessive plastic consumption. It's guilt inducing, which doesn't help my mood, but I can safely assume no one will mention holding hands, longing looks, and coffee dates someone did *not* try to ask me out on. I told Pippa about my run-in with Felix. Now she has a theory, one that made her determined to overturn my anti-dating stance. Phrases like "time to get back in the saddle" permeated our afternoon conversation. I ignored them. If there's one thing I'm certain about regarding my future, it's that saddles won't be involved.

Through my kitchen window and out past a waist-high fence, I see Theo head out his back door into his yard. Now that we're a week into summer vacation, I should check in with him about our plan. As New Hope's resident walking dictionary and all-around word nerd, he promised to help build my vocabulary in exchange for a few sewing favors. I'm retaking the SAT in August since my latest scores didn't meet the bar for a number of key scholarships. Without hefty financial assistance, my college options will be limited. I can get an economics degree from a lot of schools, but I have my heart set on Bryn Mawr. It has three distinct advantages.

One: it's an hour's drive from New Hope, so I could come home on weekends. My mom's an artist, not an entrepreneur, and she has a track record of making shaky business decisions. As anxious as I am to leave the wedding industry behind me, I'll help until we dig the business out of its financial hole and my mom can afford to hire a dependable managerial assistant. For now, the work will be good practice for running my own business one day. Also, I also love my mom, so, bonus.

Two: Dr. Lia Garcia teaches at Bryn Mawr. She created algorithms that track links between women's purchasing habits and their emotional labor output. This led to an app that helps women identify behavioral patterns before those patterns derail budgetary plans. She's not anti-shopping. She's pro-smart-shopping. I'm dying to study with her.

Three: Bryn Mawr has no boys. Period.

As a guy on the podcast rattles off stats about the world's impending demise, I extract my dinner from the microwave and pour myself an orange soda. The plastic label isn't attached properly, so the two-liter bottle slips through my hands, spilling the contents down my front and onto the kitchen floor and cabinets. Thus, I find myself on my knees for a fourth time today, only with a rag instead of a pincushion. Thank god Felix can't see me now. Not that he'd judge, and not that I should care if he did, but I feel as appealing as a dirty sock. It's Saturday night. My friends have abandoned me because I'm always working. I'm home alone, scrubbing the floor and listening to doom and gloom while the plastic wrap on my dinner becomes one with the cheese. Also, I smell like a Creamsicle.

By the time I've finished cleaning, my dinner has lost its appeal, not that its appeal was very high to begin with. As I poke at the center, trying to figure out if it's still frozen despite the scorched edges, the low drone of an accordion pierces the quiet. It's a sound I know all too well, and it can only mean one thing.

I head outside and step through an unlatched gate in the low fence that encloses Theo's backyard. I don't know who the fence is supposed to keep out, but it doesn't matter because the accordion wailing would make anyone keep their distance. It's coming from the center of the gently sloping lawn, where a giant oak tree holds a windmill-shaped treehouse in its branches. Theo's wiry frame is backed up against the trunk. His creaky old accordion is strapped to his chest. His face is raised toward the twilit sky, as though he's waiting for unseen stars to fall around him. It's a beautiful image, one that belongs on a black-and-white postcard, not in a suburban backyard.

As I approach, Theo pivots toward me. His cheeks are stained with tears. His nose is red. His lips quiver with a sob that's about to emerge. I jog forward to wrap him and his lumpy accordion in an awkward hug. He leans into me, sniffling away. How many times have we been through this? Six? Seven? Nine? If I go as far back as his first crush when we were in kindergarten, we must be in double digits by now.

"She was the one," he blubbers into my shoulder.

I'm dying to point out that she was more like the thirteenth or fourteenth, but even I'm not *that* big of an asshole. So I keep my mouth shut and let my already-damp shirt absorb Theo's latest heartbreak. We stay like that for several minutes, him limp and leaning, me trying to figure out at what point back patting gets weird. And at what point I can no longer tolerate his knobby accordion pressing into my boobs. Eventually Theo draws back and meets my eyes. His long lashes flutter rapidly. His shaggy black hair is plastered to his temples, whether by tears, sweat, or a recent experiment with hair gel, I have no idea. I pluck a strand off his face as I brace myself for an outpouring of despair.

"You're wet," he says instead.

I sputter with laughter. "So are you."

"Did you run through a sprinkler?"

"Did you *become* a sprinkler?" My question draws out a tiny smile from him. Achievement unlocked. "Want to talk about it?"

He shakes his head. Then he nods. "Windmill confession?"

"After you." I sweep a hand toward the thick rope ladder that hangs down the trunk beside us. The rope is weathered and gray, but still solid enough to hold us.

Theo unstraps his accordion. I follow him up and into the treehouse his moms made when he and I were kids. One of them is a carpenter, the other's a structural engineer, and together they can design and build anything. Theo and I have spent a *lot* of time here, first as a play space, later as an agreed-upon safe space. Within the embrace of the curved walls, we could pour our hearts out, and the other person wasn't allowed to laugh, call anything stupid, or tell anyone else what was said. This is where Theo told me about the LARPing community he joined as a freshman. It's where I told him about the brutal fight I had with my mom when she almost bankrupted her business last year. He told me about his first kiss. I did not tell him about mine. But we've both shed tears here. We gorged ourselves on junk food. We stayed up all night watching epic fantasies I wasn't allowed to make fun of and psychological dramas he wasn't allowed to yawn over. Through it all, the blades on the windmill slowly rotated in the breeze, casting shifting shadows on a pile of scavenged quilts and pillows, all of which show their age.

Theo flips on the twinkly overhead lantern. Little stars perforate the sides. As it rocks, the stars travel across the walls and ceiling. Theo watches them dance before folding himself against the wall, tucked beneath a floating bookshelf. It contains over a dozen of his favorite adventure tales and a few noir detective stories from when I was going through that particular reading phase, one of many. The shelf also holds coins, trading cards, multisided gaming dice, and a little cross-stitched Snickers bar I took forever to finish because I got bored halfway through. When Theo loves something, he loves it forever. I'm more easily distracted.

I sit across from him, wedging a velvet pillow under my butt. The sill behind my shoulder houses a pair of Funko Pop! figures, one in armor, the other in a mossy-green princess dress with swirling gold trim. Like the shelves, the sill is filled with treasures and mementos. I take them in yet again, holding in my questions while Theo tugs at the hem of his fencing team T-shirt and gusts a sigh toward the ceiling.

"She said I was too weird."

"You do own a windmill. And an accordion. And a sword."

"It's an épée."

"Whatever. You're the one with the near-perfect SAT score."

"Everyone knows what an épée is. Now, if I had a flamberge or spadroon—"

My lips twitch as I stifle a laugh. Theo notices and flashes me a wry scowl.

"Okay, fine," he says. "So I'm little bit weird, but when did weirdness become a reason to break up with someone?" He yanks a loose thread from a hole in his jeans and rolls it around between his thumb and forefinger.

"I don't know," I say. "It's not a *good* reason. Aren't we all weird?"

He flaps a hand at me. "You're not."

"Okay, so some of us are weirder than others." I cross my arms over my boring black shirt, which is tucked into my boring black pants and cinched with a boring black belt. My hair's swept up in its usual unadorned ponytail. My nails are unpainted. I'm not wearing makeup or jewelry. My only unique distinction is the smell of artificial orange soda drifting off my clothes. "My point is that if she doesn't like your particular brand of weirdness, then she's not the girl for you. Also, she sounds like a total bitch."

Theo balks. "You don't know anything about her."

"Do I need to? You're my friend. She hurt you. I hate her."

Despite my attempt at humor, Theo doesn't smile. Instead, he moans the Moan of the Truly Devastated as he flops onto his side, going limp on the blankets. I'd try to say something comforting, but I'm not sure anything I say would help right now. I've only been through one breakup and it shattered me. Any attempt to convince me that things would get better would've felt like a dismissal of my pain. I never told Theo about Liam. I didn't plan to tell anyone, hoping the less I talked about him, the more I could pretend he didn't exist. Pippa was too observant, badgering me until I fessed up about the cause of my near-constant moping. In the end, I was grateful to have her ear and her shoulder to cry on. I figure that's what I'm here for. Not to say stuff, but to listen.

Theo grabs a tattered bolster pillow and slides it under his head. The once-bright orange velvet has faded to a sunset blur of rusts and peaches. A tassel's missing, and batting busts out of a seam. Like everything else in this windmill, it's seen a lot of love.

"Breakups suuuuuuuuuck," Theo groans to the ceiling.

"I think breakups are supposed to suck. Let's face it. Very few 'Congratulations on your breakup' cards have hit the market lately." I flash him a hopeful smile. He doesn't return it, but at least he's not sobbing anymore. "How long were you and—?"

"Vicky."

"—Vicky going out?"

He rolls onto his stomach and buries his face in the pillow.

"A week." The words comes out muffled but unmistakable.

My sympathy evaporates. "A week?! And you're crying buckets over her?"

"She was different. Special."

"So were Shelley, Penny, Wendy, Cindy, Mindy, Mandy, Candy, Sandy—"

"Stop there." Theo flings up a hand. "I'm in pain. I'm grieving. My heart is bleeding. My wounds are raw. I don't need the derisive cognominating."

"Um . . . ?"

"The snarky nicknames."

"Right. Sorry." I stem my sarcasm as Theo shifts onto his side and props his head on his hand. His T-shirt pulls up past the waistband of his jeans. His jeans are normal, if in need of repair. His *Sword in the Stone* belt buckle and flying hamburger socks are another story. He's not wearing shoes, a common oversight. I don't know Vicky, but I see her point. Theo is weird. He always has been. We've been friends since our moms plunked us in the same crib while they rotated childcare duties. He's one of my favorite people in the world, and even I can't imagine dating him. He might arrive on horseback or wearing the suit of chain mail he took a year to build. He might reenact the entire Lord of the Rings trilogy with his food. He might cry over a rom-com.

Scratch that. He *will* cry over a rom-com.

"What are you thinking?" he asks.

"I'm thinking maybe you should take a break from dating for a while. At least slow down. Stop falling in love with every girl who lets you buy her an ice cream cone. Get to know someone before you name your future children."

Theo frowns. "I don't. I didn't."

"Okay, without naming your future dogs, then."

Theo opens his mouth. Then he closes it, rolling onto his back and raking his hands into his hair. It sticks out in all directions like fistfuls of licorice.

"I like dogs," he mutters. "And Gimli's a good name for a pug."

"Why a pug?"

Theo grimaces and turns away, hiding his face while still tormenting his hair.

"It's Vicky's favorite breed," he admits almost too quietly to hear.

I allow myself a pitying *Oh, Theo* eye roll while his back is turned.

"Did you send her poetry?"

"Maybe."

"Buy her flowers?"

"Only twice."

"Text her more than three times a day?"

"I wanted her to know I was thinking about her."

I swallow the sigh that wells up in my throat. This is Theo's problem. He makes a solid first impression. Then he overwhelms a girl with roses, romantic literary quotes, and an outpouring of impassioned feelings. He also plans date ten before he knows if a girl is interested in date two. I don't point any of that out. I've said it all before, so I stretch out beside him and take his hand, hoping to save his hair from further torture. His hair's insanely thick, so he could lose a few strands and no one would notice, but Vicky already punctured his heart. She's not allowed to harm his hair, too.

After a pause, Theo shifts onto his back again as his fingers curl around mine. His skin is rough. The sides of his fingers are callused, as are the backs of his knuckles from where his fist rests inside a sword hilt or guard or grip or whatever he calls it. He's the word nerd. I'm just the girl who's lucky to be his friend.

"Are we still on for vocab lessons?" I ask.

"I have your first list ready to go. I'll send it tonight."

I nudge his hip with our linked hands. "Then I'm going to need those jeans."

He rolls his head toward me. A twinkle tints his dark eyes.

"Are you asking me to take off my clothes?"

This time I don't hide my eye roll or stifle my laugh.

"Later. Your jeans need patching. That's all. A deal's a deal."

"You know, there are subtler ways to tell a guy you want to get naked with him." Theo finally smiles for real. His entire face changes when he smiles. His eyes light up. His forehead stops furrowing. An open playfulness replaces his high despair. He also has a dimple, just one, but it suits him.

"And you're prepared to teach me these methods?" I say through a laugh.

"I could if you really wanted me to."

"Well, I don't. And you could not."

He props himself up on an elbow, bristling with defensiveness.

"I could, too," he says. "I know more about dating than you do."

"You know enough to get your heart broken on a weekly basis. That's hardly a record of success." I release his hand and scoot up to face him, taking in his reddened eyes and tear-stained cheeks. "In fact, I could teach you a few things about dating. Like how to read a girl's signals. How to limit the grand gestures until you know she's really interested. How to protect yourself. How not to fall in love." The words spill out of me in response to his, but once I've said them, they seem like a decent idea.

Eyes narrowing, Theo sits up and squares off with me. The twinkle's still there, as is the dimple, but the set of his chin is all business.

"Me? Take lessons from you? You think love is a tennis score and romance is a candy-selling gimmick. You've never even been on a date."

"I've . . . dated," I hedge.

His dark brows rise. "Who? When?"

"Doesn't matter."

"It matters to me."

"Oh yeah? Why?"

"Because I thought we told each other everything. And because . . ." Theo studies me with an unnerving level of scrutiny. A breeze blows through, fluttering his hair and making stars dance across his cheeks. His face twitches as though he's struggling to sort out the rest of his reply, but a wall seems to go up as his expression settles into one of pure challenge. "Because you don't hire a coach who's never played the game."

At the unexpected force of his statement, I fall onto my heels, banging my shoulder on the windowsill behind me. With the number of times I've whacked that board, I should tattoo the bruise into my skin already. Theo winces and reaches toward me, but I wave him away. The ache spreading across my shoulder will fade quickly. My wounded pride is another story. Theo's right. I'm not the voice of experience. His words also echo Pippa's insistence that I rethink my priorities. Maybe I can go on a few dates, enjoy a guy's company, sink into a dreamy kiss or two. A summer fling isn't the worst idea, as long as I know it's a fling when I enter into it. No falling in love. No broken hearts. And Felix does have those amazing lips . . .

"So if I prove to you that I can date someone I like without getting instantly attached," I say, "you'll let me teach you how to stop falling in love?"

Theo regards me for several seconds. The intensity's

unnerving, as if he's playing chess and thinking through every possible combination of moves. He's certainly thinking through something. I'm about to press him for an answer when he extends a hand. I take it and we shake, eyes locked in twinned determination.

"You're on, Jamison."

"Watch and learn, Turner. Watch. And. Learn."

THREE

THE FOLLOWING MONDAY, I'M UP TO MY ELBOWS in paperwork. I've already put in a ten-hour workday, but the IRS is demanding documentation for all of my mom's business claims. We don't have the money to hire an accountant. We barely have the money to hire Pippa. Thus I'm sitting on the floor in the middle of the store, propped up against a throne-like chair with my laptop on the gilded coffee table and my mom's giant box of receipts, bills, and invoices dumped out in front of me. Theo's first vocab list is printed out and taped to the chaise on my left so I can study while I sort. My mom's sewing in the back room. Over at the front desk, Pippa hangs up the phone and scribbles something into the appointment book. Today she's wearing a hot pink bobbed wig. Just because.

"Last call for the day. We're officially closed." She flips the sign on the door. Then she joins me in the middle of the room, dropping onto her knees while her ruffled skirt fans out around her. "How can I help?"

I dig two overstuffed manila envelopes from the chaos.

"Sort these. Supplies in one pile. Utilities in another. Anything food or travel related in a third. If you're not sure, it goes there." I nod at the emptied box.

Pippa dumps out the first envelope and starts dividing the contents into three piles. She leans in close to me as she glances toward the back room, where the low hum of a sewing machine starts and stops.

"Why isn't your mom helping with all of this?" Pippa whispers.

"Trust me. Her time is better used back there." I peek at my vocab list. "She's aesthetically adroit but lacks accounting acumen. Also, my current agitation could make me adversarial, leading us to an acrimonious altercation."

Pippa laughs. "He's starting you on the A's, huh?"

"Apparently alphabetical arrangements augment auricular absorption."

"Damn." She shakes her head at me. "You're taking this stuff seriously."

"I take everything seriously. Don't you know that by now?"

"You're a pretty closed book, actually."

"You mean I'm aloof? Ambiguous?" I check the list again. "Ooh, how about arcane? Understood by few. Mysterious or secret. Requiring specialized knowledge."

"Now you're scaring me." She holds up a pink receipt that's faded past legibility.

I nod toward the box on my right. "In there. I'll go through all of that later."

Pippa tosses in the receipt and returns to her stack. I find a wad of blank New York City cab receipts that are being held together by a safety pin. My mom goes on purchasing trips every few months. We can write off her transportation costs, but only if she fills out her receipts. Once I've instilled the importance of accurate record keeping, maybe I can get her to stop using safety pins as her only organizational system.

Pippa glances at my vocab list. "Your SAT tutor's that cute boy who lives next door to you, right?"

"Boy? Yes. Next door? Also yes. Cute?" I scan my list. "Only arbitrarily."

Pippa drops her hands to her sides and purses her lips. I continue filling in my spreadsheet, but I can't concentrate when I know I'm being stared at, especially if the person staring at me is wearing a hot pink wig that's burned into my retinas.

"He's a LARPer," I say. Pippa gives me a *Yeah, and?* look, compelling me to continue. "He runs around with a bunch of guys in tights on the weekends, fighting for the throne of Dorkingham." I stop there, assuming I've made my point, but Pippa's still giving me The Look. "Remember that creepy scarecrow Mr. Greenblat made last year for Halloween? The one he put in front of the hardware store?" I wait for Pippa's nod. "Theo has it in his backyard. He strapped it to a tree so he could swish his sword —excuse me, his épée—at it. He walks around singing in public as though he has no idea people can hear him. Sometimes he gets so lost in a daydream, he forgets to put on shoes or a coat. Oh, and he plays the accordion."

Pippa shrugs. "Still cute."

"Still a total dork."

She gives me playful swat on the arm. I scowl and edge away, though with a bit more prodding, I'm soon laughing with her. Pippa has that effect on people. It's a gift.

"Face it, Harper," she says as our giggles die down. "You live next door to a total hottie. All that gorgeous hair, those perfectly arched eyebrows, that upturned mouth, and those dark eyes a girl can get lost in for days. If I woke up to that reflection in the morning, I'd forget to put on shoes, too."

I inch backwards onto a scattered pile of papers as I try to picture Theo the way Pippa describes him, all dreamy and swoon inducing, but he just looks like Theo.

"Please don't tell me you're trying to get me to date my neighbor now."

"Not you. Me." Pippa sits up a little straighter, smoothing the front of her skirt. "You said he just went through a breakup, so he's single, right?"

"Yeeeeaaah." I eye her sideways. "You'd date a high school guy?"

"I'm only a year out of high school myself, and a two-year age difference is hardly approaching cougar territory. So, yeah, I'd date a high school guy." A teasing smile dents her cheeks. "As long as he daydreamed, sang in public, knew how to use a sword, and played the accordion." Her smile widens as she waggles her brows at me.

I start to laugh again, but the sound quickly dies. Pippa and Theo do kind of suit each other. They might even really like each other. Then again, they're basically my only friends right now.

One inappropriate grand gesture from Theo or one inadvertently insensitive comment from Pippa, and I'd be navigating the fallout, asked to take sides.

And also . . .

"You can't date him," I say. "Not now, anyway. He's on a love detox plan. He thinks he lives in a fairy tale. Then he crashes when he doesn't get his Happily Ever After. It's not healthy, so I've offered to teach him a few things about modern dating."

"You what?!" Pippa's eyes go wide as a breathy chuckle slips out of her. "What do you know about dating? You won't even go for coffee with Flex."

I turn toward the gym. "Actually, I'm working on that."

She gasps and grabs my wrist. "You're going to ask him out?"

"I'm going to try." I attempt to look happy about this idea, but a knot tightens in my gut. Asking Felix out sounded so easy when I was shaking hands with Theo on Saturday night, full of resolve. Since then, every scenario I've played out in my head ends badly, whether Felix says yes, no, or breaks into a fit of convulsive laughter. Despite my worries, Pippa bounces on her knees, bursting with an open enthusiasm I've always kind of admired but never managed to emulate. Maybe I am a closed book, but thus far opening up hasn't done me any favors. It hasn't done anyone I know any favors, either.

For the next two hours or so, Pippa pep talks me through the worst of my fears as we sort receipts and my mom's sewing machine hums away in the background. Pippa also tells me about her summer art classes at the local community college while I continue memorizing Theo's vocab list, entertaining her by forcing each word into our conversation. I remark on the anthropomorphism of the claw-footed armchair and the archetypically aristocratic bearing of a (not really) anonymous athlete.

Pippa eventually stands and starts a stretching routine, a wise choice after hunching over for so long. I shut my laptop and work out a kink in my neck.

"You know what else starts with *A*?" She waggles her brows. *"Accordion."*

I snort out a laugh. "I've got that one down already. Along with agonizing."

"Oh, come on. Accordion music can be very romantic. 'La Vie en Rose.' Paris. A walk by the Seine. A bench made for two. A light evening rain. What's not to love?"

"I guess." I picture the scene she's describing but find myself frowning. "I just . . . I can't help but wonder if it's all worth it. Love. Romance. Dating. My mom doesn't date, and she seems perfectly happy without a love life. Why couldn't I be, too?"

Pippa peers toward the back room. "She's never dated? At all?"

"Not in my lifetime. Eighteen years ago she had a one-night stand, got pregnant, decided she was ready to have a kid, and went for it. She never told the guy. She didn't want to be tied to a drummer named Chad or Thad or Brad. The details change every time she tells the story. She's never voiced any regrets though. And she hasn't dated since."

"Wow." Pippa blinks away her astonishment as she continues stretching. "That's kind of badass, but I don't think I could go eighteen years without a bit of flirting, a cute smile across a room at a party, and . . . you know."

I nod. Yeah. I know. As many times as I've told myself I don't need a guy, my little pep talks didn't stop me from melting into Liam's embraces last summer. And they haven't stopped me from gazing across the street, hoping to catch a pair of gray eyes looking my way.

Anxious to stem all talk of love for a while, I check in on my mom and offer to make a coffee run. I give Theo's list a quick scan before heading out.

Pippa leans over my shoulder. "Did you use every word?"

"Not quite." *Avarice, aversion, avuncular.* "What do I do with *avuncular?*"

"I don't know. What does it mean?"

"Resembling an uncle in kindness or indulgence."

"Not useful. And totally sexist."

We share another laugh. Then I'm out the door and in the fresh air, striding toward Beans 'n' Leaves with alacrity. Wow, that word came into my head naturally. Well done, Theo.

My return trip is slower, as I carefully balance three hot beverages and a bag of Pippa's favorite almond biscotti. It's a pathetic payment for her help tonight, but it's all I can afford. I'm halfway back when I spot Felix in front of Teacup Pig Bakery, one of the many Instagrammable shops in town, all pastels and curlicue lettering. He has his phone out as if he's taking a photo of the storefront, and he's alone. This is my chance. I should seize it. And yet I remain frozen to my spot, predicting disaster.

I'm still staring when Felix turns my way. A breathtaking smile stretches across his face. I raise a hand to wave, but I fumble with my drinks. The cups topple, lids come off, and hot tea and coffee dowse my front. I blink down at the drips raining off my chest for the second time this week, utterly mortified.

Felix joins me in my puddle of shame. "Are you okay?"

"Yeah. No. Of course. It's nothing. Really."

He cringes as his eyes drift down my body. "Wow, you're really soaked."

"It's my June theme, apparently." I dab at my chest with my palm, to no effect.

He yanks his henley over his head, wrenching it off in that one-handed way I've never managed. He's wearing an A-line undershirt, but still, I gape.

"Use this." He holds out the henley. "I don't need it."

I stare at it, unsure how I feel about using Felix's shirt, or about how heroic he looks, standing there in the amber streetlight, all tall, broad, and beautiful, offering me the shirt off his back. Considering how warm the night air just became, I definitely feel something, and I doubt it's the coffee seeping through my clothes.

"I'll dry off at my mom's shop." I crouch to gather the fallen cups before Felix can see how flustered I am. "Thanks, though. For the offer."

"Yeah. Of course." He bends down and picks up the soggy bag of cookies. The bottom falls out, releasing the contents onto the sidewalk. He collects the chunks and drops them into one of my empty cups. I make the mistake of looking in his eyes. And not looking away. He doesn't look away, either. "We have to stop meeting like this."

"Like what?"

"Collisions. Accidents." He leans a tiny bit closer. "Zero space between us."

"I, um . . ." *am certain I'm eight shades of red and about to die right now.* "What are you doing out here, anyway? Taking pictures, I mean."

He grabs the last lid and we both stand, which at least allows me to breathe.

"I was trying to get a good angle on the *P*." He glances up at the Teacup Pig Bakery sign. "I'm taking a summer photography class. We're supposed to collage a bunch of fonts into a single image. It sounds easy, but so far mine's a total mess."

"It doesn't sound easy. It sounds interesting, though."

"Does it?" His lips tip up as he tangles his hands in his henley.

"Absolutely. And it's cool that you're taking a class this summer. All I'm doing is working. Like always." I stack the empty cups and toss everything into a nearby trashcan, allowing myself just enough time for a rapid-fire pep talk. Then I turn around, ready to ask if Felix wants to go out sometime. A sweet smile is still tugging at the full lips I'm always trying not to stare at, the ones that belong to this unnecessarily gorgeous boy with his cowlicking caramel hair and Disney prince jawline, this boy who also happens to be nice and friendly and modest and effortlessly charming and, good god, those biceps are amazing. I bet with no effort at all, he could whisk me into his arms and I . . . can't do this.

"Speaking of work, I should get back to it. I'll see you around.

Hopefully without any accidents next time." With a sinking heart, I swap a wave with Felix and walk away.

Fifteen minutes later, I'm stretched out on the green velvet chaise at Beneath the Veil, silently berating myself for my cowardice while cross-referencing my mom's bank statements with the expenditures in my spreadsheet. My laptop's open in my lap. Theo's list lies on the coffee table. More notably, I'm wearing a ruffled taffeta bridesmaid dress the color of tepid bubble gum. It's hideous but it fits, and it made Pippa laugh so hard, she forgave me for returning without her chai and biscotti. Not that she was really mad, but she was grossly disappointed in me when I told her why I returned empty-handed, and that I not only failed to bring back beverages, I returned dateless.

While I adjust numbers and my mom continues plowing through alterations in the back room, Pippa starts cleaning up for the night. She's spraying the picture window with glass cleaner when the bells on the main door jingle.

"Shop's closed," Pippa calls. "Guess we forgot to lock the . . ."

The room goes quiet. I look up. Felix stands inside the doorway with a cardboard cup holder bearing three cups, a treat bag, and a nest of multicolored sweetener packets. Pippa's jaw drops open. I feel my entire body flush, which isn't a good look when I'm dressed like an ostentatious flamingo.

Felix shuffles forward and sets the tray on the front desk.

"I figured if you were going back to work, you probably still wanted coffee. I didn't get a chance to ask what you liked, so I got basic black and hoped you could work out the sugar and stuff on your own." He thumbs through the packets. "There are three of you, right? There were three cups, but maybe someone drinks tea. Crap. I didn't think of that until just now." He glances over at me. "Should I have gotten tea?"

"No. Maybe. Pippa doesn't actually—"

"Coffee's great." She catches my eye and tips her head toward Felix. I sneak her a headshake and hold up a ruffle. She repeats her gesture with more insistence. "We all *love* coffee, right, Harper? Why don't you *get up* and go tell him how much we all love coffee?" She locks her arms across her chest and widens her eyes at me. By the way she's gripping the rag and glass cleaner, I get the distinct impression that if I'm not standing in front of Felix within the next thirty seconds, she'll drag me over there by my ponytail, tell him I've been ogling him for months, and force me at spray-bottle-point to ask him out.

I slide off the chaise and head to the front desk. Felix takes in my explosion of pink ruffles, hiding a smile behind his hand.

"You sure you don't want my shirt?" he asks.

Pippa sneaks me a vigorous nod as she pretends to clean the window. I pray my blush isn't getting worse, though I highly suspect my prayer is in vain.

"Thanks, but that's okay. We're wrapping up soon. I can change at home." I poke through the sweetener packets and creamer containers. He brought some of everything. He's thorough. I like that. "You didn't need to do this."

"I know, but I wanted to. It's the least I can do. Unless you'd like to . . ." He trails off and tugs at his ear. I try not to squirm, knowing that even the slightest movement unleashes a chorus of rustling. He looks over at the receipt chaos that covers the center of the store. Then at Pippa. "Sorry. Never mind. You guys look like you have a lot to do. I'll catch you another time." He turns away and steps toward the door.

I risk a look at Pippa. She flicks a hand toward Felix, impatiently gesturing for me to follow him. As the bells on the door jingle, I brace myself against the front desk.

"Hey, Felix?" I wait while he turns, and I mentally recite the question that's been plaguing me since Saturday night, uttered a thousand ways in my imagination, never to a good result. "The coffee. Thanks again. You're really . . . avuncular."

His brows shoot up. "I'm what?"

"Nothing. Forget I said that. I'll see you around."

"Yeah. Sure thing." He chuckles to himself as he heads out of the store.

The second he's out of view, Pippa sprints over to my side.

"Are you kidding me?" She grabs me by the shoulders and shakes me. "That gorgeous guy just brought you coffee. He obviously likes you. You obviously like him. He stood right there, trying to get up the nerve to ask you out. You didn't even have to do the asking. And you practically pushed him out the door!"

"I told him he was nice."

"You told him he was like your uncle!"

"Close enough. I'm still learning the nuances of language. And I don't have any uncles, ones I know of, anyway." I wriggle out of Pippa's grasp and rustle toward the central seating area, where I can immerse my addled mind in facts and figures.

Halfway there, Pippa grabs me again and spins me toward the door.

"Go. Now. Or I'll sneak in here overnight and paint 'Hey, Felix, Harper wants to bone you' on the window. And I'll use something that's *really* hard to wash off!"

I stumble forward. "Fine! Got it! I'm going."

I head out the door. Pippa watches from inside the shop, arms folded as if to imply she's not letting me back in unless I return with proper *Yes, I asked him* ID. Glancing around, I spot Felix's broad frame and caramel waves about a block away, receding toward Main Street. I feel weird for chasing him down, especially in my current attire, but if I'm going to embarrass myself anyway, I might as well go all in.

"Felix! Wait!" I call out as I jog toward him. He stops and turns toward me, both hands jammed in his pockets. I catch up, already panting thanks to my brilliant exercise-avoidance routine. "Sorry, I just, I wanted to . . . Do you want to go out with me?" The question falls from my mouth like an anvil into sand, not at all the way I'd hoped.

Felix blinks at me as his brow furrows.

"Are you asking me out, or are you checking to see if I like you?"

"The first one I think? I mean, yes. Definitely the first one. Felix Royce, I, Harper Jamison, am asking you out. On a date." I straighten up and attempt to look implacable.

Felix wraps a hand over his mouth and slowly draws his palm toward his chin.

"A date, huh?" The hand on his chin shifts to his earlobe, trailing a line along his impossibly square jawline. A familiar hint of pressure unsettles something in my chest. I'm not proving a point to Theo or obeying Pippa the Persistent. Well, I am, but I'm also standing in front of a guy I like, a guy I've been fantasizing about for months, asking him on a date, already caring way too much about his answer. This could go very, very badly.

"Just for coffee," I say. "A chance to get to know each other better. That's all."

"Just coffee?" Felix cocks his head. There's a hint of challenge in his eyes, and a playful quirk to his lips. He's teasing me and I like it.

"Just coffee," I repeat, fighting back a smile of my own.

He takes a step toward me, slowly, as if he's testing the waters. The little quake in my chest speeds up. A new rush of heat floods my cheeks.

"So, no flirting?" he asks.

I shake my head. He takes another step toward me.

"And no hand holding?"

I shake my head again, though the action requires more effort this time. Breathing also seems strangely difficult, as does looking anywhere but in Felix's deep-set, gray-as-granite eyes. He takes another step, stopping directly in front of me, all six-foot-whatever of crazy-hot-guy-ness. While I try to pretend I'm not insanely turned on by his closeness, he leans down so his eyes are level with mine.

"And absolutely no chance at all of any kissing?"

I shake my head a third time, barely.

A broad smile slowly stretches across Felix's face.

"Then, I accept."

FOUR

THEO FROWNS AT THE TEEN DATING SITE I PULLED up on my laptop. We're side by side on the cushy sofa in my den. The soda bottle's half-empty. The pizza box only has two slices left, one of my plain cheese and one of Theo's pineapple anchovy. I once asked him why he liked that combination. He said they were the ingredients no one else wanted and he felt sad for them. This is so Theo, empathizing with a neglected piece of fruit or an oily little fish and then making years of food orders accordingly. Feeling so much must be exhausting.

"Why is the site called Toast?" he asks.

"I think it's an acronym. Teens Only something. Or maybe carbs are back in style. Who knows? They could hardly call it Hookups for Minors. You know. Legal issues."

Theo shoves me with his elbow. I start building his profile, filling in the basics like age and location. As if bored by the whole endeavor, he bends forward and adjusts his glittery hedgehog socks. They gape at his ankles, stretched out from excessive wear. The soles are threadbare. The glitter's faded to a sparse scattering of sparkles. I had a feeling he'd like them when I picked them up for his fourteenth birthday. I should've known back then that when Theo likes something, he *really* likes it.

He takes another look at the screen. "Why'd you say I'm a Hufflepuff?"

"Girls like Hufflepuffs. They're sweet and safe."

"What if I don't want to be anything? I wasn't really into those books."

"It's an icebreaker, to give you something to talk about."

"I have plenty of things to talk about." His brow pinches, and I realize he has a point. He's read pretty much anything with wizards or quests. No need to highlight the most obvious choice, especially since mainstream has never been Theo's style.

I delete the Hufflepuff remark and scroll to Favorite Books, where I enter three titles: *The Blackest Knight, Blood on the Stairs,* and the obscure Nomads Rising series he couldn't stop raving about last summer. He nods in approval so I shift the cursor to Favorite Music, Movies, and TV. I note that he plays the accordion and type *Sons of Venus* into the section for TV shows. Then I add a few other films and bands I know he likes. Theo rests his head on my shoulder as I type. His thick hair is soft against my cheek. It smells like apples and vanilla. It's nice, like one of those plug-in air fresheners but not as sickeningly sweet.

"You don't even need me here for this," he says.

"It's your profile."

"It's your plan." He blows out a sigh as he flicks at a loose thread on my outseam.

"Well, if you're fine with anything . . ." I shift to Hobbies.

"Let's see, tilting at windmills? Maiming scarecrows? Naming your future dogs?"

He pinches my side. I jerk away, laughing while shielding my ribs with both arms.

"I hate that you know exactly where that spot is."

He wiggles his fingers as his eyes fill with mischief. "My secret weapon."

"Watch it or I'll fill in the Most Embarrassing Moment section."

Theo goes rigid as his smile drops away. "You wouldn't."

"Of course not. Sorry. I was only teasing. We'll leave that part blank."

He keeps his eyes locked on mine, watching me like a wary cat. I gulp back a swell of guilt. I shouldn't have mentioned the embarrassing moment, not that I'd ever put something like that on the Internet. We were in third grade on an out-of-town field trip. The bus was held up for over two hours in a traffic jam. Theo couldn't wait. He peed his pants. He was petrified. Our classmates would be merciless. Theo and I were about the same size, and I had my gym shorts in my backpack. We both wriggled out of our jeans at the back of the bus. I let him have mine while I wore my shorts for the rest of the day. It was November. I was freezing. Our classmates also teased us for supposedly making out on the bus, but at least I saved Theo from a much worse humiliation.

I settle my laptop in my lap again and continue filling out his profile. Theo mostly leaves me to it, but he gets irritated with any entry that's a little too generic or doesn't accurately describe his many idiosyncrasies. I remind him why we're crafting a dating profile at all: he's already gone out with every teenage medieval poetry geek and Ren-fester in a thirty-mile radius. He admitted as much before the pizza arrived. Now he just needs to meet someone nice, easy to talk to, easy to read, low stakes. She doesn't have to know that he memorized the Knights of the Round Table or once spent an entire week speaking in iambic pentameter. She doesn't have to be his soulmate, especially while he's learning to stop scattering bits of his heart all over town.

Theo picks a piece of pineapple off the pizza and pops it into his mouth.

"Are you filling out one of these for yourself?" he asks.

"Actually, I already set up a first date."

He swallows his pineapple too fast, coughing slightly as he forces it down.

"When? How? Who?" he asks once he's cleared his throat.

"Monday. On a break from work. Felix Royce."

Theo coughs again, harder this time. He bends double, pounding a fist against his chest. I swivel toward him, prepared to attempt the Heimlich, but he holds up a hand.

"I'm good," he chokes out. "Should've swallowed before I asked the question." He takes a moment to wipe tears from the corners of his eyes and clear his throat. "Felix Royce? Seriously, Jamison?"

"What's wrong with him?"

"Nothing at all, which I've always considered deeply suspect." Theo shakes his head as he blinks away his surprise. "I'm happy for you. Just don't tell him about our treehouse sleepovers. That guy could kick my ass."

"We're going for coffee. That's all." I poke at the keys, wondering how many times I have to say this before I believe it. I can tell Theo's watching me, still thumping his chest, but I lock my eyes on my laptop. If he senses my anxiety, our deal will be off. No matter what happens with Felix, I still want to help Theo avoid another heartbreak.

We take almost two hours to create a profile we're both satisfied with. By the time we finish, we've polished off the pizza and soda. We're also snuggled together, a habit we haven't outgrown since we shared a crib. My legs are twisted through his. His arms loop through mine. His cheek rests on my shoulder while mine rests on the top of his head, where I sneak a little nuzzle every now and then, drawn by the scent of apples and vanilla, like pie à la mode. I figure it's fair game since he keeps playing footsie with me. It's all friendly and familiar, a mutual comfort built on years of closeness, two only children standing in as siblings, knowing precisely what we are to each other.

The profile complete, I scroll to the top of the page.

"Now all we need is a photo."

Theo pulls out his phone. "I don't have many."

"Not even something from your socials?"

"Not like a basic headshot." Theo scrolls through his phone while I skim his socials on my laptop. He's right. The content's sparse. He's not a frequent poster. The few photos I do find are mostly fencing shots and moody-looking pics of autumnal trees overlaid with old verses. The only shot Theo finds on his phone is one of him in his full suit of chain mail, the suit he made link by link, head covering, gloves, and all. We could crop the image into a headshot, but all that metal's a little intimidating for a dating profile. Besides, Pippa was right. Theo has great hair. He might as well show it off.

We decide to take a simple photo of him on my sofa. I set aside my laptop. Theo smooths the wrinkles in the T-shirt he's wearing under his flannel. It's bright yellow with a drawing of a tall, skinny knight on a horse followed by a short, tubby guy on a mule. It's kind of perfect. Sure, I was against the full suit of armor, but we're not pretending Theo shops at J.Crew. A little bit of knighthood seems right.

He glances around the room. "Where do you want me?"

"Sofa works. This should look natural."

"Yeah, because this whole process is all about being natural." He flashes me his trademark wry smile, all arched eyebrows and tilted chin and . . . huh, I guess his lips do turn up at the corners. Pippa was right about that, too.

I find my phone and perch on the coffee table. Theo brushes his hair off his forehead. It flops back into place, every black wave curling a different direction. He tries slinging a forearm over the sofa back, but he looks too posed. He clasps his hands in his lap. Too formal. He stares directly at my phone and then off toward the bookshelves. He plants his feet. Then he rests an ankle on the opposite thigh. We cycle through a dozen poses, but he looks stiff and uncomfortable in all of them.

"This isn't working." I delete the images, one after the other.

Theo watches over my shoulder. "They're fine. It's only a photo."

"But no one will read your profile if they don't like your photo."

"That's ridiculous."

"That's reality. Face it, Theo. Most girls aren't looking for Shakespeare, Einstein, or a knight in shining armor. They just want to hang out with someone cute and fun."

"Can't I be fun *and* a knight in shining armor?"

"For me? Yes. For practice date number one, let's leave out the armor."

Theo slumps into the corner of the sofa. He kicks his legs up on the coffee table and gazes off into space, a frown deeply etched into his features. I study him, searching for a clue about how to get him to smile, not in a forced way, but like he did in the treehouse the other night, when his joy was painted across his face in big, bold strokes. I only know one surefire way to get him to smile, but it's going to cost me.

While Theo counts dust motes, I sneak my phone into my lap. In one swift movement, I straddle his shins, pin them between mine, and reach behind me to tickle his feet. He busts into a laugh and tries to wriggle away. I hold fast, madly snapping pics until he lunges at my ribs. I tilt backwards onto the coffee table. Theo moves fast, leaning over me with one hand poised beside his face and the other already finding its way to my side. Shrieking at the contact, I edge sideways. Theo comes with me. We topple onto the floor in a tangle of limbs and laughter. He jabs at my sides, my waist, my armpits, finding all of my tickle buttons, leaving me writhing and helpless.

"Stop!" I plead as he pinches my twitchiest spot again. "Truce! Please!"

He grins above me. "You attacked first."

"It was all in the name of love."

"Liar! You're a monster." He goes for my other side. He nails it.

I dodge his next stab at my waist. "You mean an aberration? An abhorrent abnormality analogous to an aquatic amphiptere?"

Theo halts his assault. I take a moment to catch my breath. As I do, the sweetest, kindest, proudest, happiest, truest, most Theo-like smile breaks across his face.

"You studied my list," he says.

Rather than confirm his statement, I whip out my phone and capture his smile. We check the image together. It's perfect.

Back in position on the sofa, we activate his profile and start scanning for matches. I wriggle into our earlier position, draping my leg over his and locking our ankles. He loops his arm through my elbow and lays his cheek against my shoulder. We're still snuggling like that, reading profiles, when my mom finally comes home.

"That beadwork is going to be the death of me!" she calls as she hangs up her jacket and dumps her keys into the bowl by the front door. Theo's hold tightens as he catches my eye, darting a nervous look at my screen. I hide the dating site by pulling up Netflix while my mom's heels click across the floorboards toward us. She pauses by the corner of the sofa. "Oh, hey, Theo. What're you guys up to?"

"Movies," we say in unison.

"Ones with lots of sex and violence?" my mom asks.

"Only the really kinky kind." I smile up at her.

Theo sneaks a light rib pinch, but I manage not to wriggle.

My mom yawns and massages her neck. "I'm going to crash. Long day. Don't stay up too late, okay? I need your help with those alterations tomorrow."

"As long as we get coffee on the way in, I'm good."

My mom promises we'll be well caffeinated. We all say good night, and she heads upstairs to her bedroom. As soon as her door closes, Theo swivels toward me.

"Do you think she ever suspects something?" he asks.

I blink at him, confused. "Something like what?"

He circles a hand over our entwined bodies. "We're hanging out alone at your place. I have a close-up view of that freckle behind your ear. You're siphoning my body heat. It could look like we're not just watching movies."

"No, it couldn't."

"Why not?"

"Because my mom knows us both." I pull up the dating site again. I'm about to make a joke about a girl's obsession with astrological signs when I realize Theo's expression has clouded over. He's not looking at the screen or at me. He's scratching at an ink stain on his jeans. "That wasn't an insult. You're like family, Theo.

My mom knows she has nothing to worry about when I'm with you. Isn't that a good thing?"

His forehead twitches as his lips pull to the side. "Yeah. Of course."

"Great. So let's find you a date already."

I start opening profiles. Theo grudgingly reengages in the task at hand. Despite expressing interest in a few girls before my mom's arrival, suddenly no one's good enough for him. He criticizes grammatical mistakes, punctuation errors, and misused homophones, finding fault with every profile. Eventually we check out a girl with a heart-shaped face, tight rows of black braids, and a great, natural smile. She's standing by a maple tree, ankle-deep in yellow leaves. The photo's promising. If nothing else, we know she shares Theo's taste for molting foliage. I scroll through her profile. Her name's Ginny. She's on her school's swim team. She likes history.

"Ooh, look!" I point at the screen. "She's a Hufflepuff. Just like you."

"Awesome," Theo deadpans. "So glad we'll have something to talk about."

We stay nestled close as we read the rest of Ginny's profile. Concluding that she'd be perfectly fine as someone for Theo to *not* fall in love with, we open the message box. I slide my laptop over. Theo types away. And types. And types, rambling on about everything he'd like to get to know about Ginny, commenting on her photo and faves, and suggesting possible date options. I leave him to it, locking my hands in my lap until he finally wraps up, ending his epic letter with a quote so corny even the Hallmark card people would roll their eyes. Before he can hit send, I snatch the laptop back.

Theo flinches. "What's wrong?"

"You're invested already."

"Yeah? So?"

"So what if she doesn't write back?"

"Why wouldn't she?"

Oh, lord. Here we go. This learning curve is going to be steep.

"Because this is the real world," I say. "People are cautious. They weigh their options. They don't fall in love at first sight like Romeo and Juliet."

"You know they died, right? So, not exactly hashtag relationship goals."

"Fine. Bad example. My point is that you can't keep pouring your time and energy into every girl you meet, assuming they're all as primed to fall in love as you are. You'll only end up crushed again. And I can't fix your broken heart as easily as I can mend your tattered jeans. My sewing skills only go so far."

Theo flutters a sad smile as he wilts against me. I trim his response to a few friendly sentences and a question that might engage Ginny in a conversation. We send the message and follow suit with two more girls, hoping at least one of them will respond and by the weekend I can coach Theo through the dos and don'ts of a first date. No flowers. No poetry. No open declarations of excitement and anticipation. No grand gestures. Keep the conversation light and your expectations low. Accept that a first date might also be a last date. Learn to walk away without caring so much.

Our more immediate task completed, Theo departs and I head upstairs to get ready for bed. Before turning out my light, I check the messages on my phone. I chime in on a group thread I've been neglecting with my friends. I reply to a message from Pippa, letting her know that yes, it's okay if she's late for work tomorrow. I take one last look at Theo's profile, confirming that his personality shines through, despite my curating. His intelligence is clear. His thoughtfulness and big heart, too. And that photo . . .

His hair tips over his eyebrows, dense and unruly. His jawline slopes gently toward the upturned lips I never noticed before tonight, quirking at the edges with a hint of irony. Even from the screen, his dark eyes light up my entire room, twinkling with pride and joy. His skin is flawless. His nose could've been carved by a master sculptor. His dimple peeks out from his left cheek, adding a compelling asymmetry to his face.

I set aside my phone and turn off my light.

Ten minutes later I grab my phone and take another look.

Shit. Pippa's right. I'm an idiot. Theo's a total hottie.

FIVE

ON THURSDAY NIGHT, I CARRY A LARGE LATTE AND a green tea over to a table by the window where Felix is waiting. Apparently he doesn't drink coffee but I won't hold that against him. We're at Gadzooks, at the far, *far* north end of Main Street. I don't come here very often, but of all the coffee shops in town, this seemed the least likely to be patronized by people I know. I realize this may be an unnecessary caution, but if this date doesn't go well, the fewer people who know about it, the better.

The coffee shop's cute and cozy. The chairs and tables are mismatched. Black-and-white photos of people drinking coffee in the 1930s, '40s, and '50s dot the paneled walls. Little lamps with gingham shades sit on every table. About a dozen other people are here. Most are on laptops while an old guy reads a paper two tables over and a trio of girls around our age chats in the corner over a frosted cookie they're sharing.

Felix thanks me for the tea as he wraps his hands around his mug, leaning down so the steam swirls before his face. His hair is damp from a recent shower, tightening the wave and darkening the tone to a deep auburn. I'm used to seeing him in workout clothes, but tonight he's wearing dark jeans and a thin, navy blue V-neck tee that's clearly not meant for jogging or lifting weights. It hugs his body in a way I stopped trying to ignore the second he walked in the door. Across from him, I've busted out of my boring black work attire into a cute rayon shirtdress and some chunky-heeled boots I rarely have a reason to wear. I even let down my ponytail and put on lipstick. It's liberating.

Felix dips a fingertip into his tea and swiftly withdraws it.

"I don't understand why they make everything so hot," he says.

"The upper palate is overrated?"

"I've never considered that angle." He smiles a little. I look away before I have to fight off my first blush of the night. While I remind myself this is a simple "get to know you better" conversation, Felix blows on his tea. "What did you get?"

"No-foam latte with three-quarters almond milk, one-quarter two percent, plus the tiniest squirt of vanilla syrup, a pinch of cinnamon, and half a teaspoon of cocoa."

Felix's smile widens. "Sounds complicated."

"I know what I like." I catch the slight rise of his eyebrows. "In coffee, I mean. Guess I can be pretty indecisive in other areas."

"We all are, probably, about some things, anyway." He shrugs as the tiniest twitch of his lips tells me he caught my subtext. "Sometimes I take forever to decide what to watch on Netflix. Or what to put on a playlist, when to get up on Sundays, when to go to bed on Saturdays, how many miles to run, where to apply for college." He bends closer and lowers his voice. "When to ask out a girl I've kinda liked for a while now."

"Mmm." I return my attention to the little bubbles forming a ring against the inside of my mug, unnerved by how swiftly he imploded our no-flirting plan, and by how good it feels. If I don't watch myself, I'll undercut everything I told Theo this week, and everything I've told myself for the past year.

After a heavy pause, I guide our conversation toward less risky territory. Felix and I compare notes on our teachers, the ones we love and the ones who annoy us. We discuss music and TV shows. We joke about growing up in a town that looks like a set from a Hallmark movie. I sip my coffee. He sips his tea. We grow more comfortable with each other, relaxing into our chairs and easing into more direct eye contact. Halfway through my latte, I stop worrying about being on a date and simply enjoy Felix's company.

"What about running?" I ask. "Is it something you've always done?"

"Sort of. Since about fifth grade. I don't know if you remember, but I was a pretty scrawny kid. I got tall too fast. I felt awkward and clumsy just walking down the street."

"I remember you being tall. I don't remember you being awkward or clumsy."

He gets all shifty and shy, looking down and tapping a thumb on the rim of his mug. I fight the instinct to take his hand. Only for reassurance, of course, though it blows my mind that Felix Royce needs reassurance about anything.

"Trust me," he says. "I was all limbs and I had no idea what to do with them. I wasn't coordinated enough for most sports, but we had those field days back in grade school, the ones where we all had to loop the track. I flew around it, beating the next guy behind me by several seconds. For the first time in my life, I felt like my body wasn't something that existed simply to house my brain or annoy me. Speed felt amazing. Strength did, too. Winning didn't totally suck, either, especially to a kid who hadn't come close to winning anything before." He shifts the handle of his mug from one hand to the other as his shoulders inch up. He made state last year and broke every school record. He has nothing to be modest about, and yet he is. "Now running's part of who I am. I still like winning, but mostly I run for the escape. I lace up my shoes and I'm in another world. It's just me, the road, and my music." He grimaces. "Sorry. I'm talking waaaaay too much. What about you? When did you learn to sew?"

"Ten years ago, maybe? But it isn't a passion like your running. My mom taught me how to sew on buttons when I was a kid. She claimed she needed the help, but she was probably trying to keep me busy so she could save on babysitting money." I laugh to myself, recalling the enormous bin of satin-covered buttons I thought looked like gnome noses. "From buttons I graduated to trims, from trims to hems, and from hems to more complicated alterations." I stop there, worried I'm rattling on too long now, but Felix is watching me as though he's really listening. It's nice. It's more than nice.

"Is that what you want to do?" he asks. "Make dresses like your mom?"

"No, I prefer to focus on the business side of things, though I like knowing I can create something with my hands. Sewing's becoming a lost art." I hold out both hands, palms up. "Sometimes I wonder how many dresses these hands have touched, how many hems, how many buttons, how many seams and dreams."

Felix surprises me by sliding his hands under mine and curving his fingers around the edge of my palms. His skin is soft and warmed by what's left of his tea.

"Is this okay?" he asks.

"You said no hand holding."

"Did I? That was stupid." He uncurls his fingers as though he's giving me an opportunity to withdraw my hands. I don't withdraw them. Instead, I relax into his hold, watching his thumbs run along the creases that curve across my palms. His touch is slow but sure. I am mesmerized, relaxing into a peculiar sensation that he's touching more than my hands, in a good way. In a *really* good way. While I try to rein in my thoughts, Felix draws my hands closer to his chest. "Do you know how to read palms?"

I shake my head, still watching his hands explore mine.

"This line says you'll live a long and healthy life." He traces a crease that ends near my pinkie. "This one says you'll run a very successful business one day." He finds the line that runs from my index finger toward my wrist. "This one says your love life is about to undergo an unexpected change." He massages the fleshy bit at the base of my thumbs, pressing gently in lazy spirals.

I swallow and find my voice. "You made all that up, right?"

"Every word." His eyes lift to mine. "Doesn't mean it can't be true."

"No. I guess it doesn't." I stop resisting my attraction and let myself gaze into his deep-set eyes. Beneath a curtain of auburn lashes, the light from our table lamp paints amber dots across two seas of wintery gray. A smile plays with his lips, revealing the briefest glimpse of his perfect teeth. God, this boy. This beautiful, oddly self-conscious boy. I am a total goner. If we were alone, I'd pull him toward me right now and—

The girls sharing the cookie a few tables over burst into giggles. Felix and I draw apart, glancing over to note that we're clearly being watched. The energy between us resets as he drinks his tea and I straighten my dress for no reason whatsoever. We ease back into comfortable conversation about his job at the grocery and my inability to get my mom to stick to a schedule, but soon enough our hands drift together again. I don't even see it happening until his pinkie brushes mine, and I tap out a tune on his fingertips.

"It's so cool that you sew," he says. "I wish I had a skill."

"You do have a skill. You can run six miles in the time it takes me to walk one."

"That's different. It's about being fast and strong. I don't create anything. These are useless." He holds up both hands and waggles his fingers. "It's why I started taking photography classes, but I'm not very good."

"How do you know?"

"Trust me. When the entire class goes silent during critique sessions, you know." His hands drop to the table, too far away for me to take them in my own.

"Can I see your work sometime?"

"I don't know." Felix shakes his head through a self-effacing chuckle. "Maybe. If you'll share something embarrassing with me."

"Hmm . . ." I consider my catalog of past embarrassments. "What would make the best trade? Tween poetry journal? Ill-conceived experiment with bangs and hair gel? Photos from my first and final attempt to drink vodka?"

"Is there an 'all of the above' option?"

"Let's take this one step at a time." I lean my head on my hand and let myself stare again, something I could do all night if he'd let me. "My mom put me in tap class four years ago. She thought dance lessons would 'build my poise.' Instead, they shattered my ego. I buried my tap shoes in the backyard so she wouldn't sign me up for more lessons. I still have nightmares about soft-shoeing across the studio."

Felix's feet bracket mine under the table. "Now *that* I want to see."

I muster the willpower to not run a toe up his calf.

"If you'll show me your lettering project, I'll do a tap dance for you."

His shyness drops away as he offers me a full-on, camera-busting smile.

"Sounds like you're asking me on a second date," he says.

"At least I'm not chasing you down the street this time."

"Think we can flirt on the next one?"

I hold out my palm. Felix lays his hand in mine, palm up. I trace a crease with my index finger, studying it closely.

"Looks likely," I say. "As long as your seventh wife never finds out."

"Don't worry. I'll tell her we only had coffee."

Felix walks me home. We take the long way, wandering by the river, toying with holding hands and then separating again as though neither of us can decide how much touching feels appropriate yet. I learn more about his family and friends. I tell him about mine, and about how badly I want to go to Bryn Mawr, even if the no-boys policy now holds slightly less appeal. By the time we reach my house, our "get to know you better" agenda has been fulfilled tenfold, and we only cheat a little with the flirting.

The lights are off as we climb the steps to my front door. Naturally, my mom is still at work. For once I find her absence highly advantageous, not because I plan to drag Felix up to my bedroom, but because she's never seen me with a guy before. I never told her about Liam. I don't know how to talk to her about guys. To the best of my knowledge, her last date was with a drummer whose name she can't remember, and whose most notable trait is that he didn't use a condom.

I find my keys in my jacket pocket. Felix waits nearby as I

unlock the door. Then he takes my empty hand and stands before me.

"Guess this is good night," he says.

"Guess so."

"Thanks for chasing me down the street."

"Thanks for letting me chase you." I make no move to release his hand, step away, or open the door. It's all I can do to hold myself upright and remember to breathe. His hair curls at the side of his temples like the top of one of those Greek columns. His lashes shift as his eyes find mine. His lips . . . Oh, god. His lips . . .

"So . . ." He inches closer.

"So . . ." I draw in a breath.

"About that tap dance . . ."

"Art first." I prod his chest with my keys.

"But I can see you again?"

"I hope so."

"With flirting?" He tips his forehead against mine.

My breath catches. "Already established."

"And maybe even kissing?"

A heady wave of dizziness washes over me at the thought of his lips meeting mine, warm, soft, seeking to undo me the way I want to undo him.

"I'll take the idea under serious consideration." I tilt my face toward Felix's.

He taps his nose against mine. His thumb strokes the soft Y of flesh between my thumb and forefinger. His breath gusts gently against my lips. The house beside me all but vanishes. There's only Felix, impossibly beautiful and intoxicatingly close.

"I look forward to learning the result of your consideration." He kisses my cheek, holding his lips against my skin for a full intake of breath before drawing away. Then he smiles, squeezes my hand, and leaves me to watch him retreat into the night.

SIX

IT'S 4:00 P.M. ON FRIDAY AND I'M ONLY ON MY
third bridesmaid dress. I let out the first. I took in the second.
The third should be thrown in the trash. The bridesmaid—who
will hereafter be known as LLPOF, short for Liar, Liar, Pants on
Fire—is not a size six. It's too late to order her a ten. Thus I'm
altering every single seam, hoping to find an extra three inches
buried in all the turquoise taffeta. These are the tasks I hate most.
They're tedious and time-consuming. Not that I blame LLPOF for
ordering the wrong size. I blame a clothing industry that makes
us all despise ourselves if we're not a size six. I got lucky. I inherited my mom's five feet nine inches of height and her slim build,
though we're probably only slim because we live on coffee and
frozen meals. "Chad" must've been fair though because my hair
and complexion are lighter than my mom's. My hair's also curlier
than hers, but no one's glimpsed a single kink since I learned how
to do a proper blowout.

Blowout. Right. My other task for the day. Learn the *B*'s.

I unearth my vocab list from beneath the dress. I'm in the
back room at my mom's shop while Pippa helps my mom with a

walk-in client. The three of them are chatting quietly somewhere near the racks. I picture the client acting bellicose and belligerent, cementing the words in my brain. For my mom's sake, I hope the client is neither. My mom doesn't need to deal with argumentative customers today. She got home super late last night. Now that we're over halfway through June, we're in the thick of wedding season. Two of my mom's custom clients are getting married next weekend. The gowns are ready to go, but one of the brides just added alterations on five bridesmaid dresses. The other bride decided to design her own veil, complete with a piped, scalloped edge and several hand-sewn lace appliqués. We need the money, but it's a lot of work for only two of us while a multitude of summer weddings loom. I'm helping where I can, with both the sewing and the tax mess, but I also have a second date to arrange and a friend to coach through his first attempt at casual dating, a friend who still considers the word *casual* to be blasphemy. There. Three *B* words down. Only ninety-seven to go.

My phone buzzes in my back pocket.

Theo: *Do I wait outside or go in and sit down?*
Harper: *Outside. Unless she's more than 10 min late*
Theo: *What if she doesn't show?*
Harper: *Get an iced cocoa. Watch a funny video. Go home. Move on*
Theo: *What if she shows but doesn't recognize me?*
Harper: *Are you wearing your fencing mask?*
Theo: *No*

Harper: *Then don't worry about it*

Theo: *Am I supposed to pay?*

Harper: *Not necessary, but it's good form since you asked her out*

Theo: *That's not "investing" too much?*

Harper: *It's not your bank account I'm worried about*

My screen goes blank. I pocket my phone, hoping I haven't stressed Theo out too much with this dating app idea. Neither of us has used one before. Everything I know about dating apps I learned from Pippa and TV shows. We did something right, though. All three girls Theo messaged got back to him. Nine others replied directly to his profile. Nine! None of them even seem sketchy. I acted like I anticipated the bombardment (*B* word number four), but the high response rate made me feel stupid for thinking of Theo as the boy next-dork for so long. Of course girls are interested in him. His problem is keeping them interested, and not crashing if they don't want to see him again.

After much debate, he asked out Ginny, the first girl he contacted. She seems nice. She and Theo have enough in common to hold a conversation but not so much that sparks will fly and he'll assume he's met his soulmate. Again. If he follows my instructions, he'll practice reading a girl's interest level and lowering his expectations. She'll enjoy his company for an hour. They can both have a perfectly lovely evening.

My phone buzzes again.

Theo: *What if she mentions Hufflepuffs?*

Harper: *Then talk about Hufflepuffs. Or change the subject if you want to*

Theo: *Is Chaucer off-limits?*

Harper: *Keep it to a minimum. You don't want to seem bombastic*

Theo: *You're studying!!!!!*

Harper: *Trying. Haven't figured out how to use bowdlerize yet*

Theo: *If Ginny lets me kiss her tonight, I'll bowdlerize that from my report*

Something prickles the back of my neck, making me twitch. Dry air, probably, though for some reason my mind wanders to the photo we put on Theo's profile, and the way he smiles with his entire being when he's happy. I picture him kissing Ginny at the end of their date. I wonder if he's a good kisser. And I despise that I wondered that and will never, ever entertain the question again.

Harper: *Bowdlerize sounds weird. Can't you just say censor?*

Theo: *Censor won't be on your SAT*

Harper: *Good point*

I'm working on a way to use *blandishment*—flattery employed for purposes of persuasion—when another text comes through.

Theo: *She showed! Gotta go. Text you when I'm home*

I pocket my phone, jittery with nerves, even though I have nothing to worry about. I'll see Theo later tonight. He'll describe his pleasant but unexceptional evening, I'll praise his ability to remain appropriately detached, and all will be well. Meanwhile, I'll finish altering this turquoise monstrosity, which is the bane of my existence. Now there's a *B* word I can use. *Bane: that which causes misery or death.*

The last client leaves shortly after 7:00 p.m. My mom offers to pick up takeout Thai food if I'll stay until all five bridesmaid dresses are finished. I have the time and I know she appreciates the help, so I agree. Pippa stays, too. She can't sew, but she'll tabulate more of my mom's receipts and invoices in exchange for some greasy noodles. Gushing with thanks to both of us, my mom heads out. I haul a dismantled dress into the main room so I can chat with Pippa while she starts her end-of-day cleaning routine.

"You're literally the best," I tell her as I sink onto the velvet chaise, half-buried under the billowing dress. "I can't believe you'd give up your Friday night to do math."

"You think I'm staying to do math?" She laughs in her giddy, infectious Pippa Pennington way. It makes her wig jiggle. Today's is a subdued maroon, styled in a high twist with a crisscrossed pair of chopsticks. "I'm here to dish about your new boyfriend."

"He's not my boyfriend."

"But your date sounded soooooo good."

"It was good. It was also only a first date." I peer over at the gym, even though Felix doesn't use it in the evenings. Less than twenty-four hours have passed since we said good night, and I already miss him. I keep thinking about his smile and his hands and how I hope he likes me as much as I like him. In other words, I'm acting like Theo. This doesn't bode well for my heart or for the bet I made.

Pippa sets down her rag and cleaner. "Is this a 'we don't do labels' thing?"

"No, but the word *boyfriend* feels big. Like we've committed to something. Though clearly it didn't mean commitment to Liam last summer."

"You sure we can't pie that guy?"

"Positive. But thanks."

"It helped me get over my exes."

"I think it'll just put me off pie." I smile to myself as I picture a stranger walking up to Liam and smashing a cream pie into his face. It's a priceless image, and Pippa's serious about it. She sent me a link to the company that does it, along with a code for her frequent user's discount. Whether or not it worked for her, I doubt it would make me resent my ex any less. The anger would still creep in when I least expect it, and the fear that I'm not worth holding on to. If I could erase *that* with a pie, I'd do it in a heartbeat.

While I continue attacking a mountain of taffeta, Pippa launches a battery of questions, filling in blanks from the brief description I provided her earlier today. I tell her what Felix wore, what I wore, what we drank, what we talked about, how often we touched, and how we left things. I answer her questions honestly, but I leave out all the heart flutters and breathlessness. If I keep that to myself, maybe I can pretend I'm still in control of the situation, even while my errant eyes drift toward the gym yet again.

My phone buzzes. I yank it from my pocket, hoping for an update from Theo. I suggested he limit his first meet-up to an hour. Ninety minutes max. It's been twice that long since he texted to say Ginny arrived. The text isn't from him. It's from Denise, a friend of mine from school, letting me know a group's going to a pool party if I want to join. I send my usual answer. *Thanks for asking. Sorry. Still working.* The invites have come less and less often over the past year. Pretty soon they're going to stop altogether.

While my phone's out, I take a moment to check Theo's dating profile, searching for signs that he might be a target for catfishing. His profile seems fine, though I'm not sure what I'm looking for. He looks confident in his photo, even with his unruly hair and his single dimple and the funny bend at the corners of his lips. I wonder if he ever—

"Hello? Earth to Harper!" Pippa flaps her hands at me.

"Sorry, what?"

"I said, but you do want to kiss him, right?"

"What?! How did you, I mean, why would you think I—?" I stop there as it dawns on me that she's not asking about Theo. "Sorry. I thought you asked something else. Yes, of course I want to kiss Felix, as long as things don't get messy."

"As in too much saliva?"

"As in too many feelings."

"Riiiiiiiiiight." Pippa elongates the word, eyeing me with an air of suspicion. Thankfully my mom returns from the Thai place so Pippa doesn't probe into which feelings I'm trying to avoid. That doesn't stop me from wrestling with them, or from wondering why, when I thought she was asking me about Theo, I didn't simply say no.

♥

Theo finally texts shortly after 10:00 p.m., six hours after his date arrived at the coffee shop. I've been going nuts, ready to assemble a search party, certain Ginny wasn't a teenage girl and Theo was being held at knifepoint until he venmoed the contents of his bank account to some thug with an eye patch and a set of brass knuckles. The instant I get his text, I throw on a pair of sneakers and run to the windmill.

Theo's lying flat on his back, staring at the twinkly lantern with his ankles crossed and his hands laced behind his head. He doesn't look my way as I sit beside him, tucking my legs in tight. A breeze drifts through the open windows, making his black waves dance across his forehead. For the first time, I notice that the Funko Pop! knight on the windowsill also has shaggy black hair and distinctly angular eyebrows. Theo told me the character was from a book he read, but now I wonder if it's a little more personal. While I look back and forth between Theo and the toy, he sighs toward the ceiling, making his belly rise and fall where his T-shirt doesn't quite meet the top of his jeans.

"You okay?" I ask.

He makes an indecipherable little murmur as his head lolls my way. His eyes are distant. His dimple's absent. His lips barely turn up at the corners. They're glistening slightly, as though he recently licked them. His lower lip is underlined by a sliver of what I assume is chocolate, a common occurrence. His upper lip looks a little chapped. His cupid's bow is more pronounced than I remembered. It dips into a . . .

Dammit. I'm totally staring at his lips. What is my deal tonight?

"Theo?" I ask gently. "Seriously. How did it go?"

"It was . . ." His eyes dart around as though he's searching for a word, a rare occurrence for someone with his verbal proficiency.

I inch forward. "Awkward? Uncomfortable? Boring? Disappointing?"

"Perfect."

I tilt backwards against the wall, banging my shoulder on the window frame, as always. While my old bruise blooms anew, I push out a squeaky "Oh?"

"Yeah." He rolls toward me. Wonder and astonishment paint his face, as if he's reliving every *perfect* moment. "I mean, it was awkward at first. We were both nervous. I was trying to remember your dos and don'ts. I didn't want to disappoint you. She was probably just shy." He presses a hand to his heart and drifts into another memory. "We were pretty quiet until Ginny mentioned the Harry Potter books. You were right. They were a good icebreaker." He nudges my knee with his fist, all chummy and proud.

I try to smile, but I can't quite manage it. Theo doesn't seem to notice my lack of response. He's still lost in his daydream. "I admitted I stopped after book three. Ginny was cool with it. Didn't care at all. She's amazing. You'll like her. My moms will, too. She swims and reads and she's so smart and she even plays the flute in her school band." Theo holds up a hand. "Don't worry. I didn't propose a duet. I'll save that for date two."

"You planned date two already?" I choke out.

"Of course!" With a burst of energy, Theo scoots onto his butt and swivels to face me, replacing wistful sighs with animated gestures, shifting with mercurial swiftness from one big emotion to the next. "If the weather's good, I'm thinking picnic. Or maybe she'll be up for a bike ride. I should've asked if she liked to cycle. I should've asked a lot of things. I don't even know if she likes berries or cheese. How do I plan a picnic when I don't know what she eats? I'll have to call her. I'm supposed to play it cool and wait a few days, right? Is tomorrow too soon? It's probably too soon. Gaaah!" He collapses into the pillows again, completely incapable of lying still.

I remain silent and motionless. I'm still trying to shake the word *perfect* from my brain. This isn't how the night was supposed to play out. Questions flash by, too fast and unformed for me to put them into words, leaving me with a vague uneasiness I can't put my finger on. All I can do is clear my throat and hope my voice stops squeaking.

"You were with Ginny this whole time?" I finally manage to ask.

"Not the whole time. Don't worry. I stuck to your ninety-minute rule."

"Then where have you been for the last four hours?"

"I took a walk on the towpath. I needed to clear my head. It was all so much, you know? Especially after—" He bites his lip and scratches at a speck on his jeans, one that suddenly occupies all of his attention. His change of demeanor jars me from my stupor.

"After Vicky *just* broke your heart?" I ask. Theo shifts a shoulder and continues picking at nothing. A laugh escapes my lips. It's uncomfortably harsh and definitely against the windmill safe-space rules, but there's no retracting it now. "You can't possibly be in love again already. You went on a date. It might lead to another one. That's all."

Theo scoffs. "That's all? Really? And how's your end of the bargain shaping up?"

"Fine. Great. *Perfect.*" I lock my arms over my chest and fight back a huff.

"So you haven't formed any kind of attachment?"

"Felix and I met up. We talked. We said good night. No. Big. Deal."

Theo stops fidgeting. His sits up straight and faces me, his dark eyes boring into mine, his stare so direct, I have to fight the urge to look away.

"Then why did Lucy from across the street say you watched Felix walk all the way down the block after he kissed you good night?"

I shoot a frown toward Lucy's house, willing her to wither, even if she's only ten.

"Felix kissed my cheek. It was sweet. Polite. Nothing more."

"But you wanted him to kiss you for real?"

"What I wanted him to do is none of your business."

"It is if you're going to sit there laughing at me for what I want."

"I couldn't help it. No one falls in love twice in one week."

"At least I feel *something*. Unlike some people." He flaps a hand at me.

My spine snaps taut. "You have no idea what I feel."

"No kidding. So tell me. What *do* you feel?"

My skin prickles with defensiveness. Sharp retorts perch on my lips. Theo scoots forward until his chocolate-scented breath warms my face. I pull myself away from the wall, rising to meet the defiance that practically steams from his skin.

"Fine. Yes. I wanted Felix to kiss me long and hard until my knees buckled and my skin was on fire and the only word I could recall the meaning of was *yes*. That doesn't mean I'm in love with him after *one date*."

The challenge in Theo's expression flickers and fades, softening into something much more complicated. His eyes travel around my face. His mouth drops ajar. The blades on the windmill shift as a breeze makes the stars dance. By the time the air goes still, all trace of Theo's softness is gone, replaced by an impenetrable glare.

"Then I hope you enjoy your second date."

"I will."

"Good."

"Great."

"Perfect."

We simmer for several seconds, neither of us breaking the ugly tension that charges the air between us. My clothes feel too tight. This room feels too small. I want to rip the shifting twinkle light from the ceiling and throw it out the window so the stars stop dancing around us, making the room seem sweet and dream-like when it's anything but. Instead, I clamber to my feet and fling open the hatch.

"Enjoy your bike-riding, picnic-eating love fest, Theo. Forget about the vocab lessons. You're obviously busy and my plans for the week won't require a lot of words."

SEVEN

BY NOON ON SATURDAY I'VE PRICKED MY FINGERS over a dozen times, dropped a bin of safety pins, and misplaced my tape measure. Twice. This is what happens when I don't get any sleep. Theo and I have fought before but not like last night. I feel awful about it. He was right to get upset. I never should've laughed at him or been such a jerk about his date. I don't know why I got so riled up about it. Maybe he and Ginny will spend the summer in a beautiful, hazy rom-com montage. He was also right about Felix. I did watch him walk out of view on Thursday. I even downed three glasses of water before I finally cooled off from that one little kiss on my cheek. What I feel for him has a lot more to do with lust than love at this point, but the potential's there, and I did break pretty much every rule I gave Theo for his first date. It's hardly evidence of indifference.

I take a break shortly before 1:00 p.m., parking myself in front of Blue Dog until Felix emerges. He smiles when he sees me. I finally feel a spark of joy.

"I only have about twenty minutes," I say. "But can I walk you partway home?"

"I'll take whatever minutes you have to spare." He holds out a hand. It's probably sweaty, but I don't care. I take it and let him lead me down the street.

"What are you working on today?" he asks as we edge past a long line outside the local ice cream parlor. The weather's gorgeous. Everyone's clamoring for cones.

"Fittings mostly. This morning was good fun. The bride came in with inspiration pics of a fluffy, organza ball gown that would fill an aisle. Twenty-seven dresses later, she decided on a knee-length satin sheath. This is the world I work in."

"You make stocking canned goods seem like a pretty sweet gig."

"Do canned goods have surly bridesmaids and picky mothers?"

Felix laughs. "Um, no. They generally arrive unaccompanied."

"Then you definitely have the better job."

We chat for another ten minutes or so before I suggest parting ways so I can get back to the shop. A large bridal party is coming in this afternoon, and I know my mom wants me to be there. Felix and I are still at the edge of town, with lots of people around, and he's too self-conscious about being sweaty to give me a hug, but he places a light kiss on my knuckles. It's sweet, like so much else about him, and it makes me think, for the briefest of seconds, that getting attached wouldn't be the worst thing in the world.

♥

Theo's out all weekend at an overnight LARPing event, but I find him on Monday after work, dancing around in his backyard, swishing his blade at Mr. Strawbody. The scarecrow's still wearing the overalls and denim jacket from the hardware store, but Theo added a plumed helmet and a little bull's-eye over his heart.

I stay out of range until Theo spots me. As he lowers his sword, I hold out the tray of treats I prepared.

"Brownies, blondies, biscotti, blueberry biscuits, and banana bread. I'd claim I baked them myself, but you might accuse me of braggadocio." I inch the tray forward.

Theo tucks his blade under his arm and peers over from his current position.

"That's a bountiful banquet of butyraceous *B*'s you're bequeathing me."

"Can I just say I'm sorry and not try to keep with your dictionary brain?"

"I don't know. You've never stormed out on me before."

"Officially I think I stumbled, tripped on a blanket, and wobbled down a ladder."

"Close enough." He wanders over and inspects the goodies while drumming his fingers against his chin. "So you think a few sweets will buy my forgiveness?"

"If it's not enough, I could"—I glance around the yard, seeking inspiration—"make Mr. Strawbody a new outfit. Something less agrarian."

"The overalls suit him, but nice use of *agrarian*."

"I can clean your room."

"I prefer it un-Harper-ized."

I spot a dog-eared book sitting on the picnic table. *The*

Nibelungenlied. It's one of Theo's favorites, full of knights and fair maidens and dragon slaying.

"How about a live reading of *The Noble Lunching Lady?*"

"Pass. You'll mispronounce all the names." He *finally* smiles. The tension I've been holding in my body all weekend starts to dissolve. I inch the tray forward, a hopeful grin plastered on my face. Theo picks out a brownie. Chocolate. Of course. "I was just kidding about remuneration. I accept your treats and your apology." He bites in with gusto, sending crumbs drifting down his T-shirt. "I'll have to hide these. Mom S. is on a diet. Mom O. is attempting to join her in solidarity, at least when Mom S. is looking." He takes the tray from me and carries it over to his picnic table. I warm at the thought of his moms supporting each other through a diet, just like they've supported each other through much harder challenges like fighting prejudices against same-sex parents and raising a kid who's broken seven bones now after fearless attempts to master the high dive or leap onto the back of a galloping horse during summer circus camp. There's so much love in Theo's family. No wonder he's always looking for "the one."

I sit on a bench beside the table. He lays down his sword, sits beside me, and makes the rest of his brownie disappear, brushing off his hands on his ragged shorts.

"Why are we always fighting?" he asks.

"Because we're polar opposites."

"Are we?"

"With your idealism and my cynicism, we're bound to create a little friction." I rest my cheek on his shoulder. It feels like home. Cliché perhaps, but true. "At least we're good at making up."

"How can we not be after so much practice?" He wraps an arm around my waist, scooting close as we wedge ourselves together, already knowing how we best fit. "I'm sorry, too. What you do or want to do with Felix is none of my business. I should've told Lucy that when she came flying across the street to tell me what she saw."

"So . . . if you think about it, our fight was all Lucy's fault."

"Totally. Should we take her down together?"

"You're the one with the swo—épée."

"Nice save." He gives me a little squeeze.

I nestle closer and blow out a sigh I feel like I've been holding in for a lifetime. The last of the daylight's fading, pinking every surface. The street we live on is quiet, leaving only the soft rustle of trees to interrupt our thoughts.

"You were right though," I say. "It's not fair of me to act like an expert if I'm not upholding my end of the bargain."

Theo takes a deep breath, making his shoulder rise and fall under my cheek.

"You really like him, don't you?"

"Yeah. I mean, I think I do." I trace a crease in my palm.

Theo's arm slips away as he releases his hold and rests his hand on the bench behind me. I sit up straight, still studying the fortune lines Felix drew across my palm.

"Can I at least say I told you so?" Theo asks.

"About what?"

"It is possible to fall in love on one date."

"I said I *liked* him. I'm not in love."

"So if he broke up with you tomorrow, you wouldn't care?"

"I'd care, yeah, but I wouldn't go serenading the moon about it."

Theo scoffs. "Only because you can't sing."

"Who says *you* can?" I poke him in the ribs.

He jerks away and wiggles his fingers at me, snapping into mischief mode.

"You sure you want to go there?" he asks.

I leap off the bench and wrap my arms around my rib cage.

"Definitely not." I back away. Theo remains seated. He lowers his tickle fingers, but I maintain my defensive stance. He has a history of sneak attacks, and the glint in his eyes tells me he's at least considering it. The glint also tells me we're okay again, with this crazy friendship that's been strained more times than I can count, but never broken. "Any chance you'll still be my word nerd? Please?"

"If you'll still be my stitch bitch."

"I never should've used that phrase."

"Needlework goddess?"

"Nah. Stick to stitch bitch. It has a ring to it. Let me know what you need mended. I'm on it." I note the frayed hem on his shorts, but I don't mention it aloud. He might make another joke about how I'm trying to get him to take off his clothes. I might not deflect it as easily this time. "What do we do with our other arrangement?"

"You mean the dating lessons? I'm no longer certain your pedagogy's sound, what with the whole knee-buckling make-out plan." He flicks a crumb off the corner of the tray. It flies into the dimming twilight while he moves on to another crumb. His motion's brusque, almost agitated, making me wish I hadn't asked my question.

"I guess we see how things go for a while. If I fall in love, you have full permission to gloat. If you and Ginny don't work out—not that you won't because I'm sure you will—I'm at your service for another lesson."

Theo gusts a humorless laugh through his nose, still flicking at crumbs with increasing force. I get the feeling we've said all we can say tonight and we might be teetering on the verge of another argument, so I tell him I'll catch him again soon. When he doesn't reply, I nudge him with my toe and nod at the tray of goodies.

"It would *behoove* you to not eat all of those at once."

"Don't worry. I'll feed some to the broticoles."

"Do I want to know?"

"Nah. It won't be on the test. Too obscure." He leans back on his elbows, looking up at me from under his tousled black bangs. The way he's curved against the picnic table makes him look oddly deflated. I can't tell if he needs a hug or if he's waiting to be left alone with his fencing partner. Hoping it's the latter, I head off the patio toward my house. I stop halfway across the lawn and look back to see if Theo's moved. He hasn't, unless he sent another crumb flying while my back was turned.

"Hey, Turner?" I call out. "Don't stress. I think this'll be a good week for both of us."

EIGHT

I MEET FELIX IN FRONT OF THE ICE CREAM PARLOR on Tuesday in the hour between my workday ending and his starting. Since he mostly works nights, restocking at the grocery, and I work days (and, okay, lots of nights, too), these little in-between moments feel precious. We instinctively link hands when we exchange greetings, as if we're already settling into patterns without having to tiptoe around what feels right.

"I hope you eat fast," Felix says as he nods at the line that snakes toward the parlor doors. "By the time we finally get our cones, I'll need to run."

"I can eat and walk at the same time if it helps."

Felix shines his gorgeous smile on me. "So many hidden talents."

I stumble through a few steps of heel-toe for him, a preview of the tap dance I've promised to perform later. He laughs and I swear my chest expands to give the sound space to settle. We ease into an exchange of anecdotes from the last few days. He tells me about one of his neighbor's cats getting stuck on a roof. I tell him about the bride who broke her arm and wanted a special sling designed to match her dress. Felix and I have known each other for years, in the way people do in small towns where we end up in the same classes and at the same events, but we haven't talked much before this past week. I'm not sure why. He's so easy to talk to, when I'm not obsessing about his lips and his shoulders and his beautiful rain-cloud-colored eyes.

He takes my hand, palm up, and traces a crease.

"It says here you'll be free for dinner and a movie Friday night."

"Interesting." I watch his thumb spiral across my skin, no longer tracing anything at all. "If it's written in my palm, then I guess it must be true."

He steps toward me, raising my hand in both of his so our tangled fingers rest just below his collarbone. I brave a look in his eyes. Despite the hum of a dozen other conversations around us, the world feels silent and still. I don't know yet how much of my draw to Felix goes beyond physical attraction, but I do know I want more of these moments, and I want to bridge the short distance between us as soon as possible.

"Good night for ice cream," a familiar voice says behind me.

I spin around. Theo stands a few feet away in baggy cargo shorts and an enigmatic T-shirt that says **That's a helmet, not a shaving basin.** He's carrying an old-fashioned picnic basket with a baguette, a red-and-white-checked cloth, and a bouquet of violets poking out. It's so adorably cliché, it's practically a cartoon. Ginny stands beside Theo, adjusting a purse that's strapped across her body. She's really pretty in person, petite with a confident stance and strong arms that look amazing in a bright coral halter dress. I think Theo said she was a swimmer. It shows.

While I assess Theo's date, his eyes go straight to the knot of fingers that bridges the space between Felix's chest and my own. His angular brows inch up as he sneaks me a look that suggests he's caught me at something. Felix and I are only holding hands. It's hardly evidence that we've fallen in love and Theo can commence gloating.

"Hey, Theo." I lower my hand but keep my fingers laced through Felix's. "And you must be Ginny. I'm Harper, and this is Felix."

Ginny says hi while Felix and Theo swap one of those silent greeting nods only guys understand, as if a tip of the chin communicates volumes.

"You're the sword fighter, right?" Felix asks.

Theo's jaw tightens. "I fence. With an épée."

"Theo's very particular about language," I tease.

He flashes me a halfhearted scowl. Felix misses it while nodding appreciatively.

"That's cool," he says. "Bet your English teachers love you."

"Appreciate, sure." Theo shrugs and adjusts his hold on the basket. "I wouldn't ascribe the word *love*. People throw that word around too easily, or so Harper tells me."

"Only because I work in the wedding industry where the word's twisted into a marketing tool." I send Theo a *Shut up* look. I have less than an hour to spend with Felix. It's a beautiful evening. The last thing I need is a philosophical discussion about love.

"How do you guys know each other?" Ginny asks.

"We all go to school together," I say. "Theo and I are next-door neighbors."

"Must be nice to have a friend so close by." Ginny's eyes drift to Felix's and my linked hands before she anchors her own hands on her purse strap. It feels like a preemptive move, making me notice how much space is between her and Theo.

"Gotta admit," Felix says. "I'm a little jealous."

I tense and avoid looking at Theo. "You are?"

"Totally. I live between an empty lot and an old couple with a lot of cats." He gives my hand a squeeze, smiling down at me without any hint of the jealousy I thought he meant. While I try not to feel like an idiot for being anxious about something so baseless, he turns to Theo. "Sorry I misspoke about the sword. It's awesome that you fence. I've seen you practice with the team. You're really good."

Theo glances at Ginny as if checking for her reaction. She smiles but in a polite way. She doesn't ask him anything about his fencing. She just plays with her purse.

"He has a big tournament at the end of August," I offer, hoping to engage her interest. "He's been practicing like crazy. He's going to kick some serious fencing ass."

"That's great," Ginny says, but without much enthusiasm.

"It's the weekend after your big swim meet," Theo says to her, eyes bright and dimple in full view. "Glad they don't conflict so I can come cheer you on. You'll have to let me know your team's colors. I can make a sign like people do at marathons. I'm also a really good yeller. I'll even bring pom-poms if you want. Or paint my face. And I can plan a celebration. How long after a swim until you can eat cake?"

Ginny's smile falters but only for an instant, so I can't tell if I imagined it.

"We should get to the park," she says. "Otherwise we'll never get through seven courses before dark."

We all wave and swap the usual parting words while Theo and Ginny head off. Of course he prepared seven courses, and not just because his moms raised him with a love of cooking. He did it because he's Theo. Go big or go home. I bet his basket also contains candles and poetry books and cupcakes with little hearts all over them.

As he and Ginny walk down the street, he raises a hand toward her lower back. She takes an almost imperceptible step away from him. He fists his hand and lowers it to his side. The interchange might not mean anything at all. Theo and Ginny are only on their second date. She might not be as comfortable with physical contact as I've been with Felix. Theo said she was shy. Yet I can't help but worry that he might have another heartbreak on the horizon. And that he has no idea it's coming.

As Felix and I inch forward in line, his thumb sweeps back and forth over the side of my hand. Yep. I'm definitely comfortable with the physical contact.

"So . . . love's a marketing tool?" he asks, brows lifted with curiosity.

I send a *Thanks a lot* glare after Theo's retreating back.

"I know it sounds harsh," I say. "But I've seen too many temper tantrums and family feuds at my mom's shop to pretend everything's candy hearts and cooing doves."

"My parents are both on their second marriages. They seemed pretty happy at their weddings. I don't remember any tantrums. Or doves." He gives my hand a squeeze, looking down at me with the teasing expression I like so much. I also like that he's taller than I am, which is a stupid thing to care about, but he feels like someone I can anchor to. I've never had that before. I've always been my own center.

"Okay, so very few people rent doves now," I say, "but they often spend gross amounts of money on trivialities. Women's obsession with physical appearance also skyrockets. Territorialism erupts. Old values and new values collide and chafe. People forget they're in love. And don't even get me started on the meaning behind bizarre holdovers like the use of veils and the creepy handoff from father to husband. Women aren't property. Why do we need to get passed from man to man or hide our faces so the groom doesn't bolt before the vows are said?"

"Not sure I can answer that," Felix says through a laugh.

I apologize for my rant as we near the front of the line. Felix swears he doesn't mind. He says he finds me entertaining, which I think he means as a compliment. It's the closest I've ever come to being called fun, so I'll take it. Most people assume I'm a dull, antisocial workaholic. I'm not, really. I just love my mom, and I want to see her business succeed. I hated watching people dismiss her last year when she was debating closing her shop for good.

She made some bad choices, sure, but mostly she trusted people and got really unlucky in whom she trusted. That doesn't mean a woman can't run a business.

Once inside the ice cream shop, I order vanilla with chunks of Snickers, my favorite. Felix orders raspberry-swirl something. We take our cones and head toward the grocery so he can get to work on time, passing by cutesy inns and artisan shops selling handmade pottery and glass yard ornaments. He stops after a few blocks to snap a photo of a book display in an antique shop, hoping to use the image in his next class project. I hold his cone while he gets the shot.

The moment is so simple, without fuss or question, but it reminds me what I liked so much about being in a relationship last summer. Sure, I was a fan of the kissing and the flirting and a few intensely steamy shared showers, but that wasn't what crushed me most about the breakup. It was the loss of the little exchanges, the ones that made me feel thought of and cared for and not alone, like when Liam would grab an extra fork for me at the cafeteria or I'd offer him a useful lyric when he was stuck with his songwriting. Like holding Felix's cone while he takes a photo, knowing, without having to say the words, that if I need him to hold something for me, he'll do it.

We reach the grocery all too soon, exchanging a quick good-bye hug near the staff entrance, once again parting where too many people are milling around to make either of us comfortable with much public affection.

"So, Friday?" Felix asks.

"Definitely." A flutter of anticipation erupts in my chest. It's so violent, I swear a thousand butterflies recently nested in there.

Felix backs away from me, hands in his pockets, smiling the smile I sought for months from across the street. The one I think about when I'm sewing, or brushing my teeth, or doing pretty much anything that doesn't occupy a hundred percent of my attention. I already feel a sense of loss at our parting, but I take consolation in the near certainty that our next date will finally involve kissing.

NINE

MY DINNER DATE WITH FELIX IS LOOKING LESS likely by the minute. It's Friday evening. I'm at Beneath the Veil, helping with the latest crisis. Today's drama: a bride's in-laws have asked/demanded that one more be added to the wedding party. This might not be a big issue, but the wedding's next weekend and the matching bridesmaid dresses were custom built. We can't overnight another by mail and bang out the alterations. The bride refuses to let anyone stand up with her if they don't match *perfectly*. She has no intention of sacrificing the carefully planned unity of her choices to appease some needy tween girl she barely knows. Members of both families are in, discussing the possibilities. Tensions are running high. The bride tries with increasing frustration to indicate that this is her wedding and everyone should respect that. Her mother-in-law-to-be insists that Cousin Cathy be part of the event, as a small concession toward the importance of family. The bride's mother plays intermediary. Poorly. The bridesmaids get involved. The in-laws get feisty. Cousin Cathy sits in silence with her eyes glued to her phone while everyone talks about her as though she isn't right there, listening to every word.

Eventually my mom offers to build another dress. Her offer effectively shuts down the bickering and we'll get a good fee for the rush order, but we don't have time to build a dress, not without canceling other commitments. The whole situation sets my teeth on edge. It's a stark reminder of how quickly love can get buried under the need for a perfect photo. Cathy could toss a few rose petals into an aisle while wearing the rainbow leggings she has on today and no one but the bride would care. This is what weddings do to people. They turn otherwise kind souls into myopic me-pleasers. And they make me postpone imminent kisses with New Hope's hottest fake palm reader.

The party finally heads out, with an appointment to return for Cathy's fitting on Monday. We only have one more client for the day. The woman wants to look through samples with no rush for an impending wedding date and no bridal party present. Pippa and my mom cover the appointment while I head into the back room.

Harper: *Can't make it tonight. Mom overcommitted us both. Need to stay and sew*

Felix: *Noooooooooooo!*

Harper: *Rain check?*

Felix: *No rain*

Harper: *Beautiful night for a date check?*

Felix: *Of course. We'll find another time. You ok?*

Harper: *Irritated. Disappointed. Kinda want to wring my mom's neck, but in a loving, I-know-you-mean-well-and-this-is-why-you-need-a-manager way. Otherwise ok*

Felix: *When will you wrap up?*

Harper: *Don't know. Whenever I stop seeing straight*

Felix: *Anything I can do to help?*

I type *Miss me* but delete it without sending. It's too much and it feels narcissistic, even though I do want to be miss-able at least once in my life. Liam said a long-distance relationship was pointless, even though "long distance" would've only been an hour's drive for either of us. He didn't even have a chance to miss me. I hate that I'm thinking about him right now while Felix's question mark blinks on my screen. Maybe I *should* pie Liam. I need to do something besides periodically revisit every hurtful word he ever said. Why do those last so much longer than the nice ones?

Harper: *Just promise me you don't take my bailing personally*

Felix: *I've read your palm. Our date will happen*

Harper: *Can't wait*

Felix sends back a smiley face emoji. It's cute and it plants a real smile on my face. I take a moment to appreciate the lack of resentment in our exchange. My friends have given me plenty of crap for bailing on social events over the past year, not in a mean way, but I can imagine it got frustrating when I rarely prioritized time with them over work. Maybe Theo's right. Felix is perfect, but if so, what the hell is he doing with me?

I shove aside that question and unroll what's left of the pale blue silk crepe my mom and I used for the bridesmaid dresses. I spend ages laying out my mom's pattern, but no matter how I arrange the pieces, we don't have enough fabric, not unless we make Cathy's dress two inches shorter than the others. If she wears flats, maybe the bride won't notice the discrepancy. Scratch that. She'll totally notice, but by then she'll be about to say *I do* and hopefully she'll stop caring about things like hemlines.

I'm still pinning the pattern for maximum fabric usage when Pippa sweeps into the room. She's wearing a vibrant green wig with blunt bangs and two pigtails at the nape of her neck. It looks awesome with her freckles, so awesome I question my boring brown ponytail, not enough to take it down and definitely not enough to dye it, but enough to wonder if I should get a more interesting haircut. After all, someone might actually notice my hair now. While I try to stop thinking about that someone, Pippa gallops over to my side, her eyes alight like a kid about to blow out her birthday candles.

"Your boyfriend's here," she says.

"He's not my—"

"Whatever. He's here. He's gorgeous. I told him I'd come get you." She tugs on my sleeve, drawing me away from the cutting table and into the main room.

Felix is standing by the front desk. He's in slim gray trousers and a plum-colored shirt that fits his body almost as snugly as his navy V-neck did last weekend. I don't know how he learned to dress so well—especially for a guy who spends most of his time in athletic gear—but I'm happy to reap the benefits. He waves when he spots me. I wave back. My mom's still talking to her client on the other side of the room, but she catches my eye long enough to raise a curious brow. I'm not sure how I feel about her knowing that I'm dating someone. Not great, I guess. Meeting the parents seems like a big step. It's too soon, like Pippa tossing around the word *boyfriend*, or Theo doing the same with *love*. Anxiety creeps up my spine. I'm trying so hard to take this whole dating idea one day at a time, to keep the stakes low, but everyone around me keeps raising them.

Pippa sets her hand on the flat of my back and gives me a nudge, propelling me toward Felix. I try to ignore my audience as I join him by the front desk, stopping a few feet away as seems only professional since a client's present. Also: the parent thing.

"Hi." I flash him another wave.

"Hi." He nods at the cardboard cup holder that's sitting on the desk. It holds three cups, just like the last time he brought us coffee, though this time the cups have writing on them. He points out each one in turn. "One plain black, one chai latte, one no-foam latte with three-quarters almond milk, one-quarter two percent, plus the tiniest squirt of vanilla syrup, a pinch of cinnamon, and half a teaspoon of cocoa."

My anxiety evaporates as my hand flies to my fluttering heart.

"Oh my god. How did you know?"

"You told me last week."

"But how did you remember?"

"Simple. I listened." He smiles down at me in a sweetly shy way that makes me want to kiss him by a fireplace or in a gazebo, as though his smile invokes every buried memory of every cheesy rom-com Theo has made me watch over the last few years. Since we're nowhere near a fireplace or a gazebo, I keep my arms to myself.

"Thanks. You're my hero." I pop the lid off the cup labeled with my name. Coffee-scented steam swirls around my face, tinged with all of my favorite notes. I breathe it in. Total heaven. "Can I pay you for these?"

"Not a chance. Just enjoy, and keep that hero idea fresh in your mind." He looks past my shoulder. I follow his gaze. My mom is sneaking a glance at us while her client looks through a rack of sample dresses. Pippa fake-adjusts magazines on the glass coffee table. Felix leans toward me and adopts a conspiratorial tone. "I think we're being watched."

"We are *definitely* being watched. Questions will ensue."

"Sorry about that. Hope it's okay that I came by. Seemed like the least I could do if you have to work all night."

"It's great. Thanks, but do you mind if I do introductions another time? My mom's still with a client and Pippa might never let you leave."

He chuckles a little, and I swear I could never, ever get tired of his smile.

"No problem," he says. "I know you guys are busy. I don't want to intrude."

I return my coffee cup to the holder. Felix steals a caress of my pinkie finger with his, tucked out of sight amid the cups. I respond in kind, letting my fingertips brush his, whisper-soft but electric. Already my pulse quickens and tiny ripples of pleasure gallop across my skin. Good lord, if Felix and I ever get a chance to touch each other without restraint, I'm going to detonate in three seconds flat.

"Think you'll be free later this week?" he asks.

"Definitely. I'll text tomorrow and we can figure out a time."

With another minute of stolen caresses that send heat rushing through my bloodstream, we say goodbye and Felix heads out. The bells on the door are still jingling when Pippa jogs over. She inspects the paper cups and whisks hers from the holder.

"I can't believe you made out with him and didn't tell me."

"I didn't make out with him. Not yet. So far we've only talked and held hands."

"Wow." Pippa cranes past me as if she's searching for Felix through the glass doors. "If all that eye sex was the result of conversation, I should do a lot more talking."

My face flames so hard, I swear my hairline's on fire.

"Can you *not* say 'eye sex' with my mom in the room?"

As if on cue, my mom escorts her client over. Pippa helps the woman make a fitting appointment while my mom spots the coffee cup labeled Ms. J. She notes the *Ms.* with an appreciative nod. Most people default to *Mrs.* and she hates that. I told Felix as much on Tuesday. Amazing. He really does listen. As if I needed another reason to like him.

"Anything you want to tell me?" my mom asks once her client's gone.

"Maybe. Eventually. It all falls under TBD for now."

"Okay." She removes the lid on her coffee, inhaling deeply. "For what it's worth, he's cute, he brought us coffee, and he obviously likes you. He's got my vote."

"Thanks, I think?" I brace myself for further inquiry, but my mom excuses herself to go take a nap on the sofa in the back room, preparing for an all-nighter. I'll get the dress cut and prepped for her, then wake her to take over. But first: coffee.

"Your mom is so chill," Pippa says when we're alone. "Mine would've launched a full interrogation. *Who is he? How did you meet? How long have you been dating? Where did you go? When? For how long? How are his grades? Does he have a job? When can we have him over for dinner so we can get to know him better?*"

I wander to the seating area and stretch out on the sofa, coffee in hand.

"I guess she understands I'm not ready to talk about him. Or she trusts me to make my own decisions. Or maybe . . ." I search for the reason something feels off.

Pippa sinks into an armchair and tucks a leg up against her chest. She's in wide-legged linen overalls and a sleeveless chiffon blouse today, all black, of course, with lots of chunky jewelry. She looks like she could go straight from work to a club. She often does, brilliantly walking the line between looking professional and looking cool.

"Maybe what?" she prompts.

"Maybe my mom and I have spent so much time *not* talking about guys, neither of us knows how to do it. Like we've waited too long and now the subject feels taboo."

Pippa frowns over her chai. "Your mom never talked to you about sex?"

"Oh, we've had the sex talk and the birth control talk. As someone who got knocked up on a one-night stand, my mom has those subjects well covered. She took me condom shopping when I was fifteen. She wanted to make sure I wouldn't be nervous if I ever needed to buy them on my own. She also had me meet her gynecologist so I'd feel comfortable talking to a doctor about birth control and STDs."

"Wow. Right. So what's missing from the equation?"

"Relationships. Dating. The non-technical stuff." I blow on my coffee, filtering memories. "I haven't had much reason to talk about any of that. My crushes all came and went so quickly, there was no point. Except for Liam, of course. You know how that went. I didn't even think to tell her while it was all happening. Liam and I were off in our little bubble, away from the speculation of everyone we knew. By the time I got home, what was I supposed to say? *Hey, Mom, while I was away at math camp, I got super horny, lost my virginity to a guy who said he loved me but didn't mean it, and now I feel like a total idiot but also really confused because I think I might've slept with him anyway, even if he'd admitted up front that he only wanted a fling?* My mom doesn't have relationships. She's an unlikely resource for advice."

Pippa rests her freckled chin on her knee. "She might surprise you."

"She might." I peer toward the back room, picturing my mom curled up on the canvas sofa in her tailored black trousers and cashmere sweater, her hair in its tidy twist, her jewelry minimal, her makeup flawless, so unlike the few photos I've seen of her at my age. "But if I tell her about Felix, the first guy I've ever mentioned, and Felix and I don't make it past a few dates, I'll feel like I took that leap for nothing. Worse than nothing. I'll have to admit the relationship failed. That *I* failed. That I wasn't fun enough, hot enough, nice enough, smart enough, interesting enough, or good enough. Feeling that was hard last summer. It's still hard. And it'll be even harder if it becomes a pattern. Telling my mom about my relationship failures would only amplify the pain."

Pippa wilts into the chair, giving me a look so filled with pity, she might be watching one of those sad pet adoption videos.

"You're still predicting disaster?" she asks.

"I'm still preparing for it. Just in case."

"Just in case, huh?" She shakes her head at me, her disapproval palpable.

I don't answer. I've lost all sense of how much to protect myself and how much to open up to the possibility of more hurt, and to embarrassing explanations of how I didn't make good choices, contain my impulses, or read a situation right. So I sip a perfectly flavored latte from a perfectly wonderful boy and dream of the day I'll just know.

TEN

TWO HOURS AFTER FELIX'S DEPARTURE, CATHY'S dress pieces are cut out, marked, and ready for my mom to sew. I'm about to wake her when I realize Pippa should've finished cleaning and headed home over an hour ago. Surely she wouldn't leave without saying good night.

I take out my earbuds, leave my mom sleeping on the sofa, and head into the main room. Pippa's perched on one of the baroque sofas in the central seating area. She's not alone. Theo's parked on a chair with his épée and a familiar bottle of glass cleaner I suspect hasn't been used yet. He's rattling on about a move he learned in fencing practice today. By the way Pippa's leaning her head in her hand and batting her eyelashes, she's more than a little interested.

"What are you doing here?" I ask as I join them.

Theo leaps to his feet. Pippa merely smiles, pivoting my way with her head still firmly planted on her hand and the dreamiest of looks on her face.

"I brought your next list." Theo holds out a folded wad of papers.

I take it from him and scan the first words: *cacophonous, cadaverous, calumny.*

"Thanks, but you could've emailed this," I tell him.

"I know, but I was looking for an excuse to stop by."

For a second I'm flattered, assuming he means he wanted to see me. Then I glance at Pippa, who's still mooning up at him.

"Do you guys know each other?" I ask.

"We do now," Pippa says. "We met about an hour ago when he knocked on the door and asked to see you. You told me not to disturb you until you finished your work"—she sneaks me a wink—"so I kept him busy until you were ready to emerge." She fans her face while Theo's not looking. I glance back and forth between the two of them, thoroughly confused. They've been chatting for an *hour?* Without coming to get me?

"If the list is only an excuse, why are you really here?" I ask Theo.

He pinches the sides of his plaid shirtfront and spreads them apart, revealing a distinct lack of buttons over his bare chest and belly. Only three buttons remain, two near his neck and one just below his belly button.

"What did you do?" I ask. "Enter a Clark Kent contest?"

Theo lets his shirt fall back into place and smooths out the overlap.

"I don't know what happened," he says. "One of the guys pointed it out when we were leaving practice. I figured you'd be here, and since you're my—"

"Yeah, yeah. Hand it over." I flap a hand at him. "Did you

bring the buttons or are they back in the phone booth with your red cape and *S* logo?"

Theo twists a black curl over his forehead, drawing a laugh from Pippa and me.

"Phone booth," he says. "But you have something here that'll work, right?"

"I'm sure I can find a few that fit. I should use bright pink ones as a penalty for occupying so much of Pippa's valuable time."

She scoots forward in her chair. "I'm not bothered."

"Great. Then you can entertain him for a few more minutes while I fix his shirt."

"Sure thing, though I suspect he'll do most of the entertaining." She waggles her eyebrows and wraps a green pigtail around her index finger.

Theo doesn't appear to pick up on her flirty demeanor, which is odd for a guy who walks through the world looking for girls to fall in love with. Maybe he really is in love with Ginny, or maybe his lack of awareness about girls works both ways. If he can't tell when they're *not* interested, he also can't tell when they *are* interested.

While I wait with an outstretched hand, Theo strips off his shirt, leaving him bare-chested in his jeans and *Sword in the Stone* belt. I don't mean to look, but I can't help myself. My eyes travel from his neck to his waistband. When did Theo get abs? And how many dictionaries did he have to bench press to get those biceps? He's lean and wiry, but he's been packing some serious muscle tone under his flannels and D&D shirts. He also has a little streak of black hair running from his belly button into his jeans. Last time I saw him shirtless, we were skipping through sprinklers, though I guess I didn't have boobs back then, so I shouldn't be so surprised he's grown up, too. Still . . .

"Want to borrow something to wear?" I ask, ignoring Pippa's sly but adamant headshake. "We have some lovely options in satin or taffeta." I pass a hand over the nearest rack of gowns. "A mermaid cut, perhaps? Or something simpler in bias?"

"I'm all right." He flops down on the ornate sofa and stretches an arm across the back. Bare-chested against deep green velvet and gilded scrollwork, he looks like a fashion model, even in his ill-fitted jeans and geeky belt. "It's warm in here, and you said it would only take a few minutes."

"Okay?" I stare at him for a moment, trying to assess if he's kidding. No normal seventeen-year-old guy hangs out shirtless in the middle of a store with a girl he's only known for an hour, with zero self-consciousness. Then again, Theo is not a normal guy. I cast one last look at Pippa. She shoos me toward the back room, mouthing, "Take your time," while Theo's not looking. This whole situation is so weird, but I might as well leave them to whatever it is they've been doing while I pay for my vocab list with a little sewing.

I find a bag of shirt buttons among the drawers of trims and notions that line half the wall space in the back room. I consider waking my mom, but her presence might make the situation even weirder. Adding the shirt buttons really does only take a few minutes, though I stick around to secure the original buttons as well. No point getting this shirt back in a week when Theo super-heroes his way out of it again.

Pippa's laughter reaches me as I'm knotting the final thread. I clip off the knot and peek into the other room from the doorway, shirt in hand. Pippa's still seated in the middle of the room, following Theo with her eyes. He's flying around the room with his épée, demonstrating a series of flourishes. He moves like a dancer, swift and agile. His balance is impeccable. Every turn is perfectly timed. Every jab is precisely aimed, and of course he's fit. He's an athlete, even if I've never thought of him that way. Until now.

He lands a lunge with his back to me, holding the position. The light shifts across his rippling back muscles as a bead of sweat trickles down his spine, pausing its journey between the dimples just above his waistband. Pippa applauds from the sofa in front of him. She stops when her eyes catch mine.

"Oops! Missed a button!" I spin away before she notices the blush that's rushing to my cheeks. Goddammit! Was I seriously ogling Theo's body? Theo?! This is why I avoid dating. My life was perfectly fine. Then I open myself up to the mere idea of being with a guy again, and all the walls I've put up crumble. I'm only lusting after Theo because I'm not out with the guy I really want to be with, the one who's easy to be with and perfect for me. This is my mom's fault. I shouldn't be here making stupid bridesmaid dresses or sewing stupid buttons for stupid boys who flounce around stores demonstrating their flashy fencing moves for moony-eyed girls in wigs. I should be standing in a garlanded gazebo, kissing Felix.

I check my reflection in the restroom mirror, ensuring all signs of my blush have faded. Then I head into the main room and toss Theo's shirt at him.

"All done," I say with exaggerated cheer. "Told you it wouldn't take long."

"Sure didn't." Pippa offers me a pert frown.

Theo lays his sword on the coffee table and puts on his shirt.

"So how did things go with Ginny?" I ask. I hope I'm not being a total jerk in front of Pippa, but I do want to know. "Did you guys get through all seven courses?"

"Yeah," Theo says, his focus locked on the buttons he's fastening. "Though we probably should've stopped at five."

"Are you going out again?"

Pippa's frown deepens. I flash her an apologetic smile. Theo slings his backpack over his shoulder, nursing a frown of his own.

"It's hard to find a time," he says. "She's busy most weekdays, and I'm out at the battlefield on weekends. But I'll keep trying until we sort it out." His gaze lowers and I can tell there's more to the story, but I'm not about to prod in front of Pippa.

She hands him his sword, holding it out in both palms. "Ginny's a lucky girl."

Theo responds with a light shrug as he takes the sword, his expression unreadable. I can't tell if he's flattered, embarrassed, ambivalent, or missing Pippa's compliment completely because he's still thinking about Ginny.

"Thanks," he says, before turning to me. "And thanks for the buttons."

"Least I could do." I sweep his vocab list off the table and hold it up.

"Enjoy the C's. I'll take my cacidrosis and my celsitude and bid you both good night." He bows low, sweeping his arm to the side as though he's whisking a plumed hat from his head. It's ridiculous. And adorable. And *so* Theo.

Pippa sees him out and locks the door behind him.

"Do you have any idea what he meant?" she asks as she spins toward me.

"None whatsoever, but maybe I will once I study his list."

I grab the glass cleaner and start on the picture window. Pippa finds a second rag in the supply cabinet and joins me.

"So he's dating someone new now?" she asks.

"I guess so. It was meant to be a practice date, but he seems really into her. I saw them together on Tuesday, but I couldn't get a good read on whether she was into him."

"Hmm."

"Yeah. Hmm."

Pippa and I pause our cleaning and look out the window together. A flickering streetlamp casts its light on the cherry trees that flank the street. A couple passes by, hand in hand. Another points at something in the chocolate shop window across the street. A light summer rain is misting, casting everything in soft focus. Normally I make fun of about how ridiculously picturesque this town is, carefully groomed for romantic getaways and busy cameras. Tonight the scene seems strangely beautiful. Maybe I'm tired. Maybe I'm confused. Maybe Theo's rubbing off on me.

Pippa wraps an arm around my waist and tips her head onto my shoulder.

"Can I ask you a favor?"

"Name it and it's yours."

"If things don't work out with Seven Courses Girl, and Theo wants another practice date, sign me up. And tell him to bring the sword."

ELEVEN

I WAKE UP SATURDAY MORNING TO THE SOUND OF my mom coming home from work. She's making toast by the time I haul myself out of bed and meet her in the kitchen. She leans against the counter while I slump against the doorframe, both of us rubbing our eyes.

"Did you finish the dress?" I ask.

"It's in one piece." She yawns into a fist, long and slow like a languid cat. "I got a couple of today's appointments moved. I'll power through the others. Then put in the zipper and make sure everything's ready for Monday's fitting. With only two appointments tomorrow, we'll still have time to focus on taxes."

"Okay," I say, too tired to muster a stronger response. I've tried for years to get my mom to close the shop one or two days a week. I've talked her down to a shortened schedule on Sundays, but I haven't been persuasive enough to gain more ground, not while she's still paying off debt. I was going to stay home today and finish my spreadsheets so we could go over everything together tomorrow, but . . .

"I can pause the finances and get the dress done today if you like."

"No. Finish up here and take the evening off. Spend some time with friends and . . . anyone else you want to see." She smiles at me with weary eyes. Her sleek, dark hair is falling out of its twist. Bits of pale blue fuzz cling to her black sweater set and wool trousers. She picks a few off and flicks them into the sink. My mom has always been impeccably stylish, even though she spends hours sitting at a sewing machine where no one can see her. I've never been able to reconcile her poise and polish with the party girl she says she used to be. And while she's never voiced any regret about having me, sometimes I wonder if she wonders. Who would she be now if she made a different decision eighteen years ago? What changes a person? Family? Career? School? Friends? Love? The books we read and the music we listen to? How do I make the right choices now so I become the person I want to be, even if I'm not sure yet who that person is?

My mom and I chat about much lighter topics while she eats her toast and I gulp back coffee. We laugh about yesterday's dress drama, and I tell her how Pippa developed a crush on Theo last night. I expect her to laugh. She doesn't. She just says *hmm* and sets her dirty dishes in the sink. Her reaction surprises me, but I remind myself how tired she is. She'll see the humor in the situation later. Theo's flashy swordplay demonstration. Pippa's over-the-top swooning. It's funny. Or maybe it's not. Maybe Theo and Pippa were just being themselves, and I'm acting like a jerk again.

I finish up with the taxes at around 4:30 p.m. As I grab a soda in the kitchen, I take out my phone to text Felix. He has relatives in town all weekend so I know we can't revisit the dinner and a movie plan, but maybe we can sneak in a quick meet-up. Before I even open my phone, I see movement out the window. Theo's jogging across his yard from the tree to the back door. Weird. I thought he was out LARPing all weekend. If he's home, maybe he'll give me a more detailed update about what's going on with Ginny, sharing whatever he didn't want to say in front of Pippa.

Harper: *Are you home this weekend? Want to come over?*

The ellipsis appears but no message comes back. I try again.

Harper: *I can make dinner. Casserole. Cannelloni. Chicken cacciatore*
Harper: *And yes, I know how to make them*
Harper: *Five minutes in the microwave, like everything else*

The ellipsis appears again. I wait for Theo to at least send a wry *ha-ha* or an eye roll emoji. Instead, my screen goes blank. I could leave well enough alone, but I'm stuck on the image of Theo trying to rest his hand on Ginny's back and her inching away. Also, his evasiveness last night about their next date. Maybe I'm reading too much into small observations, but just in case, I slip on my flip-flops and head to his place.

Olivia answers the door, enveloping me in one of her usual hugs, the kind that squeezes the air from my lungs in the best possible way. She's short and corpulent (one of my new vocab words) with tan skin and a mass of black hair she wears loosely piled on her head. Theo looks so much like her, sometimes I can hardly believe he wasn't an immaculate conception. Like me, he has a genetic father he doesn't live with. Where mine is a drummer with a forgettable monosyllabic name, Theo's is a donor named Peter Olsson. He's a good friend of Olivia and Shay. He lives in Florida now and visits once a year. They all get along really well, which I've always envied. I have one great parent, but Theo has three. Even sweeter, back when his parents were debating last names for Theo, they decided to skip the hyphenates and go with Turner since he was a turning point in all of their lives. The choice makes me wish my mom had given the matter as much thought, though I suppose Harper Jamison rolls off the tongue more easily than Harper Ormaybehisnamewasken.

"So long since we've seen you, Harper," Olivia says with a distinct roll of her *R*'s. She ushers me to the base of the stairs. "Theodoro!" she hollers up. "Harper's here. Come down and invite her to join us for dinner."

While we wait, Shay pops her head into the foyer from the kitchen, drying her hands on a dishtowel. She also has black hair, but where Olivia's is smooth, Shay's is wiry and already graying at the temples. She's taller than Olivia and her skin is fair, with ruddy cheeks and a light speckling of freckles high on her cheekbones.

"Oh, good. You're staying for dinner," she says as though this was clearly established. "I'm making my grandmother's dolmathes, and I should've halved the recipe. We have enough to feed the whole block."

Olivia hollers for Theo again. I inhale the peppery scent of home cooking, already salivating over the dinner I've been offered. No one cooks in my house, unless I count toast or frozen pizza. Theo's home life is the opposite of mine, as is his house. My mom's not big on decorating. Her effort goes into the store. Our house is comfortable, but we don't have much beyond the necessities. Theo's house is full of stuff, with paintings and textiles that mingle his Puerto Rican, Greek, and Swedish heritage. It's colorful and full of life. As a professional carpenter, Shay also built some of the furniture, adding another personal touch. The only homemade thing in my house is a set of gray curtains I sewed for the living room when we couldn't find anything that fit our old windows. In hindsight, we should've at least picked out a color.

When Theo fails to make an appearance, his moms send me to his room, warning me to knock before entering. I do knock. No one answers, so I crack the door and peek in. Theo's curled up on his bed, facing the opposite wall, wearing his giant headphones.

I open the door a little wider. "Theo?"

He flaps a hand at me without turning around. "Go away. I can't hear you."

"You sure about that?"

"Yes."

I stifle a laugh. Then I shut the door and make my way across the room, skirting the books, metalworking tools, and dirty laundry scattered across the floor. By the time I reach the bed, I realize Theo's shoulders are juddering. I climb onto his bed and curl myself around him. Without pause, he takes my hand and draws my arm tight against his chest. We lie like that for several minutes while his sniffles grow softer and further apart.

"You're not on the battlefield this weekend," I say.

"No. I'm not." He removes his headphones as he rolls over to face me. His cheeks are tear-stained. His nose is red. Bits of crust nestle in his long, dark lashes.

"What happened?" I ask.

He takes his phone from his back pocket, opens his screen, and hands it to me. I read through a series of texts from the last few days. Theo asks Ginny out again. She responds evasively about a prior commitment. He tries again. She says *Maybe another time.* He sends a *lot* of messages. They're sweet and not overtly demanding but, boy, do they accumulate. They include links to articles Ginny might like about swimming or flutes. He makes plans for bike rides, pulls up movie times, asks her if she wants to attend a reading from an author passing through town. He tells her over and over how much he enjoyed their picnic or how thrilled he was to meet someone so smart and beautiful and, and, and . . . Ginny gets terser with each reply, yet nothing dissuades him. Back and forth they go until I reach the final text from today.

It's from Ginny. She says she has a lot going on in her life right now. She's sorry but she doesn't really have time to date. She hopes he enjoys the rest of his summer. Her message is clear. She's blowing him off.

"She's still on the site, so she has time for *someone*," Theo says as I set his phone on the nightstand. "If she didn't want to date me, why didn't she just say so?"

"Because she was trying to be nice?" My voice pitches upward. I squirm atop the blankets, worried I'm going to make matters worse by defending the girl who hurt him. "Telling someone you don't like them is hard."

"So is pursuing someone who doesn't like you, but she won't say she doesn't like you, so you spend all week telling yourself you need to find the right way to impress her, flatter her, or make her laugh until you find out it's all bullshit and you've squandered hours of anticipation and curiosity on someone who thinks you're a waste of her time." Theo flops onto his back, gusting a sigh toward the ceiling.

"Were there no clues on your date?" I ask as gently as possible.

Theo rolls his head toward me as his brows pinch together. "If there were clues, would I be soaking my pillow over her? Would I have written her poems? Sourced a bike for her on Craigslist? Read that stupid wizard book again?"

"I don't know. Maybe?" My heart goes out to him. He's obviously miserable, but how could he not see this coming by now? He's been through it a dozen times.

He tangles both fists in his hair, his signature full-angst move.

"I suppose this means it's time for another lesson," he mutters.

"It can be. If you want." I try to gauge his interest in the prospect, but I suspect he'd look unhappy about pretty much anything right now, even puppies or really good chocolate. "We could set you up on another date. This time I'll watch and take note of what you're missing. Give you the signs to look out for so you don't squander all those hours again. So the next time you write a poem, it's for a girl who really wants it."

He gives me his best side-eye. Even at his most disgruntled, it holds only the tiniest hint of malice. The rest is the dignified low buzz of mustered tolerance.

"Your intentions are noble," he says. "Your methods are questionable."

"More questionable than getting your heart broken every other week?"

"No need to rub in the obvious, Jamison, but I get your point."

With a groan of reluctance, Theo sits up and joins me in scanning his matches on Toast. I briefly consider mentioning Pippa, but she's not going to help Theo learn how to read signs of a girl's disinterest. This next date is purely instructional. If he still wants to put himself out there afterward, I'll let him know Pippa's interested. Sword and all.

After almost an hour of debating Theo's options, he sends a friendly opener to Izzy, a girl with blond corkscrew curls who mentions her dogs a lot. She's one of the three girls Theo initially wrote to when we set up his profile. She responds right away. They text back and forth until it seems like there's enough of a connection to warrant a meet-up. I suggest Gadzooks. Theo sends the message, asking if she'll meet him later tonight. I worry it's too soon, but Izzy responds, *Looking forward to it.*

♥

Gadzooks is busy for a Saturday night, but after a short wait I get a spot at a small table by the windows. Theo and Izzy are on the opposite side of the room, past a group of chatty women and a bunch of people on laptops. It's perfect. I have a decent but not too obvious view of my research subject. I open the paperback I brought and wedge my phone into the pages. While Theo and Izzy chat, I take notes. Lots of notes.

Despite being only a few hours out of his most recent heartbreak, and despite my advice on the way here, Theo does nothing to temper his usual eagerness. He leans into the table, gesticulates with enthusiasm, and rarely breaks eye contact. He also acts something out with his silverware. Izzy smiles and nods for a while, engaging in the conversation, but her demeanor rapidly progresses into one of polite boredom. She dips a fingertip into her tea every few minutes. Once she appears to have deemed it drinkable, she downs it in about three gulps. She also fidgets with her hair and mug, gazes around the room, and checks her phone with increasing regularity. By the time almost an hour has passed, her nods and smiles have become practically robotic.

Soon enough, Izzy heads to the restroom. While she's gone, Theo catches my eye and shoots me a hopeful grin. I respond with a pained shake of my head. He slouches into his chair and nudges his mug toward the center of his table, fussing with the handle until Izzy returns. Within less than a minute, her phone buzzes. She says something to Theo, checks her phone, and reaches for the purse that's slung over the back of her chair. He starts to stand with her, but she shakes her head and points over her shoulder toward the exit. I can't hear their conversation, but the body language is clear. It becomes even clearer when she flashes him a brisk wave and practically runs for the door. I wait a minute to make sure she's not coming back. Then I head over to Theo's table.

"Come on." I hold out a hand. "Let's take a walk."

He frowns at my offered hand, but after a moment's hesitation, he slaps his hand into mine and lets me haul him to his feet.

"I liked her," he moans. "She has four dogs."

"Yeah, and they'll get a lot more love from her than you will."

Theo's frown deepens as his eyes catch on my paperback.

"What in the hell are you reading?"

"I'm not reading it. I'm using it for subterfuge. I got it from that Little Free Library near the school. I brought it in case you needed a laugh." I hold up the book. The title sweeps and swirls across the cover, embossed in gold: *The Rogue's Latest Mistress.* A beefy guy in an open, billowing shirt embraces a woman who can't keep her dress on. Theo smiles a little. Mission accomplished.

I drag him out of the shop and onto Main Street. A light rain is misting, but it feels good against the midsummer heat. Theo agrees, noting that the rain also mirrors his mood. He says it's the best kind of weather. It means the universe is listening, reassuring him it's okay to feel whatever he's feeling. Tears can fall. Sunshine can wait.

As we walk past a row of picturesque storefronts, I read my notes, starting with Izzy's tendency to keep her hands off the table and her elbows locked to her side, and ending with the fake text she set up to provide her an excuse to leave.

Theo balks. "How do you know that text was fake?"

"It's by the book, Turner. She holds out for an hour so she doesn't feel like she's insulting you. She goes to the restroom just long enough to tell her friend to text. When she returns to the table, she keeps her purse in hand, ready to bolt."

Theo loops an arm through my elbow and slows his already-sluggish trudging.

"That bad, huh?"

"She wasn't the girl for you. That's all."

He halts us, midstep. "Then who is?"

I slip my arm free so I can face him. The mist collects in his lashes like tiny crystals, but they don't sparkle brightly enough to combat the sadness in his eyes.

"My coworker likes you."

He scratches at the back of his neck and looks off toward the river.

"I can't date her. You guys are obviously close. It could get awkward fast."

"Even if it works out?"

"Especially if it works out."

"That doesn't make any sense."

"I just . . . I have my reasons, okay?"

"Okay." I watch the rain slide down the black waves that tip over his ears, fighting an instinct to tuck his hair off his face. I don't understand his reticence about Pippa, but I'm kind of relieved. It's easy for me to take Theo's side against all the girls who've stolen pieces of his beautiful heart, but I'll never hate Pippa. Also . . .

I shake off the thought. If Pippa and Theo wanted to make out where I could see them, I'd figure out how to deal with it. Then I'd figure out why that was even a problem for me, a question that's not worth exploring when it's all hypothetical anyway.

"You'll find your soulmate," I tell him. "You just have to be patient until you meet the right girl. And you won't have to flatter or impress her. She'll like you as you are." I offer him an encouraging smile, but he continues to slump before me, looking forlorn, with the rain glistening on his hair and moistening his cheeks. I catch a drop before it falls from his bangs. He sweeps a drop from the tip of my nose in exchange. Another forms in its place. This time it falls before Theo can stop it.

"I'm not sure I believe that anymore," he says.

"Oh, Theo." I brush the rain from his cheek the same way I've wiped away his tears so many times before. I want to reassure him how wonderful he is, and to tell him he's the most important person in my life after my mom, but these aren't the kinds of things I say. The words feel too big to be spoken, maybe because saying them feels like a risk, an opportunity for misinterpretation. Maybe because some words can only be felt.

The silence between us stretches on too long. Theo blinks at me through rain-speckled lashes. I rest my hands by my sides so I stop touching his face. I sense that I should say *something*, but I don't know what, so I don't say anything at all. Instead, I link my arm through his and guide our feet toward the bridge that spans the Delaware River.

We walk in relative silence, skirting shallow puddles and stopping partway across the bridge. Theo plants his forearms on the upper rail and stares off toward the far bank. A few cars pass behind us, but traffic's light at this time of night, leaving us to the quiet of our thoughts and the softly falling rain.

"Okay. I get it." Theo kicks at the railing. "You're right. Lesson finally learned." He pats his chest. "I need to put this thing on lockdown."

"Not completely. Just slow down. Learn to protect yourself so you don't keep getting hurt." I step up beside him, leaning over the rail and trying to catch his eye. He looks at the east bank, the west bank, and off in the distance to the north, basically anywhere but at me. "Theo—"

He holds up a hand. "No. I've got this. The old Theo is dead. The new Theo is about to be born. Henceforth you'll find me the pinnacle of disaffection, the quintessence of aloofness, the epitome of indifference. I'll be so detached, you'll need a parade to get my attention. Girls' names, tastes, and interests will fly from memory." He sweeps an arm toward the river. "Picnics? What's a picnic? Who wants to eat outside when kitchen tables are so much closer to the food and you don't have to deal with bugs?

No more plans. No more poems. No more dates. No more falling in love." He squares his shoulders and puffs out his chest, but his face twitches, belying his bravado.

"You sure you want to go off love completely?"

"I don't know." His posture droops a little. "It worked for you. Until I pushed you to go on a date, of course. That was stupid, though I guess it all worked out. I should've known you'd ask out one guy and everything would fall into place."

"It's not that simple."

"Isn't it?"

This time I kick at the railing, wondering if I should tell him about Liam, and how quickly I got caught up in the attention and the adrenaline and the insatiable craving to be close to him in every way two people could be close. And how already I can't go to sleep at night without checking my phone three or four times, hoping for a message from Felix. How I'm just as susceptible to wanting someone who might not want me the same way, or who might want me that way now, but not for long. How I'm putting up every wall I can but they keep toppling. And how I'm terrified I'm heading for heartbreak, too.

I don't say any of that. Instead, I stand next to Theo, staring at the dark and churning river, in an evening rain so gentle and atmospheric, it almost warrants an accordion song, and I will myself to be even half as brave as he is.

TWELVE

WITH FELIX'S RELATIVES STILL IN TOWN, HIS CROSS-country practices, my mom's taxes to finish, and both of our work schedules, we struggle to find an evening to get together. However, my mom suggests I come in late on Monday morning so I can meet Felix for breakfast. She still feels guilty for usurping my Friday night, though of course she didn't realize I had a date planned because she didn't know anything about Felix until he showed up at the shop. While I still feel weird about her knowing I'm dating someone, so far so good. Meeting Felix for breakfast doesn't even feel like a date, at least not as much as dinner and a movie did, but we have two whole hours together, uninterrupted. Since my mom will be at work all day, I hope Felix and I spend only one of our hours at the Cozy Café.

Felix is waiting outside when I arrive, leaning against an ivy-covered balustrade that looks like something from the set of *Gone with the Wind*. He's wearing a sexy blue henley he's kindly left unbuttoned so I can ogle his collarbone. With the sleeves pushed up past his elbow, I also have an excellent view of his forearms. I'm in a white linen dress Pippa said made my boobs look good. I recruited her for girl help this morning when I texted to explain why I'd be arriving to work late. Despite our differing tastes, Pippa's great about not imposing her look on mine. No wigs. No cartoony thigh-highs, no crinoline dresses. I love them on her, but on me they'd look like costumes.

Felix breaks into a smile when he spots me. I feel my own smile settle into place in response. I'm not sure what the proper greeting is eleven days into dating a guy I've mostly seen in public places, but he takes the lead by opening his arms. I step into his embrace, wrapping my arms around him and pressing my cheek to his shoulder. He's warm and solid, and he smells like Ivory soap. All good things.

"Hi," he says.

"Hi." I tilt my face to his. "It's good to see you."

"You, too." He tips his forehead against mine the way he did on my front patio, drawing me into a sea of dove gray. "Sorry my night shift means we have to do breakfast instead of dinner." He bunts my nose with his, maybe by accident, maybe not.

"I like breakfast. The pancakes are really good here." I rise onto my toes and let the tip of my nose arc across the bridge of his, not at all by accident.

"Pancakes, huh?" Felix's eyes sparkle as his hand slides up my back until his thumb meets my bare skin, just above the top edge of my dress. It's only a touch, an inch of skin against skin, but I feel it everywhere. "I'm thinking . . . omelet." He brushes my spine in slow, small spirals that remind me of the way he explored my hand on our first date. The night he mentioned kissing but left me with only a peck on my cheek and a heat in my body that took half a gallon of water to quench. "Eggs," he says as though it's the most delicious word, ever. "Cheese." He nuzzles my nose. "Vegetables." His nose grazes my cheek, sweeping sideways toward my ear. "Pretty much anything, really." He draws me closer and lays his cheek against mine, resting his lips near my ear so his breath tickles in the best possible way. "Guess I like breakfast, too."

My breath quickens. He must feel it. I'm pressed so tightly against him. Can he also feel the heat radiating across my skin? Or the wonderful tingly sensation that's spreading through my bones and weakening my knees? Whether he can or not, I inch higher, loosening my hold and sliding my hands up to rest against his chest.

"Felix . . ." I start, but I can't finish. I have no idea what follows.

He pulls back and meets my eyes. He doesn't speak the question, but I nod anyway. By the time his lips meet mine, my eyes are already closed and I'm melting against him. We hold like that, connected but unmoving. The electricity of our contact flies toward my fingers and toes, sparking every joint, every tendon and muscle. When my whole body is alight with the feel of Felix's kiss, I let my lips fall open.

I don't know what I become aware of first. His tongue slipping under my upper lip? Mine stretching forward to meet his? His hand sliding up my back and cradling my neck, warm and so strong? His forearm pressing against my waist and all but lifting me off my feet? I only know he kisses me, and I kiss him back with a growing hunger to erase any space that remains between us. My hands knot in his hair. The side of my dress bunches in his fist. I slip my thigh past his, feeling rough denim on bare skin. He lets out a low, happy moan and stumbles forward, holding me up as his mouth meets mine again. Tongues collide. Breath gusts out between frantic lips. I forget where we are and when and even who until a sharp voice calls out from across the street, "Get a room!"

Felix and I pull away from each other, both setting our hands to our lips as though we can hide the evidence of our kiss. I spot our heckler, a kid passing by with his friends, all of them laughing at our expense. I turn back to Felix. His cheeks are flushed. His eyes are wide. We share an embarrassed pause. Then we bust out matching smiles.

"I didn't plan to start our date like that," he says.

"Me neither." I dab at my lips. They're tender and tingly. "But I'm glad we did."

"Me too." He runs his hands through his hair and blinks through a slow breath, still laughing softly to himself. "Guess we should get you some of those pancakes."

"And we should get you those eggs." I take his hand. "Promise to eat quickly?"

"I'll ask for the check the second we place our order."

"Good plan."

♥

We don't actually rush our breakfast. That's the thing about Felix. I keep telling myself he's just a hot guy I want to make out with. Then we start talking and I really like him. He tells me about his visiting relatives. They sound like a nightmare. Felix is way too nice to come right out and say they're overbearing and they should've gone back to Pensacola already, but I can read between the lines. He also tells me his name means "lucky and successful," an idea he worries he doesn't always live up to. I tell him I was named after the fashion magazine my mom happened to be reading when her water broke. Presumably that leaves me little worry about high expectations. We laugh a lot and share bites of each other's breakfast. He even shows me a few photos of his photography projects. They're mostly collages and I don't know much about art, but I can imagine his work hanging on a wall. It would look nice. Unfortunately, now that Felix has bared his artistic soul, I'm indebted to him for a tap dance.

He lets me off the hook when we get to my place. We only have about fifteen minutes and neither of us wants to waste it. I pretty much attack him the moment we push through the front door. He kicks the door shut as his arms wrap around me. I toss my keys onto the sideboard, missing completely as my lips find Felix's. His hands are on my waist, my hips, my neck as we stumble toward the sofa. I back against it, jerking to a halt and gripping his arms to hold myself upright. They feel amazing, perfectly dented where his biceps curve toward whatever the other muscles are called. I don't care what anything's called right now. I just want to kiss him and feel his body press against mine.

His lips move to my neck. His tongue flicks against my collarbone. My nerve endings ping to attention. And not just the nerve endings in my neck. A gasp slips out of me before I have the wherewithal to stop it. Felix pulls away and smiles. Good god, he's beautiful, with his caramel waves and square jaw and big gray eyes and swollen lips. All I can do is stare at him, breathless, alive, intoxicated by his warmth and his scent and his touch and his . . . everything.

Before I realize what he's doing, he sweeps an arm under my knees, lifts me up, and lays me on the sofa, stretching himself out on top of me without a pause. I let out a breathy laugh, mostly due to surprise, but also because of how many times I've imagined him sweeping me into his arms. I wasn't wrong. He can do it, and with no effort at all.

"What's so funny?" he murmurs against my lips.

"I just like you."

His smile stretches wider. "Good. I like you, too."

We make out on the sofa, reveling in tiny confessions made by both words and bodies. We keep our clothes on, but hands have ways of sliding under shirts and inside waistbands, hinting at greater transgressions. I'm aching to feel more of Felix's skin against mine, but I'm too aware of the time. My mom has a big potential client coming in today, a rich woman on her fourth marriage to yet another rich man. She's only coming for a consultation, but according to my mom, this one custom dress could pay enough for us to cut back on a lot of the little projects she keeps tacking on to our already-full workload. I promised to be there to help, or at least to amp up the flattery.

After one last breathless kiss, I somehow manage to pull away from Felix long enough to tell him we're out of time. He draws me into a tight embrace and tells me I'm not allowed to leave. He doesn't mean it, but I enjoy the idea of being held here all day, kissed into a state of dizzy forgetfulness about banalities like work and the annoying need to pee. When he releases his hold, I run upstairs to change into a basic black skirt and blouse. As I comb my hair into its usual ponytail and check my reflection in the mirror, I decide to add a jaunty neck scarf to my attire. Pippa and my mom will probably guess what it's for, but it might stave off questioning looks from any afternoon clients.

Felix walks me to work. We stop in front of the store. Through the glass door, I see Pippa and my mom talking with a middle-aged woman over near the racks. The woman's slim and striking, with narrow features and a tidy blond updo. She wears an expensive-looking suit and a few tasteful pieces of jewelry I suspect aren't rhinestones.

I take Felix's hand. "I should go. They've already started."

"Hey, so . . . can we cash in that rain check next Saturday?"

"Depends. What did you have in mind?"

"It's the Fourth of July. Since my relatives aren't planning to leave anytime soon, my parents are throwing a party. Grilling hot dogs. Setting off fireworks. We have a lot of family in the area. It would give me a chance to introduce you to everyone."

In an instant, low-level panic replaces the warm fuzzy afterglow of our morning.

"When you say 'a lot of family' . . . ?"

"My mom and stepdad. My dad and his wife and their three kids. Five siblings. Seventeen, no, eighteen cousins. Two sets of grandparents. And don't even make me count the nieces, nephews, and in-laws. Plus whatever friends and neighbors come by."

"Wow. That is a lot of people." My voice squeaks but I can't level it. I'm pretty sure I sweated through my shirt around the time he said *siblings*. How did we go from a first date to meet the family in less than two weeks? "Can I get back to you on that?"

"No problem," he says, of course, because he's perfect and nice and not a tangle of irrational fears. "Your mom wouldn't ask you to work the holiday, would she?"

"Doubtful, but I can't remember if I had something else planned."

"I'll keep my fingers crossed you're free." He catches something over my shoulder in the shop, probably Pippa spying. "I should let you go. Text me later, okay?"

"Of course." I tiptoe up and give him a chaste kiss, the kind that won't make anyone shout at us to get a room. He blows me a bonus kiss as he turns and walks away.

I lean against the doorframe and watch until he's out of view, wondering why I'm a nervous mess right now, especially when everything's going so well. Better than well. My skin's still buzzing where Felix's hands snuck beneath my clothes only minutes ago. Though maybe that's why I'm a nervous mess. I swear something chemical happened with all that kissing. It could morph this combination of liking and lusting into a feeling I can't control. Then I'll meet his family, I'll get more integrated into his world, he'll grow bored with me, we'll break up, I'll be shattered again, and half of Pennsylvania will know me as the girl Felix Royce dumped. The girl who's still disposable.

These thoughts continue swimming through my mind as I open the door and enter the shop. My mom lights up when she sees me, waving me over.

"Harper, come meet Judy Connor, soon to be Judy Armstrong."

"As of September nineteenth." The blond woman flashes a rock on her ring finger. It's big enough to ice a pitcher of lemonade. Or feed a lot of hungry people.

I catch a wry look from Pippa as I cross the room to exchange greetings, forcing out the usual round of compliments and congratulations. Thank god I don't have to shake anyone's hand because my palms are still sweating. While I hide them behind my back, Ms. Connor spins around as if she's taking in all the gowns and accessories.

"I just *love* this shop," she gushes. "Adam — that's my fiancé — he swore I'd never leave New York City for him, but everything's so cute and personal out here." She beams at us while I wonder if she'll be as elated once the quaintness of the storefronts wears off and she can't get decent Wi-Fi. "New Hope is such a little treasure. To show how thrilled I am to embrace it as my new home, I'm hiring only local businesses for the wedding: the venue, the food, the flowers, and of course the dress!" She waves at my mom the way a game show hostess might wave at a convertible.

"We're happy to help in any way we can," my mom says, as gracious as ever.

"My family didn't think I'd leave New York, either," Ms. Connor offers for no obvious reason except she's clearly chatty and people often spill their personal details here. "They were pretty skeptical about Adam when we first met. You know families. Always assuming nobody's good enough for one of their kind."

A new wave of anxiety shudders through me. My skin turns to pins and needles while my armpits grow damp. I excuse myself on the pretense of checking on something in the back room. The second the door closes behind me, I drop onto the mushy sofa, bend double, and force myself to breathe. Pippa bursts in a second later.

"I knew something was up," she says as she plops down beside me, already rubbing my back in slow, calming circles. "What happened?"

"I'm such a mess." I lace my hands behind my neck, stretching out knots I can't find. "A confused contrarian careening toward cataclysm."

"I think I got it with *mess*," Pippa sputters through a laugh.

"Sorry. I'm on *C*." I shake my head at the irony of my situation. Here I am learning all of these SAT words while the ones I'm struggling with most are so ordinary. I force them into sentences as though I know what they mean, but I'm not using them correctly at all. *Fling*, not *relationship*. *Date*, not *boyfriend*. *Like*, not *love*. And I'm throwing around *just*s as though that one little word changes everything. *Just* coffee. *Just* holding hands. *Just* a kiss on the cheek. But there is no *just*. These interactions mean something. And the really fucked-up part is that while I'm relentlessly dodging words like *boyfriend* and *love*, they're actually what I want.

With those thoughts swimming through my brain, I finally look up, meeting Pippa's pity-filled eyes. "What is wrong with me? How can I be so afraid of something that makes me happy?"

Pippa slows her circles on my back. After a thoughtful pause, she shifts away from me and flicks her bangs off her forehead. Her wig is a royal blue shag today, winging out from her temples and the nape of her neck.

"Sounds like vertigo," she says. "People think it's the fear of falling, but it's not. It's the fear of falling combined with the desire to fall. A lot of fears work that way. That's what gives them strength. Also, and maybe more relevant, the more we value something, the more we fear its loss. So you're pretty much screwed no matter what."

"Wow. Brains suck."

"Tell me about it." She smiles, crinkling the freckled skin beside her eyes.

I get up and poke through the items on the cutting table. A cluster of rhinestone buttons, an unraveling spool of thread, a seam ripper with a pronounced hook. Behind me, Pippa perches on the sofa in a crisp taffeta skirt and a 1940s jacket with subtle military details. The jacket suits her. I swear she could lead an army into war. I couldn't even lead a termite to a rotting stump. I should probably get T-shirts printed with the word *coward* so people see me coming and know to keep away.

"Pippa? You've had a serious boyfriend, right?"

"Three, actually, though I guess it depends what you consider 'serious.' Johnny Dunham for seven glorious months of my junior year. So cute. Moved away that summer. Totally tragic. Pete Beck at the end of my senior year. Looked hot in a tux at prom, less hot in handcuffs after attempting to rip off the 7-Eleven. And Dan Cho when I first started at BCCC. He was dreamy—and secretly dating two other girls." She joins me at the table, taking the seam ripper from my hand and setting it out of reach. She moves the embroidery scissors, too. I'm unlikely to do any real damage right now, but I appreciate her awareness that my mental distress doesn't mesh well with sharp objects.

"How do you know when to stop questioning and go for it?" I ask.

"You don't *know* anything. You trust your gut."

"What if my gut says a lot of different things?"

"Roll the dice and see what happens?"

"Sounds risky."

"It's all risky. But if it's the only way to get what you want, isn't it worth it?"

Unable to answer, I lean on the cutting table next to Pippa as if we're standing at a bar, waiting for drinks, and I think about last summer. I still hate how blindsided I was when Liam ended everything, but would I really have given up those six weeks with him if I'd known the relationship was going to end? Would I give up the days I've shared so far with Felix, and whatever days remain with him, whether that's two or two thousand? I can't answer those questions any more than I can answer Pippa's. I only know I'm well past the point of indifference. And I have no idea how to handle that.

THIRTEEN

I CATCH FELIX AFTER HIS WORKOUT ON TUESDAY. I still want to see him. I also don't want him to know I'm freaking out about how fast our relationship's moving, even if I'm still feeling . . . vertiginous. While walking him partway home, he inquires about how things went with my mom's big client (good, she got the gig), how my vocab studies are going (not great, due to lack of focus), if anyone questioned my neck scarf (no, other matters took precedence, namely, my panic about you), and if I've had a chance to check my schedule yet (no, sorry, got caught up in stuff for my mom, but I'll let you know soon). He's sweet, attentive, affectionate, and flirty, all of which would be amazing if I wasn't desperate to decline his party invite. And hating myself for that desperation.

Later that night, Theo stops by my house with a pair of sparklers and another vocab list. He texted this morning and told me he was shaking things up and drawing a letter at random this time. He drew *H*. Then he decided the moment required a special celebration since my name starts with *H*. This is *so* Theo. He invents reasons to celebrate almost as quickly as he invents reasons to fall in love. He's like a joy junkie, which is certifiably adorable. I'm in no mood to celebrate, but my mom's finishing Cathy's dress, Felix is busy with family stuff, Pippa has a big art project due this week, I'm not in a position to rebuild my other friendships this summer, and I'm tired of stewing on my own. So I invite Theo in to share the humbly homogenous pot pie I've heated up.

"If I knew you were coming over, I would've picked up Hunan Wok," I say as we plant ourselves on my boring back stoop in my boring backyard and set down our boring microwaved meal. To my right, past the fence, the blades of Theo's windmill slowly spin in the breeze. The picnic table on his tiled patio is painted with Scandinavian details. A pair of cobalt blue chairs flanks the turquoise back door, conjuring images of a Greek patio. Cilantro, oregano, and Caribbean thyme sprout from planter boxes beneath the windows. As a kid, after being over at Theo's one afternoon, I asked my mom where our ancestors came from. She said suburbia. The conversation ended there.

Theo frowns as he prods the uniformly beige crust on the little pie.

"Can we at least add the sparklers?" he asks.

"Better to put that thing out of its misery as quickly as possible."

"What? No!" He bends down and tips his head over the pie. "Listen. Do you hear it? It's saying, 'Have pity, Harper. I'm only a sad little pastry. Pleeeeeease let me have a teeny-weenie itty-bitty party? Haphazardly hastening would be homologous to heresy.'"

"That's heavily hyperbolic."

"Or hilariously histrionic?" Theo forces a cheesy grin.

"Okay, fine," I say through a laugh. "Party first. Then pastry euthanasia."

With great effort, Theo jams a fork through the pie crust and makes two sloppy holes for the sparklers. I set the pie on the bottom step. He lights the sparklers. We sit on the top step and watch in silence as a thousand tiny starbursts arc into darkness. I don't know why, but sitting here with Theo, doing something as ridiculous as celebrating a vocab list with a pair of mediocre fireworks, cheers me up a little. Felix is right. I am lucky to have a friend so close by, especially one as weird as Theo. I bet no one else in the world is doing precisely what we're doing right now. This moment is entirely ours.

When the sparklers fizzle into two snaking streaks of smoke, Theo pops them out. He retrieves the pie and sets it between us. I brush off the ashes that've collected near the gaping holes. With twinned determination, we pick up our forks.

"Here's to *H*." He tips his fork against mine.

"It's hardly halfway."

"But hypothetically herculean."

We share a smile. Mine's small at first, but Theo's invites it to widen. If he can find this fun, maybe I can, too. I wait for him to dig in. He must be waiting for me to start because neither of us takes the plunge. The pot pie sits there, streaked with sparkler dust, mauled by Theo's efforts inserting the sparklers, and even more unappetizing than it was when I removed it from the box.

"Mom O. made tostones last night," Theo says.

"Don't rub it in."

"I'm not. We have leftovers. I could go get us some."

"And leave this 'poor, sad little pastry' uneaten?"

"It fought a good fight. Time for it to lay down its weary bones and journey to the big frozen foods section in the sky." Theo stands, bows his head, and lays a hand against his heart. He murmurs a prayer under his breath, maybe in earnest, maybe in jest. Then he runs off and leaves me to tend to the wounded.

While I'm dumping the pie in the trash, my phone buzzes.

Felix: *Any updates about Saturday?*

I stare at the screen without opening my phone so he won't know I've read his text. I hate that my first instinct is to tell him there's another crisis at my mom's shop. It would be a lie. The shop won't even be open since my mom's driving to New York this week to buy fabric and notions. She's also seeing a few friends, so she won't be back until late Sunday. Her taxes are even finished and in the mail to the IRS. I'll have the entire weekend to myself. Felix and I could go to his party, come back to my place, and completely ravage each other. Half of me loves the idea. The other half—or more precisely the other fifty-one percent—is still too scared. I can't write off meeting his family as "just" anything. And if we're alone together, I'll want to do more than kiss him. There's nothing "just" about that, either. I want to do it all—meet the family and have sex—but I'm not ready. I need more time.

I'm still debating my response when Theo returns with a tray of fried foods, not just tostones but empanadillas and rellenos de papa, too. I love his moms. I also love that they're not taking their diet *too* seriously. I leave Felix's text temporarily unanswered as I grab cups and a bottle of soda. Theo and I settle in to our much-improved feast on the back stoop, the vocab list forgotten, the text almost forgotten. Leaves rustle. The scent of garlic and fresh chilies wafts by on a breeze. Above us, stars pop out one by one against a darkening sky. Despite my muddled brain and my unlandscaped backyard, there are worse views in the world, and worse ways to spend a summer night.

I give Theo a little nudge with my knee. "I'm glad you're here."

"You too." He nudges me back. "I thought you might be out with Felix tonight."

I set aside the remainder of my tostones. They were delicious five seconds ago. Now they taste like greasy bananas.

"He has a family thing."

"Huh." Theo pops the last of a relleno into his mouth.

I eye him sideways. "What do you mean, *huh?*"

"I just mean, *huh.*"

"Theo—" I say in my scoldy voice.

"Harper—" he parrots back.

We hold a stare-off. I'm good at wearing people down with a look. He caves first.

"I passed you guys on my way to fencing practice earlier

today. You weren't as cozy as usual. I sensed some tension. That's all."

"Yeah. Maybe." I flick a crumb off my thigh. Then I search for another so I have something to torture. "I have a few issues to sort out. Once I do, everything will be great again." I try to flick another crumb onto the lawn but discover it's a grease spot. While I scratch at it, Theo opens his mouth as if he's about to ask a question. I cut him off. "And you? How's the 'not falling in love' plan going?"

"Fine." He slumps against the railing beside him, scowling at his sneakers. They have several holes, each one augmented by cartoon smash lines, as though Theo hulked his way through the canvas. As with his sock collection, he holds on to things forever, mending them when they're broken or torn rather than replacing them with something new. I don't fully understand the impulse, but at least he remembered to wear shoes tonight. "I haven't asked anyone out again. Guess that should be considered progress."

"You don't sound very happy about it." I scoot the tray toward the door so it's no longer taking up space between us.

Theo knots a hand through his shoelace, twisting it until the lace pinches his skin.

"I'm not like you, Harper. I need other people. Not just people. Person. I need another person. I want to feel like all of those songs on the radio. Not the sad ones but the other ones. The big, mushy *I'd do anything for you* songs. I want to fight for someone. I want a hand to reach for and an eye to catch across a crowded room. I want to get up each day knowing there's a person in the world who's as excited to see me as I am to see her." He flaps a hand at me. "You've got it easy. You're fine on your own."

My neck muscles tighten as his words echo and spin. *Fine. Easy. Simple.* As with our conversation on the bridge last weekend, I want to tell Theo he has no idea what's easy for me, but his assumptions are my fault. I hide my feelings too well.

I pivot toward him, bumping knees. "Maybe I'm not as fine as I look."

He studies me, barely blinking. His knee knocks gently against mine, tapping away like the world's softest metronome. The contact is sweet, but the rhythm starts to feel like it's marking time. I wonder if I've said too much. My confession feels bigger than I meant it to. We're not even in the windmill. I'm about to break the silence and retract what I said when the corners of Theo's upturned lips tip higher.

"You know," he says, "I kinda sensed that, too."

The tension in my neck eases as quickly as it came on. I may keep a lot of my feelings to myself, but Theo just gets me. He always has.

He doesn't probe for details about my fineness. He simply pats the spot beside him. I scoot around, pivoting into the curve of his arm and tipping my head onto his shoulder. He lays his cheek against the top of my head. For several minutes, we sit side by side in the summer night. He's probably thinking about the girl he wants to fight for. I'm thinking about the boy I want to date without being so afraid to like him. Meanwhile, for now, Theo and I are a little more "fine" for having each other.

"What are you doing on the Fourth?" I ask, hoping to lighten the mood.

"Invading Mothloria."

"The usurper queen overtaxing her subjects again?"

"The rebel forces are rallying. I think we've got this one."

I picture him running around in the forest, brandishing a broadsword, playing war games in tights. I almost laugh, but I stop myself when an idea forms . . .

"Can I come with you?" I ask.

Theo jerks away from me. "You're kidding, right?"

"My mom'll be gone all weekend. I don't have to work. I need something to do, and a place to be while I . . . sort out those issues I mentioned."

He blinks at me, his brow furrowed. "So you want to hang with the LARPers?"

"If you don't mind." I bite my lip, worried he thinks I'm setting up a joke.

He drums his fingers on his thigh, his dark eyes filled with skepticism.

"Sorry," I say. "Dumb idea. I shouldn't have—"

"Welcome to the Rebel Alliance."

FOURTEEN

HALF AN HOUR'S DRIVE NORTH AND ANOTHER twenty minutes of winding through forested parkland west of Milford, Theo pulls Olivia's SUV into an already-full parking lot. Every kind of car is present, from basic sedans to decked-out vintage VW buses painted with *Down with the queen!* slogans. Half a dozen camper vans take up the farthest spaces while several other cars have plastic storage bins strapped to their tops.

"The site's a twenty-minute walk that way." Theo nods toward a well-marked path as we get out of the car. "Hope you don't mind hauling gear."

"Sure. No problem." I peer into the back seat at the tightly packed cooler bag and the duffel filled with costume pieces, assuming that's the gear he's referring to, and that I'll carry the food. His chain mail weighs a ton, which helps explain why he has the rockin' bod I glimpsed back at Beneath the Veil. If he wears his full suit of armor every weekend, he might lift more weight than Felix. I'm trying to picture Theo fighting in all that metal when he opens the trunk and drags out a tightly packed canvas tent. My stomach lurches. "Is that what I think it is?"

Theo raises a wry brow. "Please tell me you didn't expect to stay in a hotel."

"Maybe?" I give him a cringey grin. I'm not what most people would call "outdoorsy." I'm not even outdoorsy-adjacent.

He sets a hand on my shoulder, shaking his head. "This is fifteen hundred, Jamison. You're about to step into the Land of Seven Crowns. We don't have hotels."

"What about cabins?" I crane my head toward the path. It's wide and well trodden until it curves out of sight in the underbrush. A luxury campsite is at least possible.

Theo holds out his keys. "You have two choices. Take the car and pick me up tomorrow at six, or cope without a duvet and a down pillow for a night."

I eye the bundle of tent canvas and aluminum poles. The fabric's stained and wrinkled. The metal's weathered and dented. I haven't slept in a tent since Natalie Henderson's thirteenth birthday party. That tent fit twelve girls and came with a padded floor and several strands of fairy lights. Theo's tent looks more like shipwreck detritus, but I told Felix where I was spending the weekend, claiming I'd already promised Theo I'd join him. If I back out now, he'll know I was lying.

"Keep the keys," I say. "I'll adapt."

With a few hearty words of encouragement, Theo straps the tent to my back. Then he holds out my backpack so I can slip it over my chest. I only brought a change of clothes and an overnight kit, but suddenly it feels heavier than necessary. At least I dressed for comfort in canvas shorts, a basic tee, and sneakers, though now I feel like I should've stopped by one of those stores where everyone looks like a triathlete, all fit, tan, and clad entirely in waterproof nylon. Theo lifts a hiking pack onto his back. He makes the action look effortless, but by the way the pack jingles, I'd guess it contains about thirty pounds of chain mail. He doesn't stop there. He layers over-the-shoulder bags across his chest with food and gear until the trunk is almost empty. Then he holds out two swords: his usual fencing blade and a thick broadsword sheathed in embossed leather.

"Do me the honor, m'lady?"

"M'lady?" I gesture at the grubby pack on my back and the T-shirt I'm already sweating through. "All available evidence suggests I'm firmly peasant class."

Theo's eyes sparkle with a hint of pride. He stands up a little straighter, looking taller than usual, strong, and confident, even with all of his baggage.

"You're arriving on the scene with Sir Theodoro de Montiel. You're no peasant."

With a soft smile at his rare bravado, I take the swords and tuck them under my arm. I don't fully understand Theo's boast, but I like that he feels important, especially since he's been such an outlier at school all these years.

Looking like a pair of pack animals, we trudge down the trail until we reach a large valley cut through by a narrow, snaking river. On either side of the river, people are setting up tents and picnics. We could be joining a big family reunion or a hiking tour, except for a few key differences. Hand-painted banners and flags depict family crests or list the prices of legs o' mutton and chalices of mead. Most of the people present wear some semblance of medieval attire. Some are fully dressed in ankle-length gowns or velvet tunics and capes, despite the heat. Others mix and match with T-shirts atop leather leggings or tanks worn with hiked-up peasant skirts.

"You sure it's okay that I don't have a costume?" I ask.

"Family and friends get a free pass. This is LARPing. Most of us aren't exactly in the in-crowds of our social circles. We don't want to be exclusive out here."

I consider this as a girl rolls a wagon full of flower crowns past us.

"I could pick up something here," I say. "You're letting me into your private world. An attempt to assimilate seems only fair. Or should that be faire with an *e*?"

Theo smiles, all teeth and one deeply embedded dimple.

"Don't stress about it. Just have fun. And sort out those issues you mentioned."

I nod as my thoughts drift to Felix, to the party he's probably helping set up about now, to how much I liked kissing him on Monday, to how much I like him, period, and to vertigo. Guilt creeps in about the lie I told him, and confusion about why I didn't just say I needed to slow down, though slowing down isn't the right phrase when I can barely keep my hands off him whenever we meet up. My thoughts spiral, like usual. Thankfully I'm surrounded by distractions. A juggler is teaching some kids to toss silk scarves. A burly guy's zipping up what looks like fur pants. Just past the gathering, a hodgepodge group is roping off a rectangle that's about half the size of a soccer field.

"That's where the tournament takes place," Theo says.

"You have a tournament every weekend?"

"Sort of. They're only practice rounds until the real deal happens at the end of August. They're good opportunities to suss out one's opponents. The competition's stiffer than usual this year, but I might eke out a victory next month." He describes some of the strongest competitors while I follow him to a little ring of birch trees near the river. We set everything down on a smooth, flat area that'll be perfect for the tent, while the trees divide the space from the scattered brush and open grassland, providing a hint of privacy.

"Looks like you snagged one of the best spots in the valley," I say.

"People are cool about saving it for me." He tosses this out like it's nothing, but no one else seems to have a special, secluded tree-ringed spot.

"You weren't kidding about the 'Sir Theodoro' prestige, were you?"

He shrugs and reddens as he starts sorting gear, but the answer's obvious, and it fills me with a warm, glowy, gooey, caramelly feeling. This weekend away will do more than let me clear my head and sort out my feelings about Felix. I'll get to see my best friend in his element, surrounded by people who admire him. I couldn't be happier.

As we unpack, Theo greets other participants with a range of modern *hellos* and geeky *huzzahs* complete with forearm-gripping handshakes. He introduces me as Maid Harper from the Land Beneath the Veils. I laugh the first time he says it, but by the third or fourth time, I realize it's actually pretty great. He's wildly creative, inventing a backstory for me on the spot as people inquire about who I am and why I'm here.

According to Theo, I'm betrothed to a handsome prince from a neighboring kingdom. The marriage is an advantageous political alliance for both families, but I have my doubts, namely due to the secret affair I've been carrying on with the captain of my mother's guards, Dame Pippa Pennington of the Green Locks. I've journeyed to the Land of Seven Crowns with my family's long-time ally, Sir Theodoro, for a chance to consider my choices away from the pressure of my family. I don't know what I love more, the idea of Felix being my betrothed prince or Pippa being my secret love interest. She's going to lose her mind when I tell her. By the time I finish relaying the details, she'll be begging me to set her up on a date with Theo. Maybe Theo will even reconsider the idea.

I help him assemble the tent, following his directions as I slip the canvas over the poles. Despite a concerted attempt to stem my bed snobbery, the tent stinks of mildew and it's badly patched in several places.

"Remind me to fix this for you when we get home," I say.

"I know. It's a mess." He flicks a loose patch near the top. "Too bad about the massive rainstorm that's on its way tonight."

I scan the skies, fighting an urge to grab my bag and flee.

"Please tell me you're kidding," I beg.

"You're worried about a little rain when a war's about to erupt?"

"Yes! Unless you have a really, really, *really* big umbrella in that backpack."

A broad grin breaks across Theo's face. "I'm teasing. Don't worry. Clear skies."

I give him a playful shove. He stumbles sideways, laughing at my gullibility.

I thrust a pointed finger toward his chest. "Do not piss me off, Turner, or I'll send my betrothed after you. *And* the badass captain of my mother's guards."

"You're in my territory now, Jamison. I'm not worried. I have allies."

We joke about the scene that would result if Felix and Pippa really did show up here, weapons in hand, but as I stand and inspect our work, my laughter dies away.

Theo steps over to my side. "What's wrong?"

"It's so . . . small." I keep my gaze locked on the grubby little tent, but my mind wanders back to my mom's shop, and the way I flushed when Theo danced around shirtless, the contours of his body shifting in the light, the bead of sweat that trickled down his spine, the little line of black hair that trailed toward his . . .

He sets a hand on my arm, drawing my attention up.

"We've slept together before," he says, enviably matter-of-fact.

"Yeah, but will we both even fit in there? Like, side by side?"

"I think so, not that I have concrete evidence. I don't usually have company."

My thoughts snag on his use of *usually*, but it must've been a slip of the tongue. There's no way he's shared this tent with someone else. The image is preposterous. A laugh slips out of me in response, but it comes out awkward and stilted.

Theo kicks aside the tail end of a rope, shrugging off my onset of nerves.

"Relax," he says. "If it makes you more comfortable, I'll sleep outside."

I wither a little, doubtful comfort is an achievable goal, regardless of what sleeping arrangements we decide upon.

"No," I say. "This is your tent. This is your kingdom." I sweep a hand across the unfolding scene. "If anyone's going to sleep outside, it should be me."

Theo wraps an arm around my shoulders and gives me a squeeze.

"Let's play it by ear, okay? See how you feel tonight?" He waits for my nod. "And for the record, this is not my kingdom. I'm only a knight, and we have a strict hierarchy here. C'mon, let me teach you what you need to know."

Theo takes me on a tour of the campsite — or as he calls it, the village — pointing out members of the community and explaining who they are, how they got their ranks and titles, and how everything ties into an epic tale about seven lands at war for one throne. He also explains the rules of battle. No one fights with real weapons. They save hand-to-hand combat for the tournament ring.

The war in the woods is about role-playing and bargaining for alliances, though apparently people get pretty into sneak attacks and playing dead with the use of black flags.

"How do you keep all the story lines straight?" I ask, unable to recall half of what he's told me.

"It's not that different from school. Bet you can explain every move behind the fight for last year's prom queen, or who dated whose ex, and what groups are banding together to boost each other's social media followers. This is just another battlefield."

"Fair enough," I concede. "Faire with an e, of course."

We share another laugh, one of many. Aside from the tent issue and a thread of longing for Felix I can't fully sever, coming out here feels like the best decision I've made in weeks. It's fun. It's different. It's preventing me from obsessing.

At around noon, Theo changes into his costume and prepares for battle. He wears the chain mail he made himself, though he admits it's a copy of his original set. He linked the body, hood, and leggings out of plastic rings so he could move more easily and he didn't require padding. He painted it silver so it looks like metal, but now I understand how he fights in it, and how he carried it all the way here. Over his armor, he belts on a tabard quartered into maroon and ivory squares with a crudely cut felt crest in the middle. I have to look closely before I realize the crest is a windmill silhouetted against a heart.

"Well?" He spreads his arms and does a turn for me. "What do you think?"

"I think I should make you a new tabard."

He pats down the front of his costume. "Is it that bad?"

"No, but I can do better." I attempt to brush a sooty smudge off his shoulder. It doesn't budge. "Also? I think you look amazing."

He beams at me with the pride I saw in his eyes when we first arrived. He's like a different person out here. At school he has a group of friends, but they mostly keep to themselves. He has also dealt with his share of bullying for being different or weird. It made him go kinda quiet. Out here he's confident, chatting with anyone and everyone, and he really does look amazing. Despite the glue blobs on his felted crest, he stands tall in his armor, with his broadsword belted to his side and a pair of spurred riding boots that look like they could kick some serious ass. His cheeks are rosy from the fresh air. His thick, black waves shift in the breeze, cut long over his eyebrows and ears. I'd always assumed he was lazy about haircuts. Now I realize the length and style suit his image as the noble knight from another time and place. I feel like such an ignorant jerk for making fun of his LARPing, even in my head. He's not ridiculous at all.

I give him a hug and send him off to battle. He marches into the woods with about a hundred other people — men and women of all ages, each dressed in their own unique interpretation of medieval clothing and armor. Up close, at least to a seamstress, they're a motley crew. With the help of a squint, they look like proper armies prepared for war.

Theo's absence leaves me with a few hours on my own, though "on my own" is relative. Only about a third of the gathered group joined the battle. The rest remain, setting up campfires for sausage roasts, wrangling kids with wooden swords, or working on craft projects like wire jewelry and tooled leather pouches. As someone unused to village life, I get out my phone. Naturally, there's no reception. Theo warned me, but it still sucks. I totally want to text Felix right now. I'm surrounded by a fairy tale, and I want the handsome prince to go with it. If I can't have him here, I at least want to joke with him about our impending union. Then again, bringing up a subject like that wouldn't be fair if I'm only going to panic again. I'm in or I'm out.

Anxious for more distraction, I join a group sitting around a campfire. The fire's unnecessary on an early July afternoon, but it smells nice and adds atmosphere. Three girls about my age sit to my right. One braids another's long, auburn hair while the third stencils a henna tattoo onto her bare foot. To my left, a woman hums softly to a baby dressed in a dragon costume. Across from me, a guy in elf ears splices feathers for arrows.

"You're here with Sir Theodoro, right?" the girl with the auburn hair asks me.

"We're next-door neighbors. I mean our kingdoms are adjacent or whatever."

The girls laugh in a friendly way, waving off my bumbling attempt to play along. They assure me I'm allowed to be myself. Then they introduce themselves as Kaylina of Lark's Hollow, Farlefenia of the North, and Maid Mandaliza. I stick with Harper, grateful Theo used my real name so I have less to remember.

"So, are you guys *together*, together?" asks Farlefenia, the girl with the henna tattoo. She has beautiful black hair that cascades down to her waist, and she's wearing a gauze peasant dress with a corset-like buckled belt.

"We're just friends," I tell her. "Good friends, though."

She turns an excited smile on the other girls, nudging the one in the middle and mouthing, "Ask her." The one in the middle—Kaylina, with the partially braided auburn hair—shakes her head and fusses with the belled sleeves of her brocade gown.

Mandaliza leans forward. "Kaylina has a crush."

"We all do, kind of," Farlefenia adds.

"Is he single? And straight?" Mandaliza asks. "Lina's dying to know."

Kaylina looks mortified, shooting angry looks at her friends, but soon enough her eyes turn my way as all three girls await my response.

"He's both," I say. "Single and straight."

Mandaliza nudges Kaylina. "Told you. Make a move already."

Kaylina squirms and looks at me as though she's seeking reassurance that her advances would be welcome. I don't know if they would. Maybe, but Theo did swear off love last weekend, and we don't need to extend his dating lessons into multiple realms.

"He just went through a breakup," I say. Two breakups, actually, though the girls don't need to know that. It sounds a little shady without context. "He might need time to heal before he's ready for something new."

The trio melts into a chorus of sympathetic *awww*s before launching a discussion about whose favor he'll wear at the big tournament next month. I have no idea what wearing a favor involves, but I smile as I picture Theo surrounded by pretty girls in peasant blouses and flower crowns, fangirling over him when he returns from battle. It's a fabulous image, and it makes me even prouder to be here with him. It also makes me a little envious —not of Theo, but of the girls. Their crushes seem like such fun, a means of teasing each other and building up a sense of fantasy and anticipation. They practically glow at the possibility of being chosen by a valiant knight, victorious in battle, ready to bestow one perfect kiss on the girl who catches his eye. They're swept up in the mere idea of a Happily Ever After, not obsessing about scary What Ifs. Maybe I can learn from their example.

With that thought, I vow to spend the rest of the weekend focused on the "Happily" without worrying so much about the "Ever After."

FIFTEEN

I WAS PREPARED FOR NOBLE KNIGHTS AND FAIR
ladies. I wasn't totally surprised by elf ears, belly dancers, plague
victims, a parade of jesters, or even a baby dragon. I was *not* ready
for the mead. Theo and I sit side by side on a log near the central
campfire. Forty or fifty people have gathered, seated on blankets, rocks, or folding stools. Most still wear their medieval attire,
though now that the sun has gone down, sweatshirts and jackets
are dotted among the crowd. A guy opposite us plays a lute and
sings a mournful ballad about a pair of star-crossed lovers. The
fire crackles away, sparking toward a star-filled sky.

The pitcher of mead has gone around the circle at least ten
times now. I think I've taken a swig on every pass. I don't drink very
often. I downed too much vodka at a party last fall and threw up
all over Zenya Cardin's basement. I vowed to never drink again,
but this sweet, fruity wine tastes soooo good. It also shuts down
my overactive brain and makes my muscles warm and tingly.

"Guess they don't card out here," I say as I watch one of the
girls I met earlier fill a beaded chalice from the pitcher.

"We're on an honor system," Theo tells me. "As long as no

one's disruptive, pretty much anything goes. People keep an eye on each other. No one drives. So far the worst effects have been some random streaking and a lot of really bad dancing."

"Did you?"

"The streaking? No. The dancing? Totally." He chuckles. His breath smells like oranges, cloves, and honey. He's been drinking, too.

I tip my head against his shoulder. My brain is too heavy to hold up. Or maybe my ponytail's too heavy. I can't tell what's up there anymore. It doesn't really matter. I'm more interested in what's beneath my cheek. Theo's wearing a thin leather jerkin he had on under his armor. It's practically molded to his body now, shaped by repeated use. I trace a seam from his armpit to his elbow. It's rough and ragged. Beneath it, his muscles shift as he adjusts the position of his arm. I pretend to study the stitching while I let my fingertips trace the underside of his bicep, drawn by a strange compulsion to know how he's shaped.

"I'm glad you won today," I tell him. "Are you relishing your great triumph?"

"For now. Nothing in the Seven Crowns lasts long. Alliances and animosities are mercurial out here. Today the queen is dead. The twin princes begin their reign. By the end of the month, anyone here could hold a seat of power."

"Including you?" I blink up at him.

He slips an arm around my waist, maybe out of friendly affection, maybe to keep me from falling off the log.

"I'm not interested in power," he says. "I'm in it for the fight."

"But what do you fight for if you don't care about power?"

"Honor. Pride. Righteousness." His fingers curl toward his palm against my waist. His knuckles brush up and down my side, soft and soothing. "I back the leader with the noblest cause. If greed corrupts them, I shift my allegiance. There's a freedom in that. I don't want to give it up just so I can sit in a big chair."

"Yeah. Big chairs are stupid."

Theo laughs, jiggling my forehead where it rests on his shoulder. As I search my hazy brain for something more profound to say, the trio I met this afternoon giggles to our right, sneaking flirty looks at Theo. They're wearing flower crowns with ribbons dangling down their hair. They offered to make me one a few hours ago, but I declined. It felt weird without a costume. Now I wish I did have one. I should be making more of an effort to fit into Theo's world. Also, the crowns are pretty.

"Those girls like you," I tell Theo for no reason whatsoever.

He expels a slow breath. "I know."

"I'm all right on my own for a while."

"I know that, too."

"If you want to—"

"I don't. Okay?" He withdraws his arm and scoots away from me.

I wobble, jarred by the loss of his support. And by his brusqueness.

"Theo?" I pivot his way as I right myself. "What did I say?"

He bends down and plucks a blade of grass. With his forearms resting on his knees, he proceeds to pull apart the blade as though he's separating string cheese.

"I know you think I'll date anyone who smiles at me." He eyes me sideways. I ease up a tiny shrug. He shakes his head at me and returns his focus to the blade of grass. "It's not true. It never has been. Although yes, unlike some people, I don't wait for perfection." He sneaks me another sideways glance, one tinted with accusation.

I prickle with defensiveness. "Felix isn't perfect."

"Name one thing that's wrong with him."

I open my mouth. Then I close it again. Felix can't be perfect. No one is. Maybe I don't know him well enough yet, or maybe his lack of flaws is his flaw. It makes him uninteresting—scratch that. It's not true. Now I'm inventing reasons to not like him. Maybe it's the mead talking. Or my fear of rejection. Or something else entirely.

While I wrestle with those thoughts, Theo wraps the grass around his index finger as though he's tending to a wound.

"Sometimes with my rush to fall in love," he says as much to himself as to me, "I wonder if I'm trying to distract myself."

I squint at him through my brain fog. "From what?"

He lets the grass strips scatter as he meets my eyes. We stay like that for several seconds. I sense that he's willing me to understand something he's not saying but I'm not at my most perceptive right now. Still he looks at me and I look at him, and surely he's going to tell me what he's thinking because I can't read his mind, even when I'm stone-cold sober. But he doesn't tell me, and I don't guess, so the moment gets weird.

I'm about to break the silence — though with what, I don't know yet — when he bends down and yanks another blade of grass free.

"What if what I really want is something I can't have?" he asks. "And I've known for a long time that I can't have it, but knowing that is unbearable so I keep trying to fill the empty space with anything else, hoping it'll make the space less empty?" His eyes stay locked on his hands as he spins the blade of grass between his thumb and forefinger. His question feels big, more like a prayer than a search for information. It's filled with a longing I don't understand, and yet that longing is familiar, in a distant, unformed kind of way.

As I watch Theo continue to fidget, something in my chest pinches, maybe for him, maybe for myself, maybe for both of us. Usually when a conversation gets this heavy, I deflect the tension with a joke, but this doesn't feel like a moment for humor. It feels like a moment for saying something profound. Only I don't have anything profound to offer. I'm out of my depth here. Whenever I know I can't have something, I shove it as far back in my mind as possible, relentlessly focusing my attention elsewhere until I convince myself I never wanted that thing to begin with. Things like a dad with a name, a face, and a pride in my achievements, or a mom who comes home before 10:00 p.m. on a regular basis. A home that smells like something other than microwaved burritos and loneliness. A group of friends who don't peel away while I fill my free hours with work. Love without fear. Take all that away, and my wants list dwindles to a higher SAT score, a scholarship to Bryn Mawr, and a successful business one day. All of those goals feel achievable with consistent effort. If I let the other wants surface—the ones I can't control—I'll drown under the weight of it all.

I hold out my hand, palm up. "I don't know what you do."

"Yeah. Me neither." Theo lets the grass drop as he takes my offered hand.

I draw his hand against my chest, pressing it close.

"At least we can not know together," I tell him.

"Sounds like a pretty good plan to me." He offers me a sweet but conflicted smile, one I don't even try to interpret. I just enjoy the togetherness. His thumb caresses my knuckles as we listen to the end of one ballad and the start of another. I close my eyes and concentrate on the music, letting the lilting rhythm still my circling thoughts. My head grows weary, so I rest my cheek against our knotted hands. The guy with the lute plays through a verse about a selfish knight and a forsaken maiden. When I open my eyes, Theo's watching me. Amber light plays across his prominent nose and high cheekbones. Twin fires dance in his deep brown eyes. His upturned lips twitch in the corners as though they can't decide where to settle.

"Theo?"

"Mmm?"

"About that tent . . ."

♥

We leave our shoes and boots near the rest of our gear just outside the tent. I climb in first, tucking myself between two blankets so one provides a little padding and the other cuts the slight chill of the night air. The tent canvas still smells like mildew, but it's not as bad as I thought it would be, maybe because of the fresh air, maybe because of the mead. Theo hands me his flashlight. I set it in the corner, pointing the beam upward so we get the most light. Thank god we're allowed a few anachronisms. I never would've made it to the tent from the campfire, not unless Theo tossed me over his shoulder and carried me, which he threatened to do after I stumbled for the third or fourth time.

While I lie down and shimmy backwards, Theo crawls in and lets the tent flap fall shut behind him. He pauses, scratching at the back of his neck, his expression uncertain. I hold up the edge of the blanket, inviting him in.

"You're sure?" he asks.

I nod. He awkwardly stretches out beside me in a space that's clearly meant for one. We shuffle until we're facing each other with a single pillow under our heads and our faces only inches apart. Our toes touch and our knees wedge together. We snuggle all the time, but I don't remember being so aware of his toes before. Or his knees. Or the speed at which his chest rises and falls compared to my own. Or the distinct curl of his upper lashes as they shift above his unsettled eyes. For the first time ever, I'm not sure how to fit my body against his. The mead isn't helping. Neither are lingering thoughts about want and distractions and not knowing and big, complicated words like *together*.

Almost instantly, my left arm gets pins and needles, so I free it from where it's tucked under my side, wiggling my fingers in the limited space between us.

"I don't know what to do with this," I say.

Theo rests my palm against his chest. "Here's good."

I hold up my right hand. "And this one?"

"Wherever it's comfortable."

I set it on my thigh, but I feel like a packed sausage. I tuck it in against my collarbone, but that's even worse. At a loss for other options, I set it on Theo's hip.

"Is this okay?" I ask.

He nods as he rests his arm atop mine and wraps his hand over my shoulder. I shift, searching for space that isn't there. The flashlight tips over and rolls toward the side of the tent, dimming our light. I move to adjust it, but Theo holds me in place.

"Leave it," he says. "We don't need it."

I settle back into position and realize he's right. The softer light's nice. I can still see his features but in a dreamy, hazy way that suits my state of mind. As we lie quietly, my thoughts wander to his knees and his hands and his heart beating beneath my palm. I shouldn't be thinking about any of that, so I scramble for something to fill the silence.

"I had a good time today," I say.

"Oh yeah?" Theo smiles a little. The hand that rests on my shoulder lifts long enough to graze my cheek before settling back into place. He doesn't seem to notice the gesture, but I like it anyway. "Have you sorted out those issues you were working on?"

"Not yet." My thumb finds the hand-sewn outseam on his leather leggings. I follow the stitches toward his waistband, noting every bump and irregularity with the same compulsion I felt at the campfire: an inexplicable desire to explore every available surface with my hands. "I got swept up in the fanfare. There's a lot to look at out here." My thumb meets his skin. He flinches at my touch. I withdraw my hand and tuck it behind my hip. "Sorry. I didn't mean to—"

"It's okay. Just surprising. Your fingers are cold."

"Are they?" I examine my hand as though I can see its temperature. It's a ridiculous impulse, especially when I can barely make out my fingernails.

Theo takes my hand, slips it under the hem of his jerkin, and sets it on his waist. My skin meets his, and not just my thumb this time. The contact feels dangerous, like a secret trespass, even if he's only warming my hand. I have no stitches to explore now, no seams, only the curve of his hipbone and the subtle ridges at the edge of his abs. I hold still, not wanting to take gross advantage of this situation. My breath quickens anyway as my memory fills with images of Theo lunging shirtless across my mom's shop.

I meet his gaze, searching for assurances that nothing's weird about all of this. We've held each other hundreds of times. This isn't new. This isn't different. His eyes are steady but curious and maybe even a little bit wary, as if he's twinning my thoughts.

"Can I ask you a question?" I finally manage.

"Yeah?"

"When we put up the tent, you said you didn't usually have company."

"Mm-hmm." His head tilts to the side as though he's easing out a kink. When he lays his cheek against the pillow again, his face seems closer. "What's the question?"

"What does *usually* mean?"

A teasing smile plays with his lips. "*Usually: adverb, under normal conditions.* See also *typically, habitually, customarily, generally, ordinarily —*"

I give his waist a sharp pinch. He twitches and shoots me a warning look.

"Don't start that game, Jamison. You know I always win."

"Just tell me. Please?" I gnaw on my lip, unsure why I'm pursuing this.

Theo's expression loses its mirth. He takes a deep breath and lets it out again. Then he gives my hand a squeeze where it rests against his chest.

"You want to know if I've ever had sex?"

"I guess?"

He regards me for a long moment, unmoving.

"Yes. I have. Once." He watches for my reaction. I simply nod, surprised that I'm not surprised. His brows lift as if he's surprised I'm not surprised, too. "Have you?"

"Yeah. Not with Felix," I say before he can ask. "With a guy

I met last summer when I was at camp." A rush of anxiety floods me, followed almost immediately by a wave of relief. I thought revealing my secret would unravel me, but it feels less powerful now that I've released it, and Theo exhibits no judgment at all. "Did you like it?"

He lets out a nervous laugh. "Sex? Um, yeah. I liked it."

"Me too." I laugh with him. It's not a big, boisterous laugh. It's only a release of tension, but it feels good. So does his body where it shifts beneath my hand, juddering softly with his laughter. His skin is warm and smooth. I'm dying to let my hand inch forward, or backward, or up toward his chest, or anywhere, really, as long as I can touch more of him. "I mean, I liked the way it felt at the time, but it also complicated things."

"Mm-hmm." Theo brushes a loose strand of hair off my temple and tucks it behind my ear. His eyes travel across my face. He traces one eyebrow, and then the other. As with his brief caress on my cheek, his gestures are sweet, subtle, almost subconscious, but they imply an intimacy beyond what we've shared before. Coupled with the topic of conversation and a growing attraction I can't seem to stem, the implication multiplies tenfold. Whether or not Theo realizes any of that, he draws a line down my nose from the bridge to the tip, continuing on until he rests his finger in the little dent above my upper lip. "Complicated isn't always a bad thing."

"Maybe not." I close my eyes and try to shut out the pounding of my heart. His bangs tickle my forehead, escalating my anticipation as I picture the vanishing inches between us. My grip tightens on his waist in response, drawing him closer. "But everything was different after. Not me, personally. The relationship."

"Stands to reason." His hips meet mine, jolting my whole body into awareness. Desire takes over. My knee slides between his as I draw my thigh upward. His leg wraps over my hip as we shift against each other with an intimacy that's no longer implied. His fingers lace through mine where my hand rests against his chest. We form a fist together, tightly clenched, as if we're holding on to something besides each other, or as if we're holding something back. Beneath our linked fists, Theo's heart pounds, as thunderous as mine. "Change isn't always a bad thing, either." His breath gusts against my lips, fast, rushed, scented with citrus and wine.

Wine. Right. That. I'm not thinking clearly. I'm not thinking at all. I'm getting carried away by fairy tales and too much alcohol. I came out here to clear my head, not to muddle matters further, and now I'm about to mess up my closest friendship because I'm confused and he's here and he's so beautiful and he's clutching my hand and shifting his hips against mine and my body is moving of its own accord, melding with his while his lips are so close and his skin is so warm and—

"We can't," I gasp out.

Theo goes rigid. My eyes pop open. His chest heaves against mine. Otherwise he remains dead still. Hurt floods his eyes, but I don't let myself look away.

"We drank too much," I tell him.

"I'm not drunk."

"We're not ourselves."

"Maybe we're more ourselves than ever."

"Theo." I move my hand from his waist to his cheek. "We've always been there for each other, no matter what. I can't lose that."

His brows knit. "Why would you?"

"You said it yourself. All the girls you date. What if you're only looking for a distraction? I've been on the other side of that, finding out I wasn't worth wanting for real, only for a moment. I couldn't bear knowing that's what I was to you."

"You're not a distraction. You never could be."

"You might feel differently about that in the morning. And also . . ." I brace myself to tell the harder truth, the one I know will sting. "I'm dating someone else."

Theo closes his eyes and inhales sharply. "I thought maybe, I mean, I assumed, well, I think you can guess what I assumed."

"That's my fault. I'm sorry. I wasn't clear." I wait until Theo opens his eyes again. He scans the entire tent before he looks at me, even while my hand rests against his cheek and our faces are so close, the tiniest move would draw us into a kiss. "I don't know what'll happen with Felix, but I can't do this to him. And I can't do it to us."

Theo takes my hand from his cheek and lays it on the pillow. He doesn't say anything. He just lies there looking wounded and confused.

"Do you want me to leave?" I ask.

He shakes his head and places a tiny kiss on my forehead.

"No. But I may need to unearth the accordion when we get back tomorrow night."

I wrap my arm around him and nestle against his chest, grateful our friendship is strong enough to override the painful awkwardness we created.

"Play all you like," I tell him. "I won't say a word."

SIXTEEN

"THIS IS THE LONGEST HEM EVER!" PIPPA MOANS opposite me.

I nod as I make another stitch. Pippa and I are sitting in the back room at Beneath the Veil with a massive ivory satin gown spread out on the table between us. My mom forgot about this dress while she was in New York. This isn't the first time she's blanked about a contract. It's why I want to go to college nearby. Without proper management help, she'll tank her business again. One day I hope "proper management" won't be me, but she'll have an easier time hiring someone if she can get the business back in the black first. She's a brilliant designer, but the only thing she can keep straight is an inseam.

The bride's picking up the dress tomorrow. My mom's busy with billing and correspondence to sort out, so she asked me to teach Pippa a basic hemstitch. Between the two of us, we'll finish the hem tonight, but not without canceling all other plans for the evening. Felix is working at the grocery, so my only plans involved memorizing my *H* vocab list, but Pippa has art classes to keep up with. She also has more friends than I do.

She lowers her needle and shakes out her wrist. "Okay, I've been quiet for two whole hours. Personal space. Privacy. Blah, blah, blah. But I'm dying to know. With your mom in the city this weekend, did you and Flex Netflix and chill?"

I shake my head, wishing my weekend activities were even half that simple. I also wish Pippa wasn't so curious. Then I could continue pretending I'm only thinking about finishing this dress hem and not about the big, fat mess I made this weekend.

"I went with Theo to his LARPing thing," I say without meeting her eyes.

"Seriously? The big one out at Ringing Rocks? I thought you hated all that."

"So did I. Then I went and realized it was pretty awesome. Not awesome enough for me to make myself a princess dress and go again, but I get why he likes it so much." I smile to myself as I recall Theo's practice tournament yesterday, how he danced across the field, épée swishing, crowd cheering, girls swooning. He came in third in his event. He hated that he didn't win, but he still blew me away. I showered him with compliments, careful ones, of course. We both did our best to pretend Saturday night hadn't happened. Our best wasn't great, but at least we didn't get into a fight about it. We were virtually silent when we first woke up. By midday we were awkwardly conversational. As we drove home, we sang to the radio together, teasing each other about missed notes or mangled lyrics, almost like we were back to our usual comfortable friendship.

Almost. But not at all.

Somehow instead of using the time away to delay meeting Felix's family while I stopped anticipating the inevitable demise of our relationship, I came painfully close to making out with my best friend. Even worse, I can't stop imagining what might've happened if I hadn't put a halt to things, if Theo's lips had pressed against mine and his tender little caresses turned into something else entirely. Something that makes me breathe a little faster every time I picture it. And yet I haven't stopped liking Felix. I haven't stopped worrying that he's going to dump me, either, especially now that I've piled confusion on top of confusion. In other words: backfire of the century.

Pippa squints at the dress hem as she forces her needle into the tightly woven satin.

"Are you still giving Theo anti-falling-in-love lessons?"

"That might be off the table for a while." I whip through a few more stitches, determined to get out of here before 10:00 p.m. Across from me, Pippa continues working at a single stitch. She lodges the tip of her tongue in the corner of her mouth, deep in concentration. She's not the fastest sewer, or the most accurate, but she's here and I'm grateful. "Honestly? I'm starting to think I'm the one who needs lessons."

Pippa jerks to attention. "Because you realized you're in love with Flex?"

"No. I mean, I like him, a lot, but . . ."

"But what?"

I squirm in my seat. Pippa watches me closely, way too observant for my taste.

"But what if I have no idea what falling in love even means?" I hedge.

"You knew you were in love with Liam, right?"

"Yeah. At least, I thought I knew, but maybe I was just swept up in the attention and attraction. Maybe it wasn't love at all. It certainly wasn't for him." I prick my finger as I make another stitch, pausing to suck off a drop of blood.

Pippa lowers her needle, still studying me.

"What's this really about?" she asks. "Did you bang an elf this weekend?"

"No!" I push through a nervous laugh. "I wouldn't do that to Felix. And it wasn't really an elf-centric event. A pair of rubber ears doesn't turn a guy into Orlando Bloom."

With a flurry of questions, Pippa presses me for more details. I'm about to cave and explain what happened when my mom peeks in from the main room.

"How's it going back here?" she asks.

"Fine. Slow," I tell her. "If the length of this hem is any indication of the length of the upcoming marriage, the bride and groom will have a *lot* of years together."

"We'll finish tonight." Pippa wags her needle. "I swear!"

My mom laughs. "You guys ready for coffee?"

I swap an eager nod with Pippa. "Always."

"Good. We have a delivery." My mom steps aside.

My conversation with Pippa gets filed under To Be Continued as Felix enters with a full cup tray and a goodie bag. He's in a sexy pair of vintage-wash jeans and a faded baseball tee that hugs his chest and arms. A friendly smile lights up his eyes, and I'm thrilled to note that I'm a hundred percent happy to see him.

"Our shipment was delayed," he says. "We had nothing to stock. My boss let us all off early. Thought I'd come offer my support, or at least offer snacks."

"Wow. Thanks." I get up to greet him by the doorway. He wraps me in a hug, balancing the tray behind my back. His embrace feels good, right, like I'm meant to be in his arms. I smile up at him, awash with relief. He bends down as if he's about to kiss me, but I sneak a nod toward my mom. He straightens up right away. While he tugs his ear in that nervous way I've always found so cute, I gesture at the counter on the far side of the room. "Drinks go over there. If anything stains this dress, you won't leave here alive."

He does as instructed, laying out an assortment of cookies on the flattened paper bag. My mom sticks around long enough to pick out the black coffee and ask Felix a few get-to-know-you questions about his family and interests. To her credit, she doesn't turn the conversation into an interrogation. It still feels like a big deal. If my mom's getting to know Felix, she expects him to be around for a while.

Of course she does, and so should I. It's a good thing. A great thing. A wonderful thing, and it's high time I embrace it. No more waffling about whether I'm in or I'm out. No more fear of rejection. No more hiding behind words like *fling* or *just*. Saturday night wasn't the disaster I was making it out to be. It was a collision of circumstances. Nothing more. Accordion wailing or not,

Theo will move on to another girl by next weekend, maybe even sooner. Meanwhile, I have a chance at a real relationship with Felix, one that's steady *and* steamy, one that's not complicated by a prior friendship.

This is what I want.

My mom soon heads into the main room to keep working at the front desk. Felix pulls up a stool beside me and sets a hand on my back. I love the way he reaches for me the way I always want to reach for him, even though I don't always follow through.

"Want to teach me how to sew?" he asks.

"You're kidding, right?"

"I've never been more serious in my life." Despite the gravity of his words, he smiles as he grabs a needle from the little pack on the table and starts threading it.

Pippa nods with a combination of awe and approval I'm glad Felix doesn't see.

"You really don't have to help," I tell him. "I'm just happy you're here."

"The faster we finish, the sooner I can walk you home."

I avoid looking at Pippa, certain she's still nodding at me, already anticipating the salacious stories she assumes I'll tell her tomorrow. I don't intend to tell her anything of the sort, but the thought of Felix escorting me home tonight does have a certain appeal, especially when his thigh brushes against mine. And stays there.

I teach him the hemstitch I showed Pippa. He picks it up quickly, making tidy stitches beside me. The three of us chat as the hem inches closer to completion. I ask Felix about the party. He tells a few stories and says everyone hopes they can meet me soon. Despite how okay—or at least okay-ish—I was for him to talk with my mom tonight, I quickly divert the conversation by describing the highlights of my weekend, leaving out any mention of mead or tents. Pippa chimes in, too, asking Felix all about his summer art course. She's full of way more questions for him than my mom was, and full of more sly, encouraging looks. He clearly has her support, and my mom's. He has mine, too, but between our flirty glances and gentle banter, my thoughts grow disobedient again, drifting to sparklers in pot pies, glue-encrusted windmill crests, and goofy socks that badly need replacing.

Another memory creeps in without warning: Theo's body pressing against mine, his dark eyes swimming with desire, his lips—

"Looks like we have another visitor," my mom announces from the doorway. She lingers just long enough to arch a questioning eyebrow at me before slipping away again.

Theo bursts in behind her, as if conjured by my thoughts. He's breathless and holding a massive bouquet of multicolored tulips. It's so big he can't hold the whole lot. A few escape his arms and scatter around his feet. I suck in a breath, but he speaks first.

"I know what we said, but I—" He stops short as his eyes light on Felix. His face pales. He looks at me, at Pippa, back at Felix, and down at the dozens of flowers that fill his arms. "I mean, um, I hope this isn't too forward, but . . ." He fights back a grimace. I scramble for a way to diffuse the situation as he steps around the table and plants himself in front of Pippa. "Are you free next weekend? You know, for, like, a date? With me?"

Pippa shoots me an incredulous look. "Is this your doing?"

I look to Theo for direction, but his eyes are locked on Pippa. "Um . . ."

"If you're not interested, that's okay," he blurts out. "Harper's always telling me to stop with the grand gestures, anyway. Showing up here without warning. Ignoring all reason. Buying all of these flowers. Ha! And tulips of all things. Don't look up that meaning. What was I thinking? I wasn't thinking. This is stupid. I should go. I'm so sorry." He turns to cross the room again, his cheeks flaming, his eyes downcast.

"Wait!" Pippa calls. "Saturday night? Dinner and a movie?"

This time Theo looks to me for direction. I simply blink at him, too startled by rapidly shifting events to contribute anything at all.

"Wow," Felix says beside me. "I've got to step up my game."

I let out a breathy, nervous laugh while cringing on the inside.

Theo's jaw tightens. He marches back to Pippa and thrusts the flowers at her. Several fall, but she scoops what she can into her arms and breathes them in.

"Saturday," Theo says. "I'll pick you up here at six."

Pippa beams at him. He smiles back, but his expression quickly flattens. I'm still trying to figure out what the hell I'm supposed to do, when he turns, crosses the room, nods at me and Felix, and heads out the door. And just like that, my cowardice triumphs again.

SEVENTEEN

THE WEEK PASSES TOO QUICKLY AND TOO SLOWLY. My mom commits to a mountain of work at Beneath the Veil. I help where I can while pressing her to advertise for seasonal over-hire. With my vocab studies, I speed through *H*, *F*, and *S*, contriving excuses to reach out to Theo, hoping to connect face-to-face and alone before his date. I don't have a plan, other than to find out what my gut says when I see him and I'm not acting like a startled deer.

I hate that I didn't say anything on Monday, but what was I supposed to say? He shows up with all the tulips in Pennsylvania and promptly asks out my coworker, who happens to have a crush on him. I couldn't possibly claim he came to see me. What if he didn't? He jumps from one girl to the next so quickly, maybe he did bring the flowers for Pippa. Besides, we'd agreed to forget about Saturday night and remain friends. I told him flat-out that I was staying with Felix. Did he think I was lying? Or that I'd change my mind, just like that? Even if Felix wasn't sitting *right* beside me, my feelings about Theo are too new, too raw, and too confusing for me to leap into his arms at a moment's notice. I know restraint has never been his forte —or even on his radar—but there's a way to go about things. Conversation first. Grand gestures later. Better yet, no grand gestures at all.

Theo must know all of this, but he resolutely avoids me anyway, emailing a list of *J* words with a nice but hollow *Keep up the good work!* message. Apparently I've jettisoned our friendship, jeopardizing my jocularity and leaving me feeling like a juggernaut of a jobbernowl. I can't believe that's a word, and I doubt it'll appear on my SAT, but right now it suits.

I hide in the back room on Saturday night, feigning panic about a bridesmaid dress I'm dismantling. This is a new low in my pattern of caving to cowardice. I have no right to be jealous. I halted things with Theo. I chose Felix, and we have our own date planned. Still, when Pippa showed up to work today rocking a tulle skirt, low-cut satin jacket, and white-blond spit-curled wig, I shrank a little. Whether or not Theo asked her out to save face, he's totally going to fall for her. She's going to fall for him. They're the perfect level of weird for each other. Within a week, he'll be serenading her on his accordion. She'll be in here gushing about it. Before I know it, their giddy selfies will be all over social media. I want them both to be happy, but an ugly part of me isn't ready to watch them smile at each other, especially since I looked up what tulips mean. Perfect love. I would've laughed at that a week ago. Now it's not so funny.

Pippa's giggle reaches me from the other room. I check my phone: 6:05 p.m. He's probably out there with her, which means they're already smiling. I locate my earbuds and turn on Spotify, scanning past one love song after another until I finally stumble onto a folksinger with a heavy British accent ranting about politics. I blast the song at a near-deafening volume, grateful no one's mentioning kisses or longing or the *I'll do anything for you* sentiment Theo's always chasing. As the song gets angrier and I assess my mood, I set aside my seam ripper to do some measuring and marking instead. I might be irate at my conflicted brain right now, but I don't need to take out my anger on a dress.

Several minutes later, while I'm pinning in alterations, my mom steps into view and taps her ear. I remove an earbud.

"What's up?" I ask.

"Want to talk about it?"

I turn off the music and set aside my phone. "Talk about what?"

She pulls a stool up to the table and leans her cheek in her hand. She looks tired, like usual, despite her sleek French twist and her sharp black suit.

"They're gone," she says. "The store's locked. It's just us."

"Yeah, and?"

"And I thought you might have something to get off your chest."

I glance down and brush a hand over my shirt. "Nope. All good. Nothing there."

My mom blows out a plaintive sigh, slumping further against the table. It hits me that she's trying to be helpful and supportive. I force myself to make an effort.

"I don't know how to talk to you about boys," I say. "You don't date."

"That doesn't mean I won't understand what you're going through." She inches forward on her stool. "When I was your age, I was crazy about boys. I had a new crush every week. That faded over time, but I didn't stop dating until about ten years ago."

I lower my work. "Really? Why didn't I know that?"

"I didn't want to introduce anyone if he wasn't going to stick around for a while. It wouldn't be fair to you. You wanted a dad so badly when you were little."

"No *so* badly."

"Harper." A sympathetic smile plays with my mom's lips. "You named your stuffed bunny Poppa. And you refused to drink anything but Dad's Root Beer for three whole years because maybe 'he' really did make it and you had to show your support."

I groan as I drop my head into my hands. "I forgot about all that."

My mom scoots her stool next to mine. "I tried, for a while, hoping to find someone for both of us. Eventually dating stopped being fun. It felt too much like work. Around that time, I started this business. *This* was how I wanted to spend my time." She spreads her arms to take in the whole room. "Not looking for a man. Besides, you and I had each other. I didn't need anyone else, and I didn't want to miss anything. You were growing up so fast. Sometimes I think you raised me as much as I raised you." She leans closer, her expression full of love and warmth. "I don't expect you to want the same things I want, or even the same things I used to want. But if something's out there in the world that might make you happy, you should reach for it."

I take in her advice as I frown at the mound of marigold chiffon in front of me, searching my soul for a boost of inspiration that'll push me through my lingering muddle. Inspiration doesn't come. How can it? I watch people enter this shop every day reaching for happiness, only to fight about necklines or stress about cellulite. When I reached for happiness with Liam, I ended up feeling worthless, stupid, and disposable. And now? What if I don't know what'll make me happy? Or what if I've already lost my chance?

"I like Felix," I say.

My mom sits up a little straighter. "Okay."

"I think I should see where that goes for a while."

"Okay." My mom smooths my hair over my ear.

I pick yellow threads off my pants. "It could be really great."

"It could."

"If it isn't, maybe we can revisit this talking idea?"

My mom opens her arms wide. I lean into her embrace. She rubs my back the way she used to when I was little, in the years when I still slept with a stuffed bunny.

"Of course," she says. "I'll even buy the root beer."

♥

Felix and I get take-out from the fish-and-chips place near the bridge. He offered to take me somewhere nicer, but I didn't want to end up at the same restaurant as Theo and Pippa. Also, I love fish and chips. The saltier and greasier, the better.

"I'm glad we can finally do this," Felix says as we walk the towpath, snacking on fries. The canal to our right is as smooth as green glass. Lanky branches reach toward it, wrapped in dripping moss. The evening light casts long shadows across the gravelly path that stretches into the distance, making the world around us feel like an impressionist painting. "I've been kinda worried. Thought you might be avoiding me."

"Sorry. Just busy." I catch the skepticism in Felix's eyes and force out a closer truth. "And maybe overthinking things a little. That's all."

"Anything I should know?"

I prod my fries and wonder, what should Felix know? That I'm totally falling in love with him and it scares the crap out of me, but I'm also attracted to my best friend and I have no idea how these two feelings can coexist and Felix should run screaming because I'm obviously a complete disaster, one made up of contradictions, with no social life, who's better with spreadsheets than she is with people, who needs a friend to tell her how to dress for a date, and whose last boyfriend shed her as easily as an old sweater?

"Personal stuff," I say instead. "Nothing I can't sort out on my own."

Felix nods thoughtfully, though I can't quite tell if he believes me.

"I thought my bad art might've scared you off," he says.

"Maybe I was avoiding the tap dance."

"Hey. Yeah. About that . . ." He takes my fish-and-chips bag.

His eyes glint with amusement as he backs up and folds his arms. The tension between us softens. "Well?"

"What? Now?"

"I showed you mine . . ." He lifts his chin in challenge.

I glance around. Other than an old couple pretty far down the path, we seem to be alone. I'm still in my work clothes since I didn't have time to go home and change. The black helps me feel largely invisible but the chunky heels on my ankle boots make me worry I'll topple into the canal. While I debate my next move, Felix watches me from the other side of the path. He's in linen pants and a blue-gray T-shirt that matches his eyes and clings to his amazing body. Maybe falling into the canal wouldn't be so bad. Not if he might dive in after me. I can swim, but he doesn't need to know that.

I take a bracing breath and center myself in the path.

"Okay," I say. "You ready for this?"

"I was born ready for this." His smile stretches into a grin. A flutter of joy erupts in my chest, timely evidence that I'm with the right guy.

For about half a minute, I proceed to fully humiliate myself by shuffle-shuffle-stepping my way along the path with my wrists bent back and my fingers splayed out beside my hips. I even hum a little. When I feel I've adequately paid my debt, I spin on one toe and land my turn with flickering jazz hands.

Felix applauds as best he can with his hands full. "That was awesome."

"That is why I'm planning to get an economics degree." I

tighten my ponytail, not that I jostled it much with my lukewarm performance.

Felix closes the distance between us. He pauses in front of me and bends down for a feather-light kiss, lingering close and searching my eyes.

"So, you still like me?" he asks.

I laugh to myself, grateful for an easy truth. "Of course I still like you."

"Good. I still like you, too." He holds out my dinner.

I take it in one hand while hooking the other around his elbow. Together we walk on in the beautiful summer evening. I ignore my food so I can enjoy Felix's closeness. With every step, I feel less torn about what choices to make and how and why. He's so easy to be around when I'm not predicting catastrophes or mislabeling my feelings for my best friend. He tells stories about the crazy relatives who left last week and the antics one of his coworkers is always getting into at the grocery store. I try to use a few J words on him, but when the vocab practice reminds me of Theo, I change the subject. Eventually I circle my way around to telling Felix about math camp last summer, even though it dredges up even more uncomfortable feelings, ones I do my best to hide.

"You didn't want to be a counselor again this summer?" he asks as we approach an old bridge that crosses the canal. The crisscrossing beams have been freshly painted red, making them look like the center of a Union Jack.

"There was too much to do at my mom's shop."

"Maybe she could hire someone else."

"I'm working on it, but it's a sticky subject. My mom doesn't always make the best hiring choices." I toss my garbage into a nearby trashcan. Felix does, too. We set off again at a slow amble as our hands find their way to each other. "After a long run of employees who slacked off, stole from the register, stole from the stockroom, or marketed cheap knockoffs of her designs, she finally hired an assistant manager to oversee everything but the design and sewing work. The guy embezzled her entire savings, claiming he was owed the money for fees he was never paid."

"Yikes." Felix winces. "Couldn't she sue the guy?"

"She tried. She hired a lawyer to deal with the situation. He screwed her over even further, siphoning money for work he never did. She was going to declare bankruptcy and quit the industry altogether, but a friend of a friend knew a financial planner. She got my mom on track again with a series of bank loans. My mom didn't understand it all, but I did. I made sure she stuck to the plan. Once the bad press died down, work picked up again. When we couldn't manage just the two of us, we found Pippa."

"The girl with the hair?" Felix circles a finger near the nape of his neck.

"Yeah. She's great. And now my mom and I are finally doing okay, paying off loans instead of adding new ones. I don't want to see all of that slide."

We stop under the bridge. Felix faces me and takes my other hand, doubling the link between us.

"Wow," he says.

"Too much talking?"

"Not at all." He steps closer, squeezing my hands. "I didn't realize you basically ran that place. I knew you were smart, but now I'm even more impressed."

I look away, shifting my weight, unable to find a comfortable stance. I didn't mean to brag. I didn't mean to talk that much, either, especially about embarrassing family drama. I've never told anyone but Theo—

Felix's lips meet mine. They're warm and soft, like always. He holds the kiss as he releases my hands and reaches up to cradle my face. My eyes flicker closed. The tension that's been coiled in my belly for the last two weeks unwinds. I link my hands behind his neck, tilting my face up to his. The back of his hairline is soft but bristly where it's cropped short. I brush my thumbs across it, letting the hairs slide across my skin and settle into place.

"You're too good for me," I murmur against his lips. "You know that?"

He shakes his head. "I don't know that at all."

"You're athletic." I kiss his jaw, the sharp angle that meets his neck. "You're artistic." I kiss his eyelids as he closes them for me. "You're kind." I kiss his lips, gently so I don't get carried away. "You're patient, you're thoughtful, and you listen."

He nuzzles my nose. "And that's too good for you, why?"

"Because I'm a sedentary, annoyingly sarcastic future economics major whose most notable skill is her ability to fold a fitted sheet properly."

The corners of Felix's lips twitch as though he's fighting a smile.

"You underestimate the value of a properly folded sheet."

I sputter out a laugh. "Did I mention you're also funny? I think I forgot funny."

"I think you should stop thinking." With a glimmer in his eyes and a tenacious smile still fighting to make an appearance, he draws me to him. His lips part. Mine do, too. His strong hands splay across my back. My hands cup the back of his head. From there I let the world fall away as I tumble freely into Felix's deep and dreamy kisses.

My heart pounds.

My breath gusts in shorter and faster bursts.

My gut says *yes. Yes! YES!*

EIGHTEEN

I CAN'T TAKE ANOTHER SECOND. PIPPA HAS BEEN rattling on for at least twenty minutes about how *amazing* her date with Theo was last night. He's different. He's interesting. He's so smart. He has a zillion poems in his head. He wore the sweetest little bow tie and striped socks. He's not afraid to be himself. Have I noticed how cute his throaty voice is? It's soooo cute. Especially when he hums to himself. Isn't that adorable? *So* adorable. His deep, dark eyes. His gorgeous hair. His always-smiling lips. And that dimple! Swoon!

Of course, my date was great, too, but Felix and I didn't slow dance under a lamppost or stand on the fire escape of the old, abandoned mill, reciting Byronic poetry to passersby. We didn't compete to create the tallest midnight snack at the all-night diner, and we definitely didn't play leapfrog down Main Street. These are not activities I want to pursue, but Pippa's genuine excitement makes them seem magical and inspiring, like moments out of a movie. A competitive streak I didn't know I had rises up inside me. I feel an intense urge to boast about my knee-buckling make-out session under the bridge. Fortunately, I'm not *quite* that petty.

Also, I don't want to talk about kissing. So far Pippa hasn't mentioned the topic. I'd like to keep it that way.

"How long until Ms. Connor's appointment?" I ask while I finish sorting sample gowns, ensuring everything's racked by size, style, and season.

"Hang on. Let me check." Pippa squints at the appointment book that's open on the front desk. One of these days I have to get my mom to invest in decent scheduling software. And I have to teach her to use it. "About fifteen minutes if she's on time."

I point over my shoulder toward the back room. "I'm going to go help my mom. You okay to hang out here and make sure everything's set up?"

"Of course!" Pippa slips a pen behind her ear. She's not wearing a wig today. Her red hair's looped in a simple Heidi braid. It suits her. Then again, everything suits her. I don't know how she does it, effortlessly exuding coolness whether she's in a tutu or a pair of overalls. Does Theo notice this about her?

Dumb question. Delete. Delete. Delete.

I head into the back room, determined to eject all thoughts of Pippa, Theo, their date, their future happiness, and my super-annoying resentment about all of that. My mom's draping muslin on a dress form, patterning princess seams on a new design.

"Looks great," I tell her as I grab a bin of safety pins.

"It's getting there." She takes a pin from me. "I always enjoy working on the pieces that don't get too fussy. I don't know why so many brides want all of those sparkles, trims, and flowers. A single signature detail is so much more elegant."

I watch her work, mesmerized by her ability to know where a seam should go, or which direction the fabric should face. She really is an artist. I've always admired that.

As she eases a fold into the cotton fabric, I hand her another pin.

"An economics degree will include marketing classes," I say. "If we work on branding, I bet we could get your work featured in some of the top bridal magazines. Demand for your designs would increase. You could hire more help, someone to do budgeting, equipment maintenance and supply upkeep, alterations, consultations, PR. And you'd never have to sew a fake flower again. You could make what *you* want."

My mom shakes her head at me, her eyes tinted with amusement.

"Sweetheart, that's a lovely offer and you know I appreciate all you do for the shop, but can't you enjoy being a teenager for a while? Have a party when I'm gone all weekend? Learn how to do a keg stand? Smoke a joint? Sneak your boyfriend over?"

"Sorry. Wrong kid." I set the pins near my mom's elbow and search the rack for an alteration that won't take too long. I cope with anxiety better when my hands are busy. Also, my mom was looking at me a *little* too closely while she said that last bit. I don't know what she saw and I certainly don't know what I feel, except that the word *boyfriend* seems to be on everyone's lips these days. Should Felix and I talk about what we call each other, or am I supposed to just know? "I'm not planning any parties, and weed smells like dead skunks, but I promise to drink a beer when I ace my SAT next month."

"That's the spirit!" My mom pumps a fist before returning to her work.

I laugh as I grab a maroon silk dress that needs to be cut and rehemmed from floor length to thigh length. It's one of five. Hemming them is boring but easy, and a good task to take on when I'm preoccupied. I can't believe the matching bridesmaids trend is still so popular. It's painfully outdated, but as long as brides are petrified that their friends might steal even a jot of attention, I'll be doing assembly-line alterations, and girls will be wasting money on bland and unflattering dresses they'll never wear again.

My comment about my SAT reminds me of something I meant to do this morning. As I sit down at the table with the dress and a ruler, I get out my phone.

Harper: *J's mastered. Keen for K*

The ellipsis appears right away. I almost drop my phone.

Theo: *Knead more time to prepare*

I smother a smile, glancing over at my mom to make sure she's not watching.

Harper: *That's knot like you*
Theo: *I'm trying something knew*
Harper: *Maybe by to-knight?*
Theo: *If I'm not taking a knap*

My smile's persistent. I turn away from my mom so she doesn't notice and ask questions. I'm practically buzzing with joy. After over a week in which Theo and I have barely exchanged a word —vocab lists excepted—this is a huge step forward. Maybe it's perfect that he's dating Pippa. He's obviously cheering up, and if everything works out between them, he'll be thanking me instead of avoiding me. Granted, I have some totally irrational jealousy to get over, but I'm working on it, and at least I'll have my friend back. It's great that he seems happy. Super great. Really, just . . . nothing but great.

As I lay out the bridesmaid dress to mark the new hemline, I remember the offer I made to Theo when we were out at the campsite. The maroon silk is perfect. We have loads of ivory fabric in stock. My mom won't mind if I snag a couple of yards, as long as I let her know what I'm taking. I can scavenge the other materials I need from the fabric recycle bin. If I work late all week,

I should have something together by Friday, just in time for Theo's next weekend in Mothloria.

I've barely begun the first bridesmaid dress alteration when Pippa peeks in to say Ms. Connor's arrived, and she brought the groom. This is rare. Even more rare, as the morning plays out, he doesn't simply provide lip service to how beautiful his fiancée looks in anything she tries on. Instead, the couple chats with enthusiasm about the choices they made together for the wedding, and they express genuine excitement that they can afford to invite so much of the local community. After a spectacularly non-argumentative discussion, they select the seventh of ten dresses Ms. Connor tries on as a shape for my mom to work from. It's a figure-hugging bias cut with a train of circular ruffles spilling onto the floor in the back like a waterfall. My mom is elated. She loves this style, even though it's time-consuming to cut and sew. Mr. Armstrong offers a suggestion about the placement of the shoulder straps. Ms. Connor requests a different belt style. My mom takes the notes and agrees to have a mocked-up version ready for a fitting in three weeks. It's one of our smoothest appointments ever. Everyone contributes and no one's offended by anyone else's input.

"You guys are really good together," I say as I unzip Ms. Connor in the dressing room. I've said as much many times before, but this time I mean it. "Your wedding's two months away, and you don't even seem stressed."

Ms. Connor chuckles to herself. "This is my fourth. I know

better now. You should've seen me at my first. Everything had to be *just so*. I don't know how that man stood beside me and promised to love me forever. He should've chucked me while he had the chance." She wriggles out of the sample dress. I hang it up while she puts on her own clothes. "It's funny, the things we learn as we age. Life would be so much easier if we had more wisdom when we were young, but then we'd lose the chance to make all of those beautiful mistakes." She turns a warm smile on me, one that makes me rethink every biting comment I've ever made about bitchy brides, and every time I've hated myself for making a choice that doesn't pan out perfectly.

I sweep aside the curtain, and we step into the main room together.

"It's nice of you to invite us all to the ceremony," I say. "We usually only get photographs. Unless my mom attends to make sure the dress is perfect."

"I can't invite only your mom. You're obviously a package deal."

"More than that," my mom says. "Harper's the business mind that keeps this place running. Without her, I don't know where I'd be. Probably working for someone else in another industry by now."

I busy myself by helping Pippa pack up shoes. I've never been comfortable with compliments, which is strange when I absorb criticism like an addict.

"A family business." Ms. Connor presses her hands to her heart. "Of course."

"Only until she graduates from college," my mom corrects.

Mr. Armstrong pivots toward me on the chaise. "What happens then?"

My mom doesn't answer, so I stand and try not to fidget under the attention.

"Hopefully I'll run my own business," I say. "Maybe one that's fashion related since I know a fair amount about clothes after working here. Mostly I want to be my own boss, head a company that values its workers, delivers a quality product, and caters to a female clientele in a non-pandering, nothing cutesy-and-pink-and-more-expensive-than-it-is-for-men kind of way. Also, I want to give women more pockets."

Everyone laughs as we all count our pockets. Naturally, Mr. Armstrong has more than twice as many as the rest of us. This launches a funny conversation wherein Ms. Connor tries to explain to Mr. Armstrong how women get by without the things men take for granted. The two of them really do seem good together, as are my mom and me. Pippa, too. She fits in with us so naturally. As I glance around at all the smiling faces, for the first time in ages, I can't imagine my future taking me anywhere else but here.

NINETEEN

THE DAY AFTER MS. CONNOR'S FITTING, I SURPRISE
Felix at his cross-country meet. I don't offer nearly the support
Theo offered Ginny—face painting, special signs, pom-poms—
but I jump up and down and scream my lungs out when he speeds
across the finish line well before the guy in second place. It blows
my mind that he just ran three miles. He looks less winded than I
did chasing him a single block to ask him out last month.

I find him stretching near the finish line a few minutes later.
His face lights up when he sees me. I suspect my expression mirrors his. He stands up tall and runs a hand through his sweat-damp
hair, pulling it off his broad forehead. He's totally drenched, in a
sleeveless running jersey and shorts that end at the perfect spot
on his unbelievably fit thighs. Sweat's never been a turn-on for
me, but I swear to god if we were alone right now, I'd already be
throwing Felix to the ground and yanking off his shirt.

"How'd you get the afternoon off?" he asks, still wiping at his
forehead.

"I told my mom I had something important to do. She gets it."

"Wow. Tell her thanks for me." He steps up close enough to

plant the tiniest kiss on my nose, gesturing at his body as though he's afraid to contaminate me. "I'd, you know, but . . . ick."

There's nothing "ick" about him, but I'm not sure how to say that without sounding like I'm reciting lines from that terrible bodice ripper I took on Theo's practice date. So I tell Felix how impressed I am with his running and ask if he has time to hang out. He has to check in with his coach and take a shower, but the rest of his afternoon's free. His cheeks redden a little as he says this, giving me the impression he's thinking what I'm thinking: that we won't use the time together to get ice cream.

The race ended at our school track, so I wait in the bleachers and review my vocab words while he cleans up and exchanges congratulations with his team. We walk to my house after, hand in hand, while he describes the rush of running hard and fast for three miles or more. He makes it sound so euphoric, I almost want to go for a run with him. Almost, but not quite.

We have an awkward moment when we get to my place, like we both know we're not here to bake cookies or play board games, but heading straight to my bedroom is a little *too* direct. So we decide to order a pizza and put on a movie. I grab a soda for me and a water for him while he flips on the TV. We both like plain cheese pizza, so the order is simple to sort out. I settle into the curve of Felix's arm, and almost instantly we find a film we both want to watch, one about a guy who builds an AI version of himself, only to be outdone at every turn by his fake self. Apparently Felix and I have similar taste in movies as well as food.

This moment should be perfect. There was no argument over

whether we should watch the rom-com or the action/suspense film. I won't have to sponge pineapple juice off my half of the pizza. I don't even have to worry I'm going to get tickled if I reach for the remote. But something's off, as if I've spent too many hours on this sofa with Theo. Now I'm trying to lay this version of my life on top of those memories, but the details won't line up.

Clearly, I've lost my mind. I have everything I want right now. I should be elated. In fact, I *am* elated. Snuggling with Felix must be like getting new shoes. They take a while to wear in before they're as comfortable as the old ones. That's all.

We watch our movie. We eat our pizza. As the credits roll, Felix draws me onto his lap. I take his face between my hands, still astonished that this gorgeous boy wants to be with me even half as badly as I want to be with him. Even sitting on his lap like this sends shivers of anticipation rushing through me.

"I'm really glad you came to my meet today," he says, his voice already a little raspy. "I heard you scream my name as I crossed the finish line. That was awesome."

"It was fun. And you look amazing when you're running."

"Oh yeah?" He half smiles, in that self-conscious way that always surprises me.

I nod, and then I kiss him, finding the angles of his face with my fingertips while his lips part and his tongue presses against mine. Within seconds, I'm already shifting on his lap, trying to get closer. His hands slide under my shirt and up my back. Whatever caution or restraint we were holding on to for the last two hours falls away. I grip his shoulders, his arms, his neck, as though I can draw strength from him through my hands.

Anxious to get to his skin, I ease his shirt up. He helps to draw it over his head and toss it aside. I run my hands down his bare chest, blinking through my admiration.

"What?" he pushes through a rough breath.

"Tell me you have a hideous mole somewhere. An ingrown toenail. A vestigial tail. Something besides . . . this." I flap a hand at him.

He laughs as he twists around to show me a small patch of darkened skin on his lower back, just above the hipbone that juts out from his jeans.

"Burn mark," he says. "I leaned against a stove about five years ago."

"It'll have to do." I lean forward and kiss him again, hungry for anything he's willing to share, even if his only flaw is a few inches of barely marred skin.

He draws my shirt off, helping to free it when it tangles around my wrists. I grind against him while he slips a hand inside my bra. His touch is strong and sure, making my breath catch and shooting happy little sparks across my skin.

"I didn't bring—" he pants out between kisses. "I mean, I didn't know . . ."

"It's okay. I have some upstairs."

He scoots forward on the sofa, drawing my legs around his waist. In the next second, he's easing onto his feet while I cling to him, insanely turned on by his strength, even if that's super unfeminist of me. He carries me up the stairs and into the bedroom I point out. My room's embarrassingly boring, with a plain white quilt, plain white walls, and very few personal details, but neither of us is focused on the decor right now.

Felix lays me down on my bed and leans over me. We kiss for a while, both a little nervous to take things further, despite the clear desire I both feel, myself, and see mirrored in his eyes. In time, I remove my bra. He takes off his jeans while I take off my shorts. We keep our underwear on as he rubs against me and I explore his back, his arms, his face. Soon we're touching each other everywhere. His gray eyes are so wide as he stares down at me, his lips parted and gusting out breath, his chest heaving, his thighs sliding against mine, his hand inside my underwear while I arch against him. With so little barring us from each other right now, I am a fireball of pure craving.

"Is this okay?" he asks. "Are we going too fast?"

"Yes," I gasp. "I mean no. Yes to the first one. No to the second." I kiss him again, willing him to feel, to know how much I want him.

"Have you . . . before? I just want to know how careful to be."

I nod, biting my lip. "You?"

"Yeah, but not like this, with a serious girlfriend."

My movement slows until my body goes still. I will myself to shake off the unexpected jolt of nerves, but once it seizes me, I compound it by berating myself for freaking out about something as stupid as words, especially words I want to hear, to feel, to believe in. Despite knowing I have nothing to panic about, I'm now lost in a spiral of thoughts I can't sort through. The heady blur of desire is gone. Felix notices the change. He draws back and rolls off me, his face painted with concern.

"Are you okay?" he asks.

I nod and try to smile, but my heart is racing and I'm so confused and I've never been more embarrassed in my life. I lay a hand against Felix's beautiful cheek, rotating to face him. He looks hurt, which is the last thing I want. I lean forward to kiss him again, but he pulls back and sets a hand on my chest, gently maintaining space between us.

"I'm not going to pretend nothing happened there," he says. "Seriously, Harper. Talk to me. We don't have to do this. Any of this. It has to feel right for both of us."

"It does feel right," I plead. "I want it. I want you."

"But you don't want me to call you my girlfriend?"

A chill seizes me at the knowledge that my fear is so transparent. It's so ugly, and so *not* who I want to be. He looks at me with wounded eyes, shaking his head. I rack my brain for something to say, for a way to draw the hurt from him.

"The word surprised me," I say. "I need time to adjust to it. That's all."

"We've been going out for a month now."

"I know."

"I'm not dating anyone else."

"Me neither."

"We were about to have sex."

"I *know*."

"So what did you think this was?" He waves a hand between our chests.

I swallow, fighting back another wave of panic. "I guess I'm still figuring it out."

"Wow." His brows inch up. "That's why you didn't want to meet my family."

"No! Maybe. I'm sorry. I didn't expect this to get so complicated so fast."

"It's not complicated for me." Felix sits up and slides his legs off the edge of the bed. He bows his head, raking both hands through his hair as he blows a slow breath toward the floor. And another. Then he turns toward me and regards me for a long moment. "I want you to be my girlfriend. Do you want me to be your boyfriend?"

I open my mouth to say *Yes, of course*, but at the last instant I flash to an image of Theo's body pressed against mine, our legs entwined, our linked fist bridging the space between our hearts, his breath warm against my lips. I think about Liam, too, and how I had no doubts at all about him last summer while he only wanted a fling. I hated that he lied about that, pretending it was more, pretending it was love. We made decisions based on that lie, decisions I might not have made if I'd known the full truth. I was so blindsided later. I felt so stupid, so used, so naive. I can't make myself be certain about Felix right now, but I can at least offer him the truth Liam hid from me.

"I don't know," I whisper. They're the hardest words I've ever spoken, the least simple, and the most honest. Despite the softness with which I utter them, they fall from my mouth like daggers, and they find their home.

Felix nods, shakes his head, tips his head back, and blows another breath toward the ceiling. Tears fill the corners of my eyes and start to fall. I wipe them away with the back of my hand. While I sputter and sniffle, Felix finds his jeans and puts them on.

"I think I should go," he says. "If you come to any conclusions, you know how to find me. I'm a pretty understanding guy. But I won't come looking for you, okay?"

I nod as I choke back a growing sob. Felix watches me, rubbing his face and battling his own emotions. I scoot up on the bed, desperate to throw myself into his arms, to rewind the last five minutes, or to go back even further, to the morning when we kissed by the café, when this all seemed so much easier. Instead, I hug my knees to my chest as Felix walks out of my bedroom and, a minute or two later, out of my house.

TWENTY

I'M SITTING ON THE EDGE OF MY BED, ANKLE-DEEP in wadded tissues and hairline-deep in heartbreak. My mom's sitting beside me, rubbing my back.

"I should've been able to answer him," I say for the thousandth time.

"You did answer him," my mom says, also for the thousandth time.

"Not the right way. It was a simple question. Yes or no? True or false? 'All of the above' wasn't an option." I destroy my soggy tissue and let it join the others on the floor.

My mom kicks it aside. "No one faces everything in life with total certainty. You think I wasn't terrified about becoming a mother? Or opening a business? Or letting my teenage daughter basically run that business while I screw it up at every turn?" She waits for my ghost of a smile, watching me with all the sympathy in the world. "Yes, a lack of certainty has consequences. People can get hurt. Opportunities can pass you by, but leaping into choices without careful thought has consequences, too."

I blubber softly, trying to recall the last time I did anything at all without thought, other than pick whatever crappy frozen meal I'd eat on any given night.

"Why couldn't I at least tell him how much I like him?" I moan.

"That wasn't the question he asked." My mom hands me another tissue. "And liking someone isn't enough to warrant a relationship."

"But he's perfect."

"Maybe perfection isn't the right fit for you."

I pause my sniveling to gape at my mom as though she's lost her marbles.

"You do know who you're talking to, right?" I ask.

She chuckles a little as she glances around at my carefully arranged bookshelves and the photos that are lined up with almost military precision on my dresser. My desk surface holds only my laptop and a tidy canister of pens and pencils. My white curtains and bedding are crisp and spotless. The notes on my bulletin board are all pinned up at right angles. Only the growing pile of tissues at my feet shows any sign of disarray.

"Where relationships are concerned, 'perfect' is highly subjective," my mom says. "Love isn't like a math problem. Feelings don't fit into spreadsheets or formulas with conclusive answers. We can't fold them, stack them, box them up, or file them away. We can't order them around and expect them to obey."

"They should at least make sense." I blow my nose as I relive my conversation with Felix yet again, the question that was so simple for him and so complicated for me. Then I recall what Theo said that night in his tent. *Complicated isn't always a bad thing.*

I never realized how brave he is for embracing that perspective. And how much of a coward I am for avoiding it. "I *want* to be with Felix."

"You keep saying that. Who are you trying to convince? Me or yourself?"

I try to answer, but for the second time today, an answer doesn't come.

My mom scoots closer. "I know you like Felix. I like him, too. If the two of you are meant to be together, you'll work through this, but maybe your heart is saying something else, and you need to listen." She sets a hand on my back, rubbing in slow, calming circles. "Don't try to solve this right now, while you're so upset. Give the matter some thought, or let it settle for a day or two. Sometimes the best solutions arrive when we don't force them. Try stepping away instead."

"I did step away. I spent that weekend with Theo. Look what good it did me." I point out the tissue-mageddon at my feet, hoping I haven't revealed more than I intended. My mom doesn't need to know Theo has anything to do with my current confusion. It could get really awkward at the shop now that he's dating Pippa. "I'm such a mess. I don't know the first thing about guys or relationships or anything."

"You know more than you think you do. The rest you can only learn through experience. As Ms. Connor wisely said, by making beautiful mistakes." My mom plucks a damp strand of hair off my forehead and smooths it over my ear. "Why don't I cancel tomorrow's appointments? We'll drive up to Bryn Mawr. Walk around the campus. Get lunch. Dream about a future when all the things you *do* know will carve out a life path for you, and when what you're going through right now won't feel so raw."

A new sniffle makes my nostrils waver. "You'd cancel a work-day? For this?"

"*This* is a big deal, Harper. Even if you wish it wasn't." She wipes away a new tear that trickles down my cheek. "The last time I saw you cry, you were twelve and needed six stitches in the sole of your foot. Doesn't look like this hurts any less."

"No." I reach for another tissue. "It doesn't."

While I blow my nose, my mom leans her head in her hand, waiting until I stop honking like a rusty trumpet.

"You barely knew my mom before she passed," she says, "but, wow, could she hover. I had tight curfews, rules about boys, and heavy scare tactics about drugs and alcohol. She was always asking what I was doing and when and why. It drove a wedge between us, and I made some not great choices as a way of rebelling against her." My mom takes my face in both of her hands. "I don't mean you. You know that. You're the best choice I ever made. I'm talk-ing about the partying and, yes, the boys." She laughs to herself as if she's reliving a memory she's only slightly embarrassed about now. "I didn't want to treat you with the lack of trust my mom showed to me. You've also earned that trust. You're so much more mature and reliable than I was at your age, but if you always seem fine, I don't know when you need me."

I nod, my throat thick with emotion. She adjusts another damp strand of my hair.

"So should we have a girls' day tomorrow? Just the two of us?"

"Yes, please." The words are so tiny but so big as I fall against her shoulder. She wraps an arm around me. As we huddle together, the world feels a little less painful and a little less complicated. No matter what happens with my love life, my mom's attention isn't entirely committed to her design work after all. She's had an eye on me this whole time. I just needed to invite her in.

♥

Bryn Mawr is amazing. Old stone buildings frame neatly groomed lawns. Small clusters of students read against tree trunks or gather in doorways, here for campus summer sessions. My mom and I decide against a formal tour, wandering open buildings on our own. I run a hand along wood-paneled hallways and well-worn banisters. I scope out all three libraries, giddy there's more than one. I peek into seminar rooms, athletic facilities, and one of the dining halls. It even smells good, luring me in with the promise of non-microwaved food. After checking out the buildings, my mom and I read want ads and ride-share offers on an over-packed bulletin board, getting a sense of the life of the place. We end our tour by taking a selfie near the fountain in the middle of the cloisters. The courtyard looks like a set from Hogwarts, but I won't tell Theo that.

Crap. My mind went there, didn't it? C'mon, mind, back on track . . .

Over lunch, spurred on by a new understanding about my relationship with my mom, I tell her about Liam. The conversation's awkward at first, and embarrassing, even though my mom's far from judgmental. She mostly listens and tells me she's glad I told her, without offering unsolicited advice or making me feel ashamed. She asks me how I'm feeling about it now. Amazingly, I tell her I'm okay, not in general, but considering this summer's relationship drama, Liam's no longer my biggest concern. Also, after what happened with Felix, I suspect Liam didn't lie about his feelings because he was trying to manipulate me. Maybe he lied because it was easier, or because he wanted to believe the lie as much as I wanted to believe I was totally certain about Felix. And maybe, just maybe, Liam lied because he didn't want to hurt me.

With relationship talk exhausted, my mom and I shift topics to my work at the shop, and how my friendships have trickled away this year while I've been helping her pull out of debt. She sets a new ground rule: I'm no longer allowed to work for her more than eight hours a day or forty hours a week during the summer, twenty during the school year. I realize I could've set this rule at any time, but it feels better coming from my mom. She doesn't make many rules. I understand why after what she told me about her mom, but every once in a while, it's nice to let her be the authoritarian in the household.

After lunch, my mom and I wander the area that surrounds the campus. When we pass a storefront for a palm reader, my thoughts return to Felix, tracing lines across my hand, smiling at me in a way I'd dreamed about for months. The memory draws fresh tears to my eyes as I wonder yet again how I let him walk away, how badly I hurt him, and how I can make everything right again, if that's even possible. I don't even know what "right" would involve. However, now that I've had a day to let my mom's advice sink in, I know the solution doesn't involve pretending I know what I want so Felix and I can stay together. He might forgive me for hurting him but he deserves to be with someone who's sure, just like I deserved that last summer, when I was the one who was sure.

My mom and I are halfway back to New Hope when my phone buzzes.

Theo: *K's limited. Included L. Latest lexicon at your linguistic leisure*

I open the attached list. The first two words make me sputter out a laugh.

"What's so funny?" my mom asks from the driver's seat.

"Labile: readily undergoing a change or breakdown. Lachrymose: showing sorrow especially through tears."

"Theo's vocabulary list?"

"Yeah. He's really good at these. I bet he doesn't even look up most of the words. He just pulls them from his brain." I read on. The list includes other words like *languish, lassitude, lethargy,* and *listless,* all of which relate to my current mood. Does he know what happened yesterday? Did he run into Felix? Or is the tone of his list a coincidence?

As we near the turnoff to New Hope, I recall the last time I was on this road, returning home from a war I didn't fight in and a battle I was only just beginning to wage inside myself.

"Mom?" I ask. "Can you drop me at the shop? I have a project I want to work on."

TWENTY-ONE

FRIDAY NIGHT I'M HOME ALONE, STILL DEBATING what to tell Felix and how. So far I'm certain of only two things: I should apologize for my confusion, and I should be on my own while I grapple with that confusion. My mom's working late to make up for Tuesday's campus visit. I offered to stay and help with alterations, but she insisted I head home once we closed the shop for the day, upholding the new limitation on my working hours. I'm not sure what to do with the time yet. I put out a few feelers to my friends, but rebuilding those relationships will take time. People got used to assuming I was busy. My nights will be my own for a while. My mom said if I wasn't learning how to do a proper keg stand or hosting an orgy, I should at least binge-watch a TV series full of egregious sex and violence. Naturally, I selected a documentary, this one about climate change. It's super depressing, but I figure if the world's about to end, I don't have to feel so crappy about my breakup. We'll all be drowning in unrecycled plastic before I even see Felix again, let alone figure out what to say to him.

When the film ends, I shuffle into the kitchen in my stretched-out yoga pants and my baggiest never-worn-outside-the-house T-shirt. As I put away the leftover pizza and soda, I hear grunting and clinking from the yard next door. I peer through the kitchen window to see Theo attacking Mr. Strawbody, lunging at the metal trashcan lid he's strapped on as a shield. I'm not ready to see Theo after everything that's happened, but I should fulfill at least one of the deals we made this summer. Also, I might never be ready. Probably best to seize the moment.

I run upstairs to slip on a bra and a pair of flip-flops. After grabbing the shopping bag that's under my bed, I head next door. Theo dances across his yard in the dimming twilight, spinning, swishing his blade, stepping in slow circles while he sizes up his enemy. He looks like a swashbuckler from an old movie except he's in bright green terry-cloth track pants and a sleeveless undershirt. I thought people stopped selling terry-cloth sportswear back in 1970-something, but it's true to character that Theo found an article of clothing no one else our age would wear. At least I don't have to worry about my current lack of style, though around Theo, I never have worried about that.

I wait until he nails Mr. Strawbody in the chest, poised in a perfect lunge.

"Um, hi, hey," I stammer from the edge of his yard.

He jerks upright, lowering his blade to his side. He doesn't say anything. He just stares at me with his chest heaving from exertion, otherwise unmoving.

"Thanks for the latest list," I say. "It's lusciously laudable."

He smiles a little. It's something, enough to get me to step forward.

"Look, Theo, I don't know what I'm supposed to say here or which words would make everything okay between us, but I miss you and I really want to be friends again." I hold out the shopping bag. "Also, I made you something."

He squints at the bag. "Lemon loaf? Licorice lollipops?"

I shake my head and cross the rest of the distance between us. He peeks into the bag as though he's expecting to see a bomb. As I spread the handles to give him a better view, his eyes jump to mine.

"You didn't."

"I told you I would."

"Yeah, but—"

"But nothing."

He studies my face, shoving his thick black bangs off his forehead with a slow swipe of his hand. After a long moment, he lays down his blade and draws the maroon and ivory tabard out of the shopping bag, holding it up by the shoulders to examine the crest with its carefully embroidered windmill silhouetted against a red velvet heart.

"You made this?" he asks, his face flushed with wonder. "For me?"

"Sir Theodoro needed an upgrade. Especially if you're going to kick everyone's ass at that big tournament next month."

Theo drapes the tabard over his forearm and traces the edges of the windmill with an outstretched finger. His touch is so slow and gentle, it's almost reverent. He looks at me, at the tabard, and back at me again. Then, because he's Theo, he tears up and throws his arms around me, smashing his gift and the shopping bag between us.

"Thank you," he chokes out.

I count to ten as a means of distracting myself so I don't tear up, too. My eyes prickle anyway. I can't help it, not with Theo's arms locked around my shoulders and his cheek pressed to mine as though our friendship was never strained or put on hold.

"I just, I can't, I mean, wow." He pulls away and wipes his nose on the back of his hand. It's kind of gross, but at least he didn't use the costume. Besides, after all the weeping and sniffling I've done this week, I'm the last person who should judge.

"I have something else, but it goes up there." I nod at the tree-house. It looks especially dream-like tonight. The evening air is still. The windmill blades are barely moving. Bright oranges and corals paint the stucco with the last blush of the day's sun.

Theo carefully lays his tabard and sword at the base of the tree. We head up the ladder together. He turns on the perforated lantern. I situate myself near the window, like usual, while he takes his spot by the bookshelf. At first glance, everything seems like old times. This is just another evening. The two of us are about to watch movies or share a pint of ice cream. Only there is no movie. There is no ice cream. More notably, we're both overtly cagey around each other now, a feeling I hope will fade with time.

While Theo plumps an old pillow and shoves it behind his

back, I reach into the shopping bag and take out the matching mini-tabard I made for his Funko Pop! figure. With some effort, I wrestle the costume into place and set the little guy back on the sill.

"Well?" I ask. "What do you think?"

Theo presses a fist to his lips, his lashes fluttering.

"Don't you dare cry again." I stare him down. He swallows and lowers his hand, blinking away whatever tears were about to emerge. When I'm sure he's going to hold himself together, I fold up the shopping bag. "That isn't a character from a book, is it?"

He shakes his head. "It's from a custom-order site. Mom O. found it for me. You plug in the details and attach photos. They send the figures a few weeks later."

I'm half tempted to ask who the girl is, but he's had these things for years. That's so many girls ago, he probably doesn't even remember. The figure's kinda generic white-girl-looking, with long, wavy brown hair and narrow, gently curved brows. I think Theo was into a girl who looked like that back in junior high. Cindy or Mindy something. She liked goats and wore scrunchies. That's all I remember about her.

While I speculate, Theo clears his throat and tugs at the rumpled toe of his threadbare sock, his eyes locked on the task. Naturally he's not wearing shoes. Why he doesn't also skip the socks in the summer, I'll never know.

"So, um, Pippa told me you and Felix had a fight," he says.

I slouch against the wall, wishing we were chatting about

virtually anything else. I told Pippa about Felix on Wednesday. I couldn't *not* tell her. She saw it all on my face.

"I had a feeling she might say something."

"She seemed to think you could work it out, if you wanted to."

"Maybe. I don't know." I find a loose thread on the hem of my T-shirt, suddenly as preoccupied with my clothing as Theo seems to be with his. "He deserves more than I can give him right now. That's pretty much all I do know." I wrap the thread around my finger and yank it free. "Seems like things are going well between you and Pippa."

Theo inches up a shoulder. "She's cool. And fun. I like her wigs."

I swallow a thick lump of jealousy. I've never been called cool or fun. Smart, capable, driven, organized, productive, impressive, mature, and helpful, but never fun.

"I had a feeling you guys would hit it off," I manage.

"Well, if you had a feeling . . ." Theo teases.

"Whatever." I roll my eyes, not in the mood. "I'm glad you like each other."

"Are you?"

"Um, yeah? Of course. Why wouldn't I be?"

"I don't know. You tell me."

I blink at him through tired eyes, uncertain what he's driving at and why a familiar sense of challenge tints his expression. A silence builds. He stops fussing with his clothes. I stop fussing with mine. We launch a weird round of looking at each other and then looking away again, as though we've lost our ability to communicate as normal humans.

Unable to bear the growing tension, I turn my attention to the window. The last of the daylight's fading fast, making the stars from the overhead lantern pop against the curved plaster walls. I should probably go. I did what I came to do. I'd love to spend the rest of the evening with Theo instead of alone with my angst and my remote control, but I don't want to talk about my relationship. Or his. We'll get there, but not tonight.

I'm scooting onto my knees when Theo breaks the silence.

"Want to give me another lesson before you go?"

I stifle a laugh. "You still want me to teach you how not to fall in love?"

"Wouldn't hurt. Might at least save you a night of accordion music." A twinkle appears in the corner of his eye, a twinkle I've missed desperately.

"In case we haven't clearly established this, I'm a disaster at relationships." I meet his eyes, pleading for sympathy with mine. "Just ask Felix. He'll tell you."

"Did you fall in love with him?"

I reel. "How did we get to *that* question?"

"Seems like logical information to pursue if I'm soliciting a continuation of my anti-amorous edification. Consider it an attempt to reestablish your credentials."

I eye him sideways, searching for signs that he's kidding. He doesn't smile. He doesn't wink. He doesn't even lift his chin. He simply holds my gaze, watching me with an unnerving intensity.

"How about we skip the lessons?" I say.

"How about you answer the question?" Theo raises his brows, direct and defiant.

I prickle the way I always do when he gets my defenses riled up. My jaw tightens. My shoulders twitch. Sarcastic retorts wait on my tongue, ready to spring to life, but he's asking a simple question. I even have a simple answer, one I've given a lot of thought to this week, though that thought always led to the same maddening conclusion.

"No," I say, knowing it to be true. "I'm not in love with Felix."

"Then you still have something to teach me after all." The twinkle in Theo's eye returns. Now I know he's baiting me. He even squares his shoulders as though he's prepping for a face-off. They're really nice shoulders, though I wish to god I didn't notice that.

"What exactly do you think I can teach you?" I ask.

"On second dates, do expectations change?"

"I don't know. Depends."

"On what?"

"How the first date went?"

"If it went well?"

"Then yes, probably."

"If it only went okay?"

"Still probably."

"Do I pay?"

"If you asked her out, yes."

"If she asked me?"

"Then no, though it's always nice to offer."

"If she wants to hold hands?"

"Then hold her hand. Unless you don't want to. Then don't."

"What kinds of compliments are okay?"

"Focus on the neck up and you'll be fine."

"If she wants to take a walk?"

"Then walk."

"Or slow dance?"

"Same rules apply."

"And if she wants to kiss me?"

I jerk backwards, hitting the corner of the goddamned windowsill yet again. I crane around as though I'm checking to see if a bruise is forming, even though I can only see about two inches of my back. Theo watches me contort myself, amusement still tinting his eyes.

"How do I kiss a girl without getting—what was your word? Attached?"

"I don't know." I throw up my hands. "Keep your tongue in your mouth, and you'll probably be fine. Oh, and don't get naked. That never helps."

Exasperated to find myself discussing the absolute last topic of conversation I wanted to touch on tonight, I tuck the folded shopping bag under my arm and crawl toward the door. Theo halts my progress by meeting me in the middle of the windmill. Both kneeling, we're almost exactly the same height, though I slouch a lot more, so I have to look up a little to meet his eyes.

While I search them for signs of his intentions, he slides the bag out from under my arm and tosses it aside.

"So what you're saying is if I do this, it's safe?" He leans forward and places a sweet little kiss on my cheek, straightening up and studying me as if he's trying to gauge my reaction.

I keep my face blank, but a zillion tiny bubbles course through my bloodstream.

"Y-yeah. Sure. Seems fine."

"What about this?" He places a second kiss at the corner of my jawline.

"Mm-hmm. Still okay."

"Or this?" He brushes a few loose strands of my hair aside and follows the curve of my ear with his lips. He's barely making contact, but I feel his touch in my toes, my fingertips, my suddenly wobbly knees.

I lower myself onto my heels. "I, um, yeah, what was the question?"

Theo lays a hand against my cheek. I lean into his touch and close my eyes. He kisses my other cheek. His kiss is so brief and tender, I might've missed it, and yet every cell in my body is buzzing right now, zapping out little messages of craving, yearning, begging for more. After four sleepless nights and as many restless days, my gut in knots and my brain whirring, his touch feels so good, so right, as if something went on pause that night in the tent and it's finally continuing now. His thumb shifts against my cheek, and I draw in a sharp breath. Questions start to form in my mind, but they fade before finishing, over-powered by intense waves of desire. How did we . . . ? What are we . . . ?

"Zero attachment," Theo murmurs against my ear, nuzzling it with his nose.

"Absolutely none." I lay my palms against his chest, feeling his truth in his galloping heartbeat. I brave a look in his eyes. They're so dark right now, I really could get lost in them forever. His thick lashes twitch as his eyes shift from my left eye to my right and back again. I don't know what he's looking for or what he sees, but as he wets his lips, the bubbles in my bloodstream multiply a thousand-fold. I know only one thing: if he doesn't kiss me in the next three seconds, I'm going to explode.

"Only practice," he says, practically panting.

"Part of the lesson plan."

"Edification."

"Exactly." I can't stand it anymore. I close the distance, setting my lips against his. We hold like that while my hands slide around to the back of his neck and his hands cup my face. His lips part before mine. My head tilts to the side as I find the perfect angle to fit our mouths together. A peck. A nibble. Then a hint of warmth and wetness as his tongue taps at my lower lip. I draw back, but not very far. "Theo, I . . ."

He watches, waits, his breath coming fast and short.

"You what?" he asks.

"I completely forget what I was going to say."

"Thank god." His lips press against mine, harder this time,

with an insistence that shatters any resistance I was still cling-ing to. My mouth falls open. My tongue finds his. He draws me against him, chest to chest. I tangle my hands in his hair, grateful there's so much to hold on to. His hands are on my face, my neck, my back, strong and warm. We practically dive at each other, kissing so deeply, I lose all sense of what's his and what's mine. As soon as I ask myself the question, I realize I don't care.

I have no idea how long we make out, but at some point amid all the kissing, gasping, and gripping our fists into each other's clothes, we topple sideways onto the pillows and blankets. I wrench a hand into his undershirt, desperate to tear it off and get to his skin. He frees my ponytail, letting my long hair fall around both of our faces. I'm on top, then he is, then we're side by side, wedging our thighs together, sneaking hands past the edges of clothes, devouring necks, ears, lips. Kissing no longer feels like enough. Nothing feels like enough. I want all of him, and I want to give him all of myself.

He starts grinding against me, holding my hips against his with both hands. I roll on top of him and draw my T-shirt off over my head. He slows his motion, gaping up at me with what I can only call awe. It mirrors the wonder that overtakes me as I look at him. This boy—this beautiful, brilliant boy—is here, shar-ing himself with me, laying himself bare, utterly fearless. I feel him shift between my legs. He wants this as much as I do. The thought makes me want him even more. I take his hand and set it on my breast. Then I kiss him again before I start worrying about what might happen tomorrow. I don't want to think about that right now. I only want this intoxicating, brain-numbing, body-electrifying desire, and I want it to last forever.

Theo rolls me onto my back, kissing my neck, the inner curves of my breasts, and the ticklish spots on my sides. While I writhe against his hips in the best possible way, he inches the waistband of my pants down, teasing me with feather-light kisses that span from one hipbone to the other. I arch against him, my entire body on fire.

He grips the sides of my pants. "Can I?"

"As long as yours go, too."

A grin splits his face. It draws out my own smile in response. He slides my pants off, leaving me in my bra and underwear, which sadly weren't picked out for this occasion. Thankfully the thought's fleeting as I watch him kick off his socks and shove his track pants down, struggling as they catch around his ankles. I take the opportunity to check out his underwear, half expecting random goofball print boxers. Instead, he's in simple black boxer briefs, and he looks so goddamned sexy, I can't believe he's the same guy who used to hang out on his own at recess, his nose buried in a book, hiding from bullies. And the same guy I thought of as a brother for so many years. He is *so* not my brother. Thank god. I know we can't have sex right now. I didn't plan for it and I doubt Theo did, either, but there are a lot of other things we can do and I want to do it all.

As he finally frees his ankles and flings his pants aside, his phone falls out and lands beside me. It's buzzing. The name on the screen is clear as day. *Pippa Pennington.*

Reality crashes in. I bolt upright, already scrambling for my shirt.

"Oh my god," I gasp out. "Oh my god, oh my god, oh my god." I find my shirt and yank it over my head. It's inside out, but I don't bother righting it.

Theo kneels before me, holding out both hands the way people do when they walk toward an animal they think might be dangerous.

"Harper. It's okay. Calm down."

"Calm down?!" I wrestle my yoga pants out from under his knees. "As if I haven't made enough bad choices lately. I had to go and do this?!"

"Whoa. Wow." Theo drops onto a hip, knotting a hand in his hair. "Is that how you really feel? That I'm nothing but a bad choice?"

"Not you. This." I flick a hand back and forth between us. "It's wrong. It never should've happened. I have, like, two friends in this whole stupid town, and I'm rapidly working my way toward none." I jam my legs into my pants.

"No surprise with an attitude like that."

"Don't get lofty with me, Turner. You're as guilty as I am."

"Guilty about what?"

"Seriously?" I fling a hand toward his phone.

He sinks in on himself, looking hurt and confused. "Do you really think I'd —?"

"Pippa loved your first date. She couldn't stop raving about it."

"I'm glad, but that's beside the point."

"It shouldn't be. Not with all the questions about your second date."

Theo frowns at that, as though he finally realizes what we've done. It's not like him to miss how his actions might affect someone else, unless making out with me meant absolutely nothing to him. One more game played in the privacy of our hideout. The thought hurts like a son of a bitch, but I push through it as I yank my pants over my butt.

- "Don't worry," I say. "You've got the meaningless kissing down."

Theo balks. "Meaningless?"

"Zero attachment. Only practice. Your words. Not mine."

"And you took that literally?"

"You told me yourself. You're always chasing the next distraction."

"Yeah, but not from—"

"There's no point arguing about this." I crawl toward the door through a tangle of blankets, wishing my exit wasn't taking *forever*. "Maybe you were a distraction for me, too. I've had a shitty week, though apparently I can make it even shittier."

"Ouch," Theo murmurs as I pass, pressing a hand to his heart.

I spin toward him as I start down the ladder, tears stinging my eyes. I want nothing more than to climb back into his arms and pretend the last minute didn't happen, but his phone's still buzzing, Pippa's name is permanently etched into my retinas, and I have to go to work tomorrow knowing I betrayed her. Worse than that. I didn't even think about her. I embraced what was in front of me without question. I haven't even talked to Felix yet. I didn't think about him, either. I've never hated myself more.

"This was a m-mistake," I stutter through a sob. "A stupid, hasty, mistake. We said it didn't mean anything. Let's stick to that plan. And please, *please* don't tell her."

TWENTY-TWO

I'M CURLED UP ON THE SOFA WATCHING A SLASHER movie when my mom finally comes home. I hate horror films, but this was the least romantic thing I could find. I close my eyes at all the gory parts, meaning I've spent most of the last two hours with my eyes squeezed shut. Trouble is, once my eyes are closed, I lose myself in memories of Pippa bouncing around the shop after her date last weekend, blathering on about Theo. I also think of Felix, staring at me with wounded eyes, waiting for a *yes* that never came. I can't believe I locked them both out of my mind once Theo knelt before me, planting the tiniest little kiss on my cheek. That was all it took for me to fly to Selfish Town.

One. Tiny. Kiss.

Theo's right. No wonder I don't have any friends.

"What are you watching?" my mom asks as she nudges my feet aside to wedge herself onto the sofa.

"Midnight Massacre Part Something."

"I thought you didn't like this kind of thing."

"I don't, but so far no one's kissed anyone, broken into song, held a hand, batted an eyelash, or uttered the word *love*. It's perfect."

My mom scoots closer and sweeps my hair over my shoulder, lining up the strands so they blanket the back of my neck, poker straight and silky smooth.

"Did you see Felix tonight?" she asks.

"No." I pause the film and sit upright. "Why?"

My mom waves a hand over her neck. I take a second to register what she means. Then I leap off the sofa and run to the bathroom, groaning as I get a look at my reflection. My neck is speckled with telltale purple blotches. A lot of them. I draw aside the neckline of my T-shirt. More little blackberry-shaped spots dot my shoulders and cleavage. Good lord, Theo covered some serious territory.

The thought turns me on, which is the opposite of what it should be doing. I can't help it. I want him, in all the ways it's possible to want someone. Nothing I experienced with Liam or Felix compares to those precious, stolen minutes in the treehouse. Liam always seemed like he was trying to prove something, showing off, looking for approval or praise. Felix was my fantasy boyfriend. Being with him was like being in a joyous bubble of what I thought a relationship should feel like, all dreamy and romantic, but nothing felt totally real. It was *too* perfect. Theo and I simply fit together. We shouldn't, but we do, and I never realized how much until tonight.

I slink back to the den, where my mom's waiting cross-legged on one end of the sofa. I take the other side, drawing a blanket onto my lap so I feel less exposed. I hope I don't look like a child, clinging to my security blanket. I also hope I remember to wear a neck scarf to work tomorrow.

"You know I trust you," my mom says. "I'm not going to lecture you about the choices you make with boys. I heard an earful at your age. It only made me rush out and do everything my mom told me not to. I just need to know you're being safe. And I need to know you understand what being safe means."

I almost laugh. If I wasn't so tied up in knots right now, I probably would laugh.

"I think we covered it with the condom shopping and gynecologist appointment."

"Right. Well, I'm glad all that sank in, but being safe also means being thoughtful about who you share your body with and how you share it." She leans closer, waiting until I meet her eyes. She has no humor in hers. Only worry and care. "I know you're upset about your breakup. Flying into something physical with another guy might fill that emptiness for a few minutes, maybe even a few days or weeks, but that feeling won't last. You could be stuck negotiating the fallout of your intimacy with someone you don't want to be entangled with. I don't mean only physical repercussions. I mean emotions, too. The body and the heart are connected in mysterious ways. So if you're going to fool around, make sure it's with someone you like and someone you trust." She draws my hair back and lays her fingertips against my neck. "So was all this with someone you like?"

I swallow hard as her question begs me to expose a truth

I've been denying for hours, days, weeks, maybe even years. A truth I've been grappling with since I fled from the treehouse, maybe even since the morning I woke up in the tent, my body tangled with Theo's, my heart full of uncertainty. I called my feelings attraction, but I misused my words yet again. Now the right words seem as evident as the nose on my face.

"No," I say. "It was with someone I'm stupidly, crazily, madly in love with."

My mom's gaze flickers toward the kitchen. "Theo did this?"

I stiffen, clutching the blanket with both hands. "How did you know?"

"Oh, Harper." The tiniest hint of a smile lifts the corners of my mom's lips as her eyes well with sympathy. "The way you fussed and fidgeted every time Pippa so much as mentioned his name. I've never seen someone so eaten up by jealousy." She glances at my hands. I release the blanket from my death grip. "Besides, that boy's been in love with you for as long as I can remember. I always figured at some point you'd realize how special he is. When you were ready."

My breath rushes out of me. I fall backwards into the corner of the sofa, releasing the blanket as my body goes limp, robbed of everything that once held it together.

"He . . . what?"

My mom shakes her head at me as her smile widens. She gets off the sofa and fetches a photo book from our shelves, holding it out to me as she takes her seat again.

"It's all there if you take the time to notice it."

I flip open the book. The first few pages are pics from a road trip my mom and I took when I was in first grade. After that comes a trio of shots of Theo and me from the same summer. In the first one, we're biting into a single slice of watermelon together. In the second, he's holding the slice away from me while I fume with indignation. In the third, I'm eating the last bite while Theo shines a toothless grin at me. Other pages depict Halloweens spent trick-or-treating together, with shots of our annual candy swap. Theo gave me all of the Snickers because they were my favorite. I gave him pretty much everything else because even the crappiest candy made him absolutely giddy. We show off the gifts we gave each other at Christmas, each one thoughtfully selected and often handmade. Theo also poses with his spelling bee trophies while I wrap my arms around him and look on with intense admiration. He does the same for me when my team wins the area math competition. Sure, there are pictures where one of us looks annoyed or disinterested, but mostly we smile at each other. A lot.

I flip through the book again before I shut the cover. So when Theo told me he was trying to distract himself from what he really wanted, did he mean . . . ?

"He's dating Pippa," I say.

"Dating or went on a date with?"

"The first, I assume. They had something planned this weekend, I thought for tonight. He was asking for all kinds of advice about second dates. And she really likes him." I run a hand over the book. My mom sits beside me, characteristically withholding her opinions, even though I kind of wish she'd yell at me for being selfish and stupid. It would save me the effort of doing it, myself. "Guess I should talk to her, huh?"

"It's a place to start."

I press the photo book to my chest. "I said some terrible things to Theo tonight. I got carried away and then I panicked about how I got carried away. Why do I do that?"

My mom chuckles to herself. "I think you come by that trait honestly. It was pretty much my trademark when I was your age. All of your responsibility and maturity must've come from Ted."

"You mean Chad?"

"Was it Chad? Maybe it was Tom. Oh, Lord." My mom waves off the conversation as though it's a mildly annoying odor. "Just use a condom."

♥

I'm sitting on the chaise at Beneath the Veil when Pippa arrives for work on Saturday. My mom's in the back room doing last-minute adjustments on a gown we're fitting in about an hour. I've already downed two enormous lattes, which only partly explains why my knee is bouncing and I've torn my cup cozy into a thousand pieces. A large chai and a bag of Pippa's favorite biscotti sit on the table before me like sacrificial offerings. I can only hope they make this conversation slightly less painful.

Pippa swishes across the store, looking fabulous as always, this time in lavender topknots and blunt bangs. She's wearing a funky black halter dress and sparkling jet jewelry that looks hand-made. I'm in my usual boring black dress shirt and boring black trousers, plus a ton of concealer. An ugly pang of jealousy stabs me in the gut, or maybe the ache is due to the gallon of coffee I drank, the breakfast I didn't eat, and the sleep I didn't have. But seriously, how can he not be crazy about her? She's like rainbows and unicorns and everything fun. I'm like the crusty loaves of white bread they put on sale after a day because it's already stale. Though that's probably my sleep-deprived, guilt-ridden brain talking. On a good day, I'm at least a decent pretzel bun.

Pippa sweeps up the cup marked with her name. "Ooh! You got my chai. Thanks, Harps." She takes a sip and glances around. "What are you doing just sitting out here? Catching up on hairstyles for summer brides?" She nods at the neatly stacked magazines.

"I'm waiting for you, actually. There's, um, something we need to talk about."

Pippa lowers herself into one of the throne-like chairs, instantly wary.

"Am I being fired? Please tell me I'm not being fired."

"No. God, no. This place would collapse into chaos without you. My mom would schedule every fitting at once." I chew on my lip, force myself to stop chewing on my lip, and smooth out a nonexistent wrinkle in my pants. "It's about Theo . . ."

Pippa flaps a dismissive hand. "Oh, that. So he told you?"

This time it's my turn to be wary. "Told me what?"

"We were supposed to go out last night, but he texted around five and asked if he could meet me right after work instead of later at the restaurant. I got all excited, thinking he couldn't wait to see me. Turned out he wanted to tell me he liked me a lot and he had a really good time last weekend and blah, blah, blah, but he couldn't keep dating me because he was into someone else."

"Wait. What? He said that right after work yesterday?"

"I *know*. Surprise!" Pippa flings up a set of jazz hands. "Though at least he didn't wait until we were halfway through the appetizers. Or ordering dessert."

"Um. Yeah. That was decent of him." I rapidly sort the timeline in my head, stunned into stillness by this new information. So he broke things off *before* I saw him? Why didn't he tell me? I asked, didn't I? Or did I? Oh god. Maybe I didn't. But then what was with all the second-date questions?

As I try to recall the details of our conversation, Pippa spins toward me, narrowing her eyes and gripping the arms of her chair.

"Do you know who he's into? Wait. Never mind. Don't tell me. I don't need to know. I'll end up stalking her online, searching for things I can hate about her." She flops back in her chair, expelling a dramatic, put-upon sigh. "You were right. I never should've tried dating a high school guy. They have zero commitment, but whatevs. It was one date. I'll live." She blows another sigh into her lavender bangs, making them flutter.

I drop my head into my hands and massage my forehead. I'm relieved she's not heartbroken, and I'm glad Theo wasn't still dating her when we made out, and yet . . .

"I do know who the girl is," I say, barely. "And you don't need the Internet to figure out what to hate about her. That's what I wanted to talk to you about, though less about him liking her and more about her liking him." I stare at my toes, waiting for a cue to move. Pippa doesn't give me one, so I peer up at her between my fingers. She's glaring at me with her lips pursed and her arms locked across her chest. My guilt redoubles itself, but I force myself to straighten up and meet her eyes. "I'm sorry. I didn't realize how I felt until last night."

Her brows inch upward. "What happened last night?"

I drop my head into my hands again. Pippa gasps and shuffles forward.

"You didn't!" she says.

I peer at her sideways, shrinking into myself. "No, but we were getting there."

She gives me a swat on the arm. "Bitch stole my man."

My entire face rumples into what must be a truly hideous grimace.

Pippa laughs in that way that always makes the world seem brighter. "Kidding, Harper. Take a joke. I didn't stake a claim on the guy, especially after only one date. He has a right to make his own choices. I mean, I'm still going to hate you, but only so I can guilt you into buying me chai for the rest of the summer."

I finally stop hiding my face as I sit up and scoot toward her. "I'm so, *so* sorry. I only went next door to drop off that costume I made him. I didn't know how he felt or how I felt, but we started talking and next thing I knew we were—"

Pippa thrusts a palm at me. "Stop there. On the talking."

I search my pants for wrinkles again. They're the kind of pants that are designed not to wrinkle, but I need something to do with my hands. I reach for the bag of biscotti. Pippa sweeps it away as though she knows I'm about to massacre the contents.

"One question," she says.

"Anything."

"So, you didn't know he'd ended things with me when you . . . 'talked'?"

I shake my head, tongue-tied by a new swell of guilt.

Pippa snaps off the end of a cookie and pops it into her mouth.

"Every morning. Large chai latte. Two, no, three almond biscotti. Waiting at the front desk. And on Fridays you have to clean the windows."

"Done."

"C'mon, then. Over here, man-stealer." She waves me into a hug. I squeeze her hard, filled with gratitude that she's so forgiving, even if her form of forgiveness will run me a hefty tab at Beans 'n' Leaves. She won't really hold me to it, but it's the least I can do. I wouldn't be as generous if our situation was reversed. On the surface, maybe, but I'd be seething inside. I held a grudge against Liam for an entire year. Granted, different circumstances, but I could definitely use lessons in how to be chill.

Pippa polishes off her cookie while I sweep the shredded coffee cozy into a trashcan. We finish tidying up together, prepping the seating area so it's spotless for the next bride-to-be. As we set up for the first fitting of the day, I fill Pippa in on how I left things with Theo, leaving out a description of his state of undress and sticking to the key facts about how badly I panicked when I saw her call come through. She tells me she only called him because she'd misplaced her credit card. She thought he might've picked it up at the coffee shop where they met earlier that evening. Turned out her card had fallen from her phone holder into her pocket. I'd love to blame crappy phone accessory design for last night's catastrophe, but I was the one to freak out and flee the second the situation became complicated. I was the one to tell Theo he was a mistake.

"So what happens now?" Pippa asks.

"Now I have to learn to be brave."

TWENTY-THREE

THEO WON'T SEE ME OR ANSWER MY TEXTS. HIS moms won't even let me into the house, though Olivia sneaks me a plastic container of leftovers, and Shay encourages me to try again once he's had time to cool off. I get the distinct feeling all three of our moms have been waiting for us to get together for years. They probably placed bets on when it would happen. I hate that everyone else saw something I didn't even consider, but I can't do much about it now except hope Theo's eventually willing to accept one more apology.

While I wait for him to break his silence, I move forward with the other uncomfortable conversation I need to have. As soon as we hit a day with a break in the fitting schedule, I time my exit and park myself in front of Blue Dog CrossFit. Felix emerges a few minutes later, as punctual as ever. He's sweaty from his workout. His T-shirt is damp and his skin shines in a disconcertingly sexy way. His caramel cowlicks form parentheses at the sides of his forehead, and his pale lashes flutter as he blinks away the bright sun. He looks gorgeous, as always, which makes me question my sanity a little. I can't help that I'm attracted to him. I also can't help that I'm in love with someone else.

His eyes go cold as he spots me. I suck in a breath, mustering courage.

"Hi." I flash him a choppy wave. "Can I walk you home?"

"It's over a mile."

"I have the time." I attempt a smile. I fail miserably.

Felix looks around as though he's seeking an excuse to say no.

I lean forward and try to catch his eye. "Do I need to tap dance?"

He snorts out a hint of a laugh. "Please don't."

"I was that bad?"

"You were . . . entertaining." His hint of a laugh turns into a hint of a smile.

I finally let out the breath I was holding.

"I'd like a chance to explain," I say. "Actually, that's not true. I want to hide from you until graduation so I can pretend nothing bad happened between us, but I think you deserve better, and I'm trying this new thing called *not being a coward.*"

"Oh yeah? How's it going so far?"

"Well, my stomach's in knots, I think I've sweated more than you have in the last hour, and I'm dying to fake a fainting spell, so, pretty good, I think?"

He nods thoughtfully as he hikes his gym bag up his shoulder.

"Okay." He tips his chin to the left. "I'm this way, but if you faint, I'm leaving you to the crows."

"Totally fair."

We head down the street together, weaving our way through the tourists who populate the area every summer, mostly couples on romantic retreats, but also families, artists, and New Yorkers who need an escape from the city. Felix and I break the ice with small chat about his latest cross-country meet and my recent run-in with a bridezilla who excised her sister from the wedding party for not being as pretty as the other bridesmaids. The conversation's halting and we both try too hard to sound casual, but gradually we ease into more of a natural camaraderie. It helps, and it allows me to get into the hard stuff. Slowly, carefully, searching for words that don't come easily, I explain how my breakup last summer made me afraid to like a guy again, and how it made me look for reasons *not* to be with someone rather than look for reasons *to* be with someone.

"I got used to liking you from a distance," I tell Felix as we head out of the busier part of town and onto a side street. "It was comfortable, uncomplicated, risk-free, though I was starting to feel creepy watching you through the windows for months on end."

Felix gives me a little nudge. "It was kind of cute, actually."

"You noticed?"

"You didn't? I thought you must have. I was totally doing the same thing."

"Yeah, I guess I did notice." I smile to myself as I recall some of the fleeting glances we exchanged, each of us waiting for the other to make the first move. "I was so happy when we finally started dating. The more time I spent with you, the more I liked you, but all the while this little voice in my head kept saying, 'It's not real. It won't last. Don't trust it. Avoid words like *boyfriend*. Don't get attached. Don't let too many people know you're dating so you won't have to explain why he stopped liking you.'"

Felix halts and turns to face me, taking my hand.

"But I didn't stop liking you."

"I know, but the possibility was always there, tapping at my brain, reminding me I wasn't cool or fun or interesting enough. I told myself to ignore it, and I was starting to, but then . . ." My words die in my throat. I slide my hand away, unsure how to say what I need to say. I recall what Pippa told me about what Theo said to her. He didn't couch it in generalities like *It's not you, it's me.* He came right out and said it. "But there's someone else. I didn't realize it until recently. I'm not even sure where things stand with us, but I like him. I . . . more than like him." I back against a picket fence, gripping the knotted wood in both hands. Felix watches me from the other side of the sidewalk, one hand linked through the strap of his gym bag, the other raking through his hair.

"The guy with the sword?"

"It's an épée. But yeah."

Felix nods again, that way he does, as if he's deeply concentrating, sorting one thought from another until he reaches a clear conclusion. I pick at the fence behind me and try not to crawl out of my skin. I can't tell if he's hurt, mad, or unsurprised by what I told him. Maybe I'm the only one in New Hope who didn't see it. Well, me and Pippa.

"I'm really sorry," I say when I can't stand the silence for another second.

"I know. It still sucks." He studies me, his eyes narrowed. "I've gotta ask. Are you sure? Because he doesn't really seem like your type."

"I would've said the same thing a few days ago, but maybe that's what I like so much about him. He isn't a type at all." I start to think about that, but I catch a flash of hurt in Felix's eyes. "You're not, either. I didn't mean that. After all, how many star athletes are going to have their photographs displayed in galleries one day?"

"They won't be."

"They might. You're better than you think you are. At a lot of things."

"Apparently not at the things that count. Between us, anyway."

We both go quiet. He drums his fingers on the strap of his gym bag. I release the picket behind me and try to anchor my hands somewhere less awkward: my hips, my pockets, each other. I want to reassure Felix that he isn't the problem. He did everything right, but how do I put weight behind that statement when I'm telling him I prefer another guy, one who might not even want to be with me? A tension builds until a pair of giggly girls passes between us, eyeing us as though they've stumbled into a juicy bit of gossip.

Felix tips his chin down the street. We head off again toward his house.

"Do you think we can be friends?" I ask. "Like, could we still hang out, get fish and chips, praise each other's artistic mastery, only without the flirting and kissing?"

"I don't know. I liked the flirting and kissing."

"Yeah. I did, too." My hand inches toward his, but I tuck it behind my back before it misbehaves. Felix and I carry on in relative silence until we reach his house. It's a two-story brick home that looks a lot like mine, with an empty lot on one side, a fat black cat sunning himself in the next yard over, and two tabbies parked on the front porch.

Felix steps onto his driveway. "Thanks for walking me home."

"Thanks for letting me. And for listening."

"I need some time to consider the friend idea."

"Okay." I kick at a weed in the sidewalk crack. "You'll let me know?"

Felix nods as he backs up a few steps. A lump of emotion builds in my throat, threatening to rise to my eyes. I hate watching him retreat. I'm aching to run after him, to fling my arms around him and beg him to forgive me and kiss me and make all of these ugly feelings go away. I always thought breaking up with someone would be so much easier than being broken up with. Maybe it does hurt less than being unceremoniously dumped. At least it's not laced with shock and powerlessness, but it still feels awful. The guilt for hurting someone I care about gnaws at my chest, embedding its claws so deeply, I'm not sure it ever plans to leave. Grief hits me almost as hard, hollow and haunting like a gust of frigid air. I don't want to give Felix up. He made me happy. I want him to be happy. He didn't do anything wrong. I haven't stopped liking him. I don't even know what'll happen with Theo, but I guess that's what I have to figure out next.

TWENTY-FOUR

"HE WENT TO STAY WITH HIS DAD IN FLORIDA," I TELL
Pippa as we prep a fruit tray for today's first client. "His moms
told me last night. He won't be back until the end of August."

Pippa pauses, mid–melon slice. "He'll be gone for a whole
month?!"

"Apparently I blew it even bigger than I thought." I arrange
the strawberries in a perfect arc at the corner of the tray.
"Unless he really is down there to study with his fencing hero.
That's what Olivia told me he was doing, but from the look
on Shay's face, I'm pretty sure he's playing a hardcore game of
Keep Away from Harper." I take Pippa's melon slices and add
them to the tray, making a happy fruit rainbow for a bride we
already know is only going to complain about it. She was awful
at her first fitting. Pippa, my mom, and I have a bet going for
how many things she'll gripe about today. My mom aimed low
at seven. Pippa went for a nice, even ten. I shot high at sixteen.
The biggest loser has to walk down Main Street in the bridesmaid's dress we inherited from the girl who got booted from last
week's wedding party. It's a hideous pea green polyester chiffon,

strapless with a butt bow and a satin bolero. It's going to look great on my mom.

"Maybe he'll change his mind," Pippa offers. "The situation isn't all your fault. He implied we were still seeing each other. He must've known that'd be weird for you."

"Weird or an invitation to tell him he'd made my shitty week shittier?"

Pippa sets aside her knife and plucks grape clusters off the main stem.

"So you made a few hasty comments," she presses. "He can't be *that* upset."

"He cried over a girl he only went out with twice. He played that agonizing accordion for six hours straight after a LARPing maiden turned him down last fall. He can't even bear a piece of pineapple being lonely. If he liked me even half as much as I like him, and if he took anything I said to heart, then yeah, he can be that upset."

Pippa sneaks a piece of cantaloupe. It's the same color as her wig. I love that.

"You said he's good at accepting apologies, right?" she asks.

"He has been, but that was when we were firmly entrenched in the friend zone. I get the feeling the stakes are higher now." I drag over a trashcan and dump all the rinds. A trail of juice drips onto my skirt. "Dammit. We haven't even started the day, and I've already maculated my clothes."

Pippa's eyes go wide. "You've *what?*"

"*Maculate: to spot or stain.* I'm on M now."

"You got a new list? That sounds promising."

I sigh as I scrub juice off my skirt. "I found a list online. It's not the same. I have no motivation to study without Theo's help." I toss aside the dishtowel. As Pippa finishes the cleanup, I add a few decorative silk flowers to the tray. Might as well give the bride another thing to complain about. I really don't want to wear that dress. "I'm starting to think I took on this vocab challenge as much to get inside Theo's brain as I did to boost my SAT scores. Not that I realized it at the time, but now it's pretty obvious I did a lot of things in order to be closer to him."

Pippa picks up the tray, perfectly balancing it on one hand.

"Have you told him that?" she asks.

"I haven't exactly been suffering in silence." I get out my phone, hold it in front of Pippa, and rapidly scroll past the many, many messages I've sent without answer. Apologies, explanations, pleas for forgiveness, attempts to make him laugh. Ironically, it's a very Theo approach to the situation, and one that's as unsuccessful as ever.

"Wow. Can't say you haven't tried." Pippa heads to the door, tray in hand. "Maybe the time apart is good. It'll give you a chance to miss each other."

"Or it'll give Theo time to realize he's better off without me." I hold the door and follow Pippa into the main room. My mom's arranging the gown and undergarments in the dressing room. She flashes us an *I'm not listening* smile before returning to her task.

"You really think there's no chance he'll come around?" Pippa asks.

"I don't know. The look on his face was awful." On instinct, I pluck a piece of lint off the sofa. Then I put it back in case it prompts another complaint from the bride. "If I was Theo, I'd fly to Florida with an armload of roses and a serenade prepared, but I'm not as brave as he is. Especially where big feelings are concerned. He wants to be away from me. I need to respect that, don't I? Or do I keep trying, hoping he'll come around?"

"Might as well keep trying. What do you have to lose?"

"A month of useless optimism?"

"Small price to pay, don't you think?"

I don't think, but I don't tell Pippa that. Frankly, an entire month of feeling like I feel right now sounds excruciating. All the anxious hoping and waiting, only to be met with silence or rejection. It's like water torture for the soul.

While Pippa adjusts the fruit layout, I send a few more texts.

Harper: *Miss your melodramatic mellifluousness*
Harper: *Might you manumit me from my monumental malaise?*
Harper: *Or mitigate my mulish melancholy?*
Harper: *Maybe?*

No ellipsis. No response. Has he blocked me? Would I even know? I'm probably driving him crazy, and I really do need to leave him alone. A month isn't that long. He'll be back before the school year. He also has that big tournament. Surely he wouldn't miss his chance to be dubbed victorious. I just need to be patient. Yep. Totally. Give him space. Give him time. Let him do his thing.

Also, a month is basically FOREVER.

I pocket my phone and stand at attention as Stacy, the bride-to-be, bustles in with her mom and two friends. She's a petite brunette with a button nose and aggressively plucked eyebrows. Her friends pick at the fruit platter while Stacy notes that the melon has been cut larger than bite size and the silk flowers look gross with juice on them. Two complaints down and we haven't even started on the clothes.

My mom takes Stacy into the dressing room, where the gown, shoes, and undergarments are already set up. Usually Pippa or I help with the dressing, but my mom is kind enough to let us off the hook this time. I linger close by on the pretense of being available to help. Really, I'm tallying Stacy's complaints. A steel bone pokes her underarm. The fullness at the top of the skirt makes her hips look fat. The white should be closer to eggshell. Ivory's awful against her complexion. Is this really the fabric she approved, or did my mom swap it out for something cheaper? (My mom did not swap it out for something cheaper.) Wasn't the waistline lower at the last fitting? It looks wrong now. (It's exactly where it was at the last fitting.) These are *so* not the shoes Stacy had on last time. (They're totally the shoes she had on last time.) They pinch her feet but the next size up can't be right because she's *always* a six and she'd never wear a six and a half and why would the shoe company mislabel their product? It's simply poor marketing.

We're at seven complaints by the time Stacy emerges. I'm already tasting victory, imagining pinning my mom into the ugly bridesmaid dress so it'll fit over her boobs. While I stifle a triumphant smile, Stacy flounces over to the trifold mirror. Her friends leap up from their seats, gushing with praise. She really does look beautiful, like a model on a magazine cover, even if she's not six feet tall. Her dress has a corseted satin bodice with visible casings for the steel. The matching skirt has a slight bustle to the back and three rows of tiny pleated ruffles peeking out at the hem. The shape's old-fashioned, but the finish is sleek and modern. The pleated ruffles took me three days with the iron. My mom did most of the remaining construction. She was really proud of this one. She also knew the bride would be less than thrilled. Some days I don't know how she does it. All this work, just to hear someone find every little fault. Thank god I've never wanted to be an artist. After watching my mom for years and even seeing Felix beat himself up over his class projects, putting creative work into the world seems like total torture.

A phone rings from the dressing room.

"Can you grab that?" Stacy asks her friend.

One of the girls scurries over with Stacy's purse. We all wait a few feet away, looking busy while the bride answers her call. Her first few phrases are friendly. Then they get tense. Within two or three minutes, she's swearing and pacing. The call ends with an abrupt "Fine. I'll be there in twenty minutes to take care of it myself!" Phone in hand, she marches over to the fitting room, her voluminous skirt trailing behind her. "We have to reschedule," she says to her mom and friends. "Kurt can't get the orders right. There's a mix-up in the shipments. Clients are clamoring and we have no product on the shelves. I work with a bunch of incompetents. Next thing I know, they'll expect me to cancel the honeymoon so I can stay home and deal with this crap."

Without a word, my mom slips into the dressing room to help Stacy change. Pippa heads over to the front desk with Stacy's mom. Together they look for an opening in a new online appointment system we're trying out. It confuses my mom, but Pippa's thrilled. I offer the girls a last chance at the fruit tray and sparkling cider before I clear it. By the time I return to the main room, Stacy's exiting the dressing room. She's on her phone, her previous agitation softened into mild annoyance.

"You're right, of course," she says as she crosses to the seating area and drops onto the chaise. "I'll talk Cheryl through it and then step away. You and I are going to have the best time in Fiji. No work. No stress. Just us." She exhales slowly, listening to her phone as her friend rubs her back. "Love you, too, hon. Can't wait to be your wife." She blows a kiss into the phone before putting it away, tipping her head onto her friend's shoulder. "Isn't he the best? He's totally the best. God, I'm lucky."

I hold my position near the racks while she rallies and joins her mom by the front desk. Her sudden shift of tone gives me pause. She's no longer the insanely picky bride we all made fun of, the epitome of everything I hate about the wedding industry.

She's a girl in love with a guy, turning to him for advice and support, excited to be his partner in life. It's sweet, and it takes the edge off my cynicism. Maybe I've been treating this industry the same way I've been treating my dating life: looking for reasons to *not* see love rather than looking for reasons to embrace it. I've lumped every bride together into a collective of bitchy egotists. I'll never buy into the image in the magazines, the one that depicts marriage as total conflict-free bliss, but weddings do promote sincere human connection. They also foster commitment, trust, and care. If I stop ignoring or denying that, I'll enjoy my work here a lot more. I might even stop avoiding my own human connections.

The bride and her party soon exit with the fitting rescheduled for next week. I check my phone again. Nothing. I almost throw it across the room, irritated at its constant reminders of Theo's silence. If we communicated via smoke signals or carrier pigeons I could pretend bad weather or poor avian navigational instincts foiled our connection. Instead, I'm stuck knowing Theo's intentionally shutting me out.

I can't stand it, so I sneak him a few more texts.

Harper: *Making motion for muteness moratorium*
Harper: *Must metamorphose misunderstanding*
Harper: *Meagerly managing morass of moods*
Harper: *Mostly moping*
Harper: *Mayday!*

I'm trying to come up with a way to use *malapropism* or *mercurial* when my mom's voice breaks my concentration.

"I guess we all know what this means." She joins me by the racks, nodding toward the picture window. I follow her gaze to see Stacy get into a swanky silver Porsche that's parked out front.

"Lightning-fast turnaround on the final alterations?" I ask.

"That dress fit her like a glove. It won't require much work."

"Even if she claims it does?"

"I'll talk her through it. She's just nervous. It's natural before a big life change."

"Okay, then what is it we 'all know'?" I exchange a curious look with Pippa.

She shakes her head, as lost as I am, but as she glances out the window, a smile of recognition dents her freckled cheeks, taking its time to ease into full position.

"I tallied nine," she says.

"I only caught eight," my mom counters.

I stiffen. "No way. The bet's off. She canceled her appointment."

My mom shrugs, all *c'est la vie.* "I don't recall that stipulation, do you, Pippa?"

"I sure don't!" Pippa flies across the shop and into the back room, skipping out a minute later with an armload of the most nauseating pea green fabric I've ever seen. "Thanks to Stacy's cancellation, we have an entire hour to ourselves. Plenty of time to make a spectacularly attired coffee run. I'll even do your hair and makeup!"

I groan at the thought. My mom laughs and gives me a quick squeeze. Pippa drags me into the dressing room by the wrist, practically humming. And while I've never been a fan of publicly humiliating myself, at least this time, no boys are involved.

TWENTY-FIVE

HALF AN HOUR AFTER STACY'S DEPARTURE, I'M fully clad in a cloud of vivid green chiffon with an armpit-pinching satin bolero that makes me sweat and a butt bow that makes sitting down impossible. The bride must've wanted her bridesmaids permanently upright and at the ready. Pippa has styled my hair into a towering bouffant she decorated with scattered silk flowers. I look like I belong on the cover of a 1950s girl group album that's full of songs with the word *baby* in them. My mom can't stop laughing. Pippa can't stop fussing. She gives me lace gloves and presses me into using her coral lipstick. It looks awesome on her with her cantaloupe hair and rockabilly halter dress. I look like I kissed a kumquat.

My mom stays behind while Pippa and I head down Main Street to Beans 'n' Leaves. I get a lot of stares and funny looks. I swear people are whipping out phones to snap pictures, but it's hard to tell in New Hope. People are always taking pictures. On the way back from the coffee shop, I pass a group of my friends heading to lunch. They take in my attire and ask if my mom's getting married. I laugh at the absurdity of the idea. We chat for a few minutes as I explain the bet and ask how everyone's summer is going. The conversation's nice, friendly, like how my life used to feel before I started working all the time. My friends even invite me to a party next weekend. For the first time since my mom's near-bankruptcy, I don't tell them I'm busy. I get the details and say I'd love to come. A little seed of joy sprouts in my chest as we wave goodbye. My social life no longer seems like a thing of the past. It's repairable. I can help my mom's business thrive and still have a life outside of her shop. Next step: hiring more staff.

Pippa and I are almost back at the shop when I spot Felix chatting with one of his running buddies in front of the gym. He goes still when he sees me. His friend claps him on the shoulder, laughing hard enough to bust a gut. Felix simply gapes. I hike my dress up past my ankles and do a quick soft-shoe for him, ending the routine with a saucy wiggle of my butt bow. He smiles a little as he tugs on his earlobe, blushing ever so slightly, maybe for my embarrassment, maybe for his own. In that tiny interchange, a weight lifts off my shoulders. We're not friends in this moment, but we might be, in time, when the sting dies down. I didn't necessarily lose him forever. Only for now.

My optimism lingers as I change into my own clothes and remove the flowers from my hair. I have social plans for the first time in ages. Felix and I are one step closer to reconciliation. I'm even beginning to appreciate the wedding industry. Also . . .

Once again I do the thing I always tell myself not to do right before I do it, only this time I don't feel the agonizing push and pull. I simply open Instagram and pull up Liam's page. The latest shot is of his band on a crappy stage in a crappy bar. For the first time since our breakup, he strikes me as ordinary. Sure, he's talented, smart, and good-looking, even with the haircut I always thought was kind of pretentious. He's also just a guy. And this time, I think I'm using the word *just* correctly.

Pippa leans over my shoulder, draping her arms around my neck.

"The pie offer still holds," she says.

"Thanks, but I don't need it. Not anymore."

"Even after he dumped you, like, two minutes before you guys left town?"

"Maybe he was avoiding a bigger confrontation. And maybe he was so dismissive because he didn't know what to say, like I didn't know what to say to Felix or even to Theo. Relationships are hard. Breakups suck for everyone."

"They suck less when your ex is wiping whipped cream off his eyebrows."

I laugh a little, grateful for Pippa's fiercely dedicated friendship.

"I don't need revenge," I say. "I need to let my resentment go."

I scroll through Liam's photos until I find a few from last summer. A sunset walk in the woods. A selfie we took in a meadow, both of us wearing dandelion crowns. Another with cones in our hands and smudges of ice cream dripping off our noses. A kiss in the rain. Together, they paint a picture of a perfect summer romance. Yes, he tossed me aside without a second thought, but that doesn't mean the relationship wasn't worth having. It *was* beautiful, for a while. Maybe a while is enough. Maybe the possibility of things ending shouldn't scare me as much as it does. Maybe it shouldn't scare me at all.

While Pippa watches, massaging my shoulders like a boxing coach prepping her fighter to enter the ring, I scroll back up to Liam's latest band shot. I type into the comments. *I hope the gig went well. Bet you rocked it. Good luck with the band and with senior year.* I barely hesitate before hitting send. I don't know what he'll do with it. Hopefully nothing at all. I didn't send it for him. I sent it for me.

♥

At home alone after work, I peel the plastic off a tray of pad thai and settle in on the sofa. I'm about to click on a suspense film about a manipulated political campaign when another title catches my eye. *Love, in Other Words.* It's Theo's favorite rom-com. I've seen it — or at least parts of it — a dozen times. He can't get enough of it, especially the end when the couple comes together for a big, mushy kiss. It's a massive cheese fest and *so* not my thing, but I watch it anyway. I cringe through the clichéd meet-cute at the library. I also sass-talk the TV all the way through to the final swell of music as the couple says the L-word. Except I'm not cringing anymore. I'm caught up in the moment.

Okay, so there is something I haven't said to Theo yet. A word that won't show up on my vocab lists, even though it's harder to define than any of the words he's given me.

I get out my phone. I put it away again. I can't do it. Not yet. It's too big, too scary. What if he stays silent? Or if he tells me he doesn't feel the same way? I don't think I could bear it. No matter what my mom said about him or what I saw in our photographs or what I sense in my heart, I don't really know how he feels, so I set aside my phone.

My mom comes home about an hour later to find me staring at it again.

"A watched phone never rings," she says.

"I know."

"Give him time."

"Everyone keeps saying that."

"Then maybe you should listen." She's smiling, so I know she's teasing, but I frown at my phone anyway, and at my long thread of unanswered texts.

"What if time doesn't help? What if he hates me?"

"He doesn't hate you."

"He might. How do I know if he never responds?" I set my phone on the photo book that's sitting beside me, the book I *might* have been obsessively looking through since the movie ended and I got tired of staring out the window at a vacant treehouse.

"I have time to listen, if you want to talk." My mom holds out a grocery bag.

I take it and look inside. It contains a two-liter bottle of Dad's Root Beer.

"Thanks," I say, my voice breaking on the word. "Talking would be great."

♥

Hours later, I climb into bed and set my alarm. I think I've been through every emotion at least three times today, but talking through it all with my mom helped. She's always been a good listener, even if I'm still learning how to be a talker.

Before turning out my light, I type the message. *I love you.*

I stare at the screen, unable to hit send. I delete the text. I type it again. I delete it again. It's still too big, too risky. Besides, if I'm going to say it, it shouldn't be by text. I should stand in front of him and say the words aloud, even if he doesn't say them back. I suspect that thought will give me nightmares, but I go ahead and turn off my light.

My phone buzzes a few minutes later.

Theo: *Your magniloquence is mawkish and meretricious*
Theo: *Mirth minuscule*
Theo: *Miss me*

I hold the phone to my chest and inhale, long and deep.

Harper: *You have no idea*

TWENTY-SIX

I CHECK MY PHONE AGAIN. IT'S ONLY 3:15 P.M. IT'S
August twenty-third, the day Theo's expected back in town.
Olivia said his flight would arrive around seven tonight. I'm los-
ing my mind. I haven't heard a word from him since he sent those
three texts the week after he left. They were enough to keep me
from despair, but now that he's returning and I've had a month
without him, I have no idea what to expect. My mom banished
me to the workroom for the day. I was making everyone nervous.
Pippa's running the fittings with my mom while I alter dresses
with Jane, my new coworker.

As I finish the beading on a neckline, Jane stands and stretches
over by the sewing machine. She's twenty-one and lanky with a
round face and sleek black hair she wears in braided knots. She's
been with us for a week now and, wow, what a difference. I didn't
even have to place an ad. Everything came together at that party
I went to a few weeks ago, yet another reason to cultivate a social
life. I was explaining to my friends why I've been AWOL all year.
Denise, the girl who was hosting the party, said her older sister
sewed and she was even looking for work. We met, Jane showed

me some of the dresses she'd made, and I asked her to come in and interview with my mom. She was hired on the spot for twenty hours a week. Now I don't know how we managed without her. She's twice as fast as I am, and she complains a lot less, too. If she settles in and likes the job, we might even be able to hire her full-time, which would allow my mom to take on more design work while I focus on the business end of things.

Jane hangs up the bodice she finished letting out. "What should I alter next?"

I shuffle over to the rack. "I organized them by priority. Start on the left and work your way back. If any of my notes don't make sense, let me know or move on to the next one."

She examines the wedding gown on the front of the rack, trailing a hand down the cascade of white ruffles at the back.

"I hope all of these ruffles don't need rehemming," she says.

"Nope. The shoulders need to be taken up. That's all. My mom made sure it was practically perfect already. It's for the Connor-Armstrong wedding next month."

"That big one at the boathouse? The one practically everyone's invited to?"

"That's the one." I picture Ms. Connor—soon to be Mrs. Armstrong—crossing the lawn in this gorgeous dress, beaming at her husband-to-be. Her second and third fittings went as smoothly as her first, reinforcing my earlier realization about the nuances within the wedding industry. I've witnessed plenty of screaming matches this month, and plenty of tears over body issues or budgets, but I've also seen a tremendous amount of love, care, support, and joy. I think I get it now, at least partly. After all, if life is a series of beautiful mistakes, at least one of them should involve a really great dress.

My phone pings on the table in front of me. I jump. My elbow knocks my tray of beads to the floor. They scatter every direction. I swear under my breath as I kneel and collect them while sneaking a peek at my screen. The text isn't from Theo. It's from Denise, asking if I want to join the group for ice cream after dinner tonight. I can't, of course, though depending on how things go in a few hours, I may need a *lot* of ice cream.

Jane helps me gather the beads and we both ease into our respective projects, but as the afternoon wears on, I spill the pins, misplace the buttons I was using, sew a sleeve in upside down, break a zipper, and prick my fingers so many times I need half a box of Band-Aids to ensure I don't bleed on the dresses. Eventually my mom halts my haphazard anxiety-fest by sending me home early. I appreciate that I'm not functioning at my best, but as I trudge up my driveway twenty minutes later, lacking manual labor to distract me, time seems to slow to a truly painful crawl.

The next few hours are excruciating. I try to watch TV but I can't concentrate. I surf my socials but end up stalking Theo's instead, pausing on a gorgeous shot of him smiling over his shoulder on a busy beach. He's tanned and beautiful with the wind in his dark hair and his lips quirking at the corners. A seagull hovers above him against a bright blue sky. An ocean wave crests near the shore. The girl beside him gazes out to sea.

Wait . . . a girl's in the shot???

I take another look. A lot of people are on the beach. Theo and the girl aren't necessarily together, but they're not *not* together, either. He's had a month. Why wouldn't he start dating someone? He has no reason to wait for me the way I've been waiting for him. He has no reason to wait for me at all. The girl's gorgeous. Of course she is, in a cute string bikini and with boobs twice the size of mine. She even has great hair, sweeping blond locks she holds off her face like a mermaid on a book jacket. She looks smart, nice, fun, way more interesting than I am.

I realize I'm obsessing and I can't possibly tell any of that from an out-of-context photograph, so I turn off my phone. I clean. I put on makeup. I remove the makeup. I let down my hair. I put it back up. I try on several outfits but decide I look like I'm trying too hard in all of them, so I put on my work blouse and skirt, hoping the outfit masks my neuroses. Then I clean again. It's the only thing that passes the time.

Shortly after 9:15 p.m., headlights flash outside the kitchen window as Olivia's SUV rolls into the driveway. I draw in a breath and hold myself up against the counter, conjuring patience. Theo hasn't seen his moms in a month. They'll want to catch up without me usurping his homecoming. He might not want to see me at all, especially if he's in love with the girl in the bikini. Besides, if I run out there, I'll only say the wrong thing.

When the car door slams, I can't help myself. I fly onto my patio. After so many days of silence, of hoping but trying not to hope, of not knowing, I can't wait any longer. Theo's closing his car door with a duffel bag slung over his shoulder. He goes still when he sees me. Shay walks around from the driver's side while Olivia climbs the stairs toward the front door, carrying Theo's sword case.

"Theo?" Olivia calls. "You got everything?"

"Yeah, um, can you guys give me a minute?"

Shay and Olivia look my way. I manage an awkward wave, which at least gives me something to do with my hands while my heart tries to leap from my chest.

Shay sets a hand on Theo's shoulder. "Take as many minutes as you need."

She and Olivia head inside. Theo lets his bag slide off his shoulder and drop to the driveway. He skirts the car while I head toward him, pausing a few feet away. His hair's a little longer, spiking out over his ears. His tan is darker. He looks taller somehow, though that may be because I'm shrinking in on myself. At least he's wearing a faded D&D shirt and pair of outdated cargo shorts, so he hasn't changed *that* much.

"Can I hug you?" I ask. "I really want to hug you."

Theo smiles a little and nods, letting his arms fall open. I practically slam into his chest, flinging my arms around him and pressing my cheek against his shoulder. His arms slide around me, but his embrace is weak, limp, barely an embrace at all.

"I'm so sorry," I say into his shoulder.

"I know. It's okay. I needed to leave town for a while, anyway. Have a think. Clear my head." He drops his embrace and starts to pull away.

I tighten my hold. "A few more seconds. Please."

"Okay. A few more seconds." His arms settle back into place around my shoulders. We stand there for what feels like at least a full minute, unspeaking, but eventually he releases me and I'm forced to do the same.

"Theo." I reach up to touch his face, but I sense him tensing so I roll my fingers toward my palm and tuck my fist against my riotous gut. It shouldn't be in turmoil. I've practiced this a hundred times. I'm supposed to start off casual, ask how he is, how his dad is, how he liked Florida, if the fencing practice is paying off, if he feels ready for his tournament. Unfortunately, none of those questions rise to my lips. "I didn't mean any of it. You know that, right? I thought Pippa was calling because you were supposed to be with her that night, and I was mad at myself for forgetting all about her and I panicked."

Theo shoves his hands into his pockets and backs up a step. "I know. I shouldn't have let you think we were still dating. That was my fault." His shoulders inch up as he toes at a pebble on his driveway. "When you asked about her, you sounded jealous. It felt good. It shouldn't have, but it did. Maybe if I hadn't—"

"It's not your fault." I reach forward again, this time letting my fingertips graze his cheek. "And I *was* jealous, like, crazy insanely jealous. I still should've given you a chance to say something before I freaked out and said all of those mean things."

Theo takes my hand from his cheek and lowers it to my side.

"It's all good," he says. "We won't let that night get in the way of our friendship."

I stagger back a step. "Our friendship?"

He leans against the side of the car, shoving his hands into his pockets again as he stares out toward the road, lost in a thought. I look down at my hand, the one he removed from his face. Oh god. He doesn't want me to touch him. He doesn't want to touch me. He keeps putting space between us. I did ruin everything.

"I can't do it, Harper," he says as he finally looks my way again. "I thought about it, a lot, but I don't want to be the kind of guy who waits until he knows his feelings are returned before he does or says anything. I don't want to keep my accordion in the closet. I don't want to walk through the world with armor on, afraid I might get hurt. I want to love boldly and bravely or not at all." He thumps a fist against his chest. I open my mouth to assure him I don't expect him to change who he is or how he loves, but he holds up a hand. "You were right last month. Hooking up was a mistake. We don't fit as a couple. We're better as friends. It took me a while to see it, and some distance, but it's true. You need someone tough. I need someone . . . not so tough."

My chest seizes. I can't breathe. I hold out a hand to steady myself on the hood of his mom's car. It's warm, solid, but I feel like the whole world could shatter right now.

"I'm not that tough." The words fall from my lips, so quiet and strained, they're almost inaudible.

Theo takes a deep breath and slowly releases it. He watches me for a moment, thinking god knows what. Then he circles the car and picks up his duffel bag.

"I know we made things awkward, but we've pulled through plenty of other friction or miscommunication. We'll get past this, too. Before we know it, you'll be teasing me about whatever book I'm reading. I'll correct your grammar. Or I'll cry about a girl. You'll tell me why I shouldn't. You know. Like old times."

My lower lip quivers. My whole chin quivers. I try to say something, but I can't. My throat has closed. My lungs won't expand. The world around me is spinning and blurring. So I stand there, staring at the driveway, trying not to collapse.

"So . . . friends?" Theo asks.

I manage a nod, unable to say the word. He takes a step away. Then another. And another, until his front door opens and closes.

And just like that, I'm alone.

TWENTY-SEVEN

MY MOM FINDS ME SOBBING INTO MY PILLOW AT around midnight. She sits on the edge of my bed and plucks my tear-dampened hair off my face. I sputter away, unable to speak for several minutes. She patiently aligns strands of hair until I'm able to take a full breath.

"He only wants to be friends," I choke out.

"I'm so sorry." My mom draws me into a hug. "That's not what I expected."

"Me neither. It's not what I wanted, anyway." I wipe away my latest round of tears and fill in my mom on the painful reunion, squeezing out the story between the sobs that continue to rack my body. "I don't know how to be his friend now."

"You take it a day at a time, I guess."

"Can we move? Please? Pittsburgh? New York? Another block?"

"Oh, Harper." My mom takes my soggy face in both hands. "Running away won't make this hurt any less."

"Can we at least get really thick curtains? And put up a much taller fence?"

"Curtains, maybe. A new fence is out of our budget."

"Okay. Curtains will help. I can stay inside a lot."

My mom chuckles even though I'm not trying to be funny. I can't bear the idea of watching Theo bring another girl home, especially if he takes her up to the treehouse, to *our* treehouse. I can't even bear the thought of seeing him fence Mr. Strawbody. I want to be there when he wins his tournament. I want him to wear my favor, even though I still have no idea what that means. I've fostered so many dreams of what we'd share, even while I told myself not to. Practicing my last few vocab lists with him while he whips out sample sentences, already knowing every word by heart. Adjusting his costume before he heads into battle. Sharing his tent again. Arranging another alphabetical tray of sweets. Reading his favorite books and watching his favorite rom-coms together without my usual sarcastic play-by-play. I was finally going to earn the love I'd taken for granted. Until today those dreams were at least possible. Now they're vanishing.

"Kevin Barnes," my mom says, apropos of nothing.

"Who's Kevin Barnes?"

"My junior year prom date. I was so in love with him, I would've flown to the moon if he'd asked me."

I grab a tissue and wipe away a lingering sniffle. "What happened?"

"He met someone else that summer. Told me he wanted to 'play the field.'"

I groan. "Sports metaphors are the worst."

"True, but they didn't make the breakup hurt any less. My god, how I cried over that boy. Sobbed for days and days on end. I thought my parents were going to ship me off to boarding school, just to get some peace." My mom sets a hand to her mouth, shaking her head as though she's reliving the memories.

"What made you stop crying?"

"Time. Being with my friends. Finding new dreams. Letting the old ones go."

My sputters kick in again. "I don't want to let my dreams go."

My mom renews her embrace. "I know. And I'm not encouraging you to rush anything. Give these feelings the space they deserve. Gradually, when you're ready, start filling the space with new experiences and relationships. Spend more time with your friends. Start an early application for Bryn Mawr. Teach me how to do spreadsheets. Do the things that make you happy. You and Theo may not get your old friendship back, but you can build a new one. You love each other so much. I'd hate to see you let that go."

I attempt to say, "Me too," but I erupt into another round of sobs instead.

My mom stays with me for another hour or so, regaling me with funny stories of her sordid youth. It helps somehow, knowing she's happy where she is now, despite being slammed with heartbreak, falling in love, falling out of love, experimenting with casual sex, dealing with an unplanned pregnancy, going on terrible first dates as a new mom, deciding she wasn't that interested in romantic partnership anymore. I also appreciate the distraction. My own thoughts are too heavy, too dark and dismal. My mom's levity adds a bit of brightness. I can't picture a future that doesn't have Theo in it, but my mom's right. We can build something new. Eventually.

TWENTY-EIGHT

PIPPA LOWERS HER CHAI. "HE SAID *WHAT?!*"

I repeat my sad tale while Pippa and Jane split the last biscotti. I didn't have any cookies. I didn't even bother with my usual coffee. The idea of consuming anything still nauseates me. Hours of sobbing last night didn't do my body any favors.

"He can't get away with that," Pippa says when I finish. "You did not wait a month just so he could play the friend card."

"He can play whatever card he wants," I say. "I wish he couldn't, but he can."

Pippa huffs. "It was one stupid fight. You've apologized a zillion times. You even gave up Flex for him." She flings a hand toward the front of the store.

Jane eyes us sideways. "Who's Flex?"

"Harper's super-hot, super-nice, totally amazing ex-boyfriend."

"That guy who uses that gym across the street?" Jane cranes around and peers toward the picture window. "The one who's always looking over here?"

I flop sideways on the chaise, curling myself into a ball. "That's the one."

Pippa spins my way from the armchair at my feet. "Maybe he'll take you back."

"I thought about it, but it wouldn't be right," I moan. "I still want Theo."

Pippa springs to her feet. "That's it. He's getting pied."

I bury my face in a pillow. "No one needs to get pied."

"He can't ditch me, try to bone you, fall apart over a few harsh words, ignore you for an entire month, let you assume he's going to sweep back into town and adore you, only to blow you off! It's bullshit." Her hands fly out, jangling a multitude of bracelets.

Jane looks back and forth between us. "I think I'm missing something."

Pippa fills her in on my history with Felix and Theo, and even Liam, since the pie reference works best with the full saga. I remain in the fetal position while she rattles off the details of my painful love life, but I soon tuck the pillow aside. It's stiff and it has a decorative button in the middle. Like everything else in this shop, it was made to look pretty, not to be comfortable, and definitely not to absorb severe agony.

"Maybe he's testing you again," Jane offers when Pippa finally takes a breath. "Like when he was gauging your jealousy. Or maybe he's testing himself?"

"He didn't seem particularly 'testy.'" I close my eyes and relive our agonizing reunion for the thousandth time. "What would he even be testing?"

"I don't know." Jane shrugs. "It's just a thought."

I consider her suggestion while we all volley speculations

across the coffee table. We debunk the theories as quickly as we make them. Theo was clear. Friends and only friends. I start to laugh, in an awkward, sputtering, not-really-amused way.

"What's so funny?" Pippa asks, swapping a worried look with Jane.

"This is *my* fault. I taught Theo how not to fall in love. I told him to keep his feelings in check. I ordered him not to get attached. Apparently I taught him well."

My mom soon relegates me to the back room since I look like a bloated blowfish, though that metaphor's probably flawed or redundant. I know who'd be able to confirm which of the two, but he's unavailable. Meanwhile, we have a ton of work at the shop, though at least we're over the summer rush, and with Jane's help we're no longer in a daily panic.

Thus, shortly after 6:00 p.m., I find myself trudging home, attempting to engage with the *V* list I pulled up on my phone. So far, it's perfect. *Vacillate: to be undecided. Vagary: an unexpected and inexplicable change. Vicissitude: a variation in circumstance or fortune.* I can use all three of those in a single sentence. My SAT is in five days. I'm still cramming. Despite the weird grief cloud I live under right now, I'm not giving up my dreams of Bryn Mawr and of holding on to the one partnership I haven't completely mangled this summer, the partnership I have with my mom.

I'm heading up the driveway when I hear clinking and thudding in Theo's backyard. I glance over to see him sweep across the lawn and lunge at his foe. I flee into my house as fast as possible. My mom should seriously rethink my moving suggestion.

Sure, our house is convenient, comfortable, familiar, and affordable, but living next to Theo is going to make the whole "find new dreams" plan uniquely challenging. It's like trying to start a diet while living next to a chocolate factory, though that's a dumb metaphor because Theo's the one who's crazy about chocolate. The thought makes me want to bring him sweets, the way I always have before when I needed to apologize. This time I don't think cookies or candy will bridge the chasm between us.

I turn on the TV but soon realize I'm standing there with the remote in my hand, staring vacantly, with no comprehension of the menu on the screen. Suspecting I'm as low on blood sugar as I am on sleep, I leave the TV on and head into the kitchen. There, I stare again, this time at the open freezer and its well-ordered stacks of boxes. Lasagna? Burrito? Lo mein? Vegetable korma? Who needs to travel when a cornucopia of international cuisine is only five minutes away? *Cornucopia* was on Theo's C list. I hate that I remember that. I can't wait until *everything* stops reminding me of him.

Unable to imagine eating anything at all, I shut the freezer and pour myself a root beer. I'm not sure why, but I still like the idea that it connects me to my dad, no matter where he is, who he is, or what his name is. Funny the importance we place on objects, though this may be my overtired and undernourished brain talking again.

I'm putting the cap back on the bottle when the doorbell rings. I flinch, dropping the soda. It splashes my front and spills out onto the floor. I scramble to right the bottle and mop up the mess while flashing through a vivid episode of déjà vu.

The bell rings again.

"Harper?" Theo calls from the front doorstep. "You okay in there?"

I freeze as my body goes cold, then hot, then cold again. I'm not ready. It's too soon. What is he thinking, showing up here the day after he gave me the brushoff? He got a month to process whatever he was going through. He can't give me a week?

"I saw your lights on," he calls. "I know you're home."

I shoot a glare at the kitchen window. Tomorrow: curtains. Priority number one.

"Please?" Theo calls. "I only need a minute."

I scan the room for an excuse to avoid facing him.

"Can't," I call toward the door. "Oven problems."

"You don't bake."

"Stove problems, then."

"Or cook."

"Microwave problems?"

"Just come to the door, Jamison."

I close my eyes and muster strength. It's the *Jamison* that does me in. The familiar ease with which we always tossed around last names. The best of friends, no matter what.

I blot my soaked shirt as I head to the foyer and open the door. Theo's leaning against a support beam on the patio. His sleeveless undershirt hugs his chest while his cotton shorts hang loosely around his hips, right below what I assume is his sword belt even though he isn't wearing a sword. As usual, he's also decided against shoes, revealing stretched-out socks with roller-skating cats on them. Once again, I marvel at his inability to toss the most threadbare clothing, even if I'm also flattered he keeps my gifts forever.

He straightens up when he sees me. "Hi."

I flash him a wave as I cling to the door, ready to shut it at any moment.

He nods at my shirt. "Sprinkler problems again?"

I squint at him until I get the joke. Right. The night I offered to teach him how not to fall in love. He was bawling his eyes out about what's-her-name. I arrived with a soda-soaked shirt. Funny that he remembers that. Though I guess I do, too.

"What do you want, Theo?"

"The treehouse. You fixed everything. I wanted to say thank you."

I tip my temple against the door. My head's too heavy to hold up, though I could say that about my entire body right now. I forgot about the treehouse. While Theo was in Florida, I repaired all of the pillows, quilts, and blankets. I made curtains. I even padded that damned windowsill I'm always hitting, not that it matters anymore. I also fixed his tent, but he'll figure that out later when he's alone. Or not alone. Thank you, brain.

"My stitch bitch contract was ending this month," I tell him, frustrated at the uncontrollable bite in my tone. "I wanted to make sure you got your money's worth."

"Well, it was nice. Really nice. Thank you." He smiles a little but it's one of those smiles that doesn't get very far before it fades again. "I'm sorry about yesterday."

"You have nothing to apologize for." I shrug the same way he smiled. "You said what you felt. It's on me to deal with it."

"I didn't mean to be so brusque, or to leave you standing there like that. I worried . . . I wanted . . . I was trying to make sure I didn't give you mixed messages."

"Then consider the conversation a rousing success." I start to shut the door. "Your *thank-you* is appreciated. Your apology is unnecessary but also appreciated."

"Also"—Theo steps forward—"I brought you a souvenir." He holds out a small, rectangular package wrapped in brown paper.

I frown at it. "You sure that's not a mixed message?"

"Just take it. Please?"

I open the door all the way as I toss my towel onto the sideboard. With a growing knot of apprehension in my gut, I take Theo's gift, unwrapping it to find a dog-eared paperback with a swoony hero and heroine on the cover. They have windblown hair, billowing costumes, and expressions of tormented rapture.

"*The Rogue's Next Mistress*," I read on the cover. My eyes shoot to Theo's as a little spark of unexpected joy ignites in my chest. "There's a sequel?"

"Apparently. I came across it at a big used-book sale. Thought you might want it, you know, in case the first one ended on a cliffhanger."

I turn the book over in my hands, smiling despite myself.

"I bet he got the girl. Or she got the guy. I'm not sure whose story it is. I didn't get past the title page." I skim the back cover, not because I want to know the plot, but because I don't dare look at Theo right now. He's not allowed to be wonderful when he's also breaking my heart.

"So . . . what're you having for dinner tonight?" he asks.

I sweep a hand over my damp shirt. "You can't tell?"

"Besides the beverage."

I risk a glance at him, unsure why he's making small chat. He shifts his weight from one foot to the other, looking all cute and awkward with thick hair I want to run my fingers through, dark eyes I want to gaze at forever, really amazing arms I want around me right now, and thumbs tucked into his empty sword belt.

"I didn't plan a menu," I tell him. "Besides, I'm on *V.* I don't think vichyssoise or venison comes in a microwave variety."

Theo's shoulders droop as his eyes trail to his socks.

"Wow, right, the vocab. You had to do half the alphabet without me."

"It wasn't the same, but I did my best. I'll find out if it's enough next weekend."

His angular brows knit together as his shoulders shift, rise, and settle into place.

"Saturday?" He waits for my nod. "That's the same day as my tournament."

"Then let's hope it's a good day for both of us." I set my hand on the doorknob and start to shut the door again. I can't stand here chatting about everything we no longer share with each other. It hurts too much, drawing the threat of tears to my eyes. "Thanks for the book. And the thanks. I should go make vegetables or vermicelli or whatever."

"Wait. Dinner." Theo steps forward again, still shifty and unsettled. "I was asking because my moms made a massive homecoming feast. We have leftovers, including some of your favorites. I could box them up and bring them over if you like."

As if I haven't sped through enough emotions in the last few minutes, a streak of exasperation shoots through me, causing my grip to tighten on the doorknob.

"What are you doing?" I ask.

Theo blinks at me, all innocence and confusion. "What do you mean?"

"You can't shut me out for a month, tell me you're 'just not that into me,' and then show up here the very next night with a thoughtful gift and a dinner offer and sad puppy dog eyes about the separate lives we're living now. Talk about mixed messages." My entire face pinches. I try to relax it, but it won't budge.

Theo wilts before me. His lips twitch and his eyes well with remorse.

"I'm sorry," he says, his voice small. "I know. You're right, but . . ."

"But *what?*"

"I missed you."

The tears I've been holding back creep into the corners of my eyes. I tuck myself behind the half-open door. It's the only way I

can stop myself from throwing my arms around Theo and bawling while I grasp at any scrap of longing that mirrors mine.

He kicks a toe against my doormat as his expression grows
so dejected I can almost hear accordion music, and this time I
wouldn't even mind.

"It's been a month, Harper. A really long month. I tried to be
cool and distant, to detach and focus elsewhere, on fencing, reading, spending time with my dad, learning to surf, joining a local
gaming community, anything but you. It worked okay when I was
in another corner of the country, and I tried not to muddle things
last night, but now that I'm over there"—he nods at his house
—"and you're over here, I don't understand why we can't both be
in the same place." He catches something in my expression and
backs up a step. "You know. As friends."

The answer is so obvious. The words dance around my lips.
Because I'm in love with you. I don't say it. I can't. It'd only make
things even more awkward between us.

While I search for something to say, Theo leans forward,
studying my face.

"You've gone blotchy," he says. "Are you okay?"

I start to say *yes* but as soon as I meet his eyes, regarding me
with a kind of love but not the kind I want, my breath catches and
my chest shudders. As much as I hated his swift dismissal yesterday, this is worse, the push and pull, the way he tells me not to
want him but makes me want him more than ever.

"I'm good," I somehow manage. "Allergies or whatever." I fan
my face with the book, hoping it dries any impending tears before

they fall. Theo and I stare at each other for a long moment, me with staggered breath and watery eyes, him worried and watchful.

"What do you want me to do?" he asks, his voice as gentle as a cozy sweater.

Tell me you're madly in love with me, I think. *Tell me you didn't mean what you said yesterday. Tell me you're using the word* friends *as a shield when what you really want to do is hold me and kiss me and love me forever.*

"Just give me some time," I say instead. "And some space."

He nods thoughtfully as he takes a really, *really* slow breath.

"Okay," he says at last. "I'll steer clear until you give me a green light. I don't want to make this any harder than it needs to be, for either one of us." He scratches his head, leaving his black waves poking in all directions. "So . . . that's a no on dinner, right?"

"Theo—"

"Right. Sorry. Time and space. Got it." He steps off the patio, but he pauses at the base of the stairs, looking back at me where I stand frozen in the doorway, unable to inch the door closed and shut him from view. We get stuck in another uncomfortable silence, as if neither of us can muster a word as simple as *goodbye.*

I hold up the book. "Thanks again for this."

A smile dents his cheek as the tiniest glimmer of joy finds its way to his eyes.

"You might find it vapid or vacuous," he says.

"Don't start with me, Turner." I purse my lips, trying not to take the bait, but I can't help myself. "Your venerable verbosity is veritably vainglorious."

His smile widens as he backs away from me. "You're going to ace that test."

"You're going to win that tournament."

"We've got this."

I nod, holding myself up against the doorframe. Barely.

"Yeah. I guess we do."

TWENTY-NINE

ON THE MORNING OF MY SAT AND THEO'S TOUR-
nament, I sneak into the treehouse. The Funko Pop! figures are on
the windowsill, like usual. Mini-Theo is still wearing the little tabard I made. I put a tiny crown of flowers on his head and sprinkle
confetti around him. I don't know what the real prize is for winning a joust or a swordfight, but I assume Theo will understand
my gesture when he returns home tomorrow.

We haven't spoken since the night he brought me the book.
He's been good about giving me time and space, no longer assuming I can settle back into a comfortable friendship right away. We
wave whenever we see each other. The smiles we exchange are
forced and painful, but I guess even stilted communication is better than absence and silence. I bought super-opaque kitchen curtains anyway. I even clothes-pinned them shut. Still, this is Theo's
big day. Ignoring it felt wrong, so here I am, kneeling on pillows,
bag of confetti in hand.

The princess figure stands next to Mini-Theo, positioned so
close they look like they're holding hands. It's so cheesy but so

Theo. He's probably using them like voodoo dolls, willing a great romance into being. He doesn't need the help. The LARPing girls will be all over him today. I bet one of them gets him to wear her favor. I really hope that's not a medieval euphemism for sex. I'm not ready to find out he's sleeping with someone else. I'm not even ready to find out he's holding hands with someone else.

With a vicious streak of envy for what I realize is only a toy, I snatch the princess from her knight. As I wedge her into the opposite corner of the sill, facing away from Mini-Theo, I notice a freckle behind her ear. A freckle just like mine.

I slump onto the pillows and blankets as I take a closer look. The plastic doll is hardly a realistic representation, but upon close inspection, her eye color matches mine, as does the shape of her lips. If I ever left the house without blowing out my hair until it was poker straight, the brown waves that ripple down the figure's back would also match my hair. The last time I wore my hair with its natural wave I was twelve or thirteen, which was around the time Theo got these figures.

I could scream right now. Why didn't I like him back then? Why did I have to wait until he got over his crush to develop my own? And why does it feel like so much more than a crush, no matter how many times I repeat the word *friend* to myself, drilling it into my brain, hoping I eventually accept it?

My phone buzzes in my pocket, drawing me from my speculation. It's a message from Pippa, wishing me good luck and confirming she'll pick me up from the testing site at 3:00 p.m. Right. It's my big day, too. Time to focus.

Back at home, I guzzle enough coffee to ensure I'm awake but not so much that I'll have to pee every hour. Still in my PJs, I debate what to wear. I read somewhere that people do better on tests and at interviews if they feel confident and put together. It's probably a load of crap, but I pick out a cute summer dress that's close in color to the one the Funko Pop! princess was wearing. I feel crazy caring about something like that, but apparently I do and since nothing else in my closet begs to be worn, I run with it. I even consider leaving my hair unstyled, but I can't stand the wave and frizz, so I compromise and loop it into a braided coronet. It works, and it reminds me of one of Pippa's favorite styles, one of the few I can sort of pull off.

My mom drives me to the testing site at a school in the next town over.

"You sure you're okay with Pippa picking you up this afternoon?" she asks.

"Totally. Get through your fittings. We can celebrate tonight, if a celebration is in order. If it's not, I'll still split a beer with you." I pull up my final vocab list, cramming in one last review session. *Zealot. Zephyr. Zygote.* A text comes through on my screen.

Theo: *You're going to rock it*
Theo: *Thought you should know that. In case there was any doubt*
Theo: *Or any vacillation, quandary, dubiousness, polysemy, or tergiversation*
Theo: *I believe in you*

The ellipsis doesn't come again. My screen goes dark. I stare at it anyway, just in case, with my thumb hovering over the bottom button as I fight the urge to respond.

"Theo?" my mom asks.

I turn my phone upside down. "How did you know?"

"Did you really think he'd let you take the test without at least saying good luck?"

"Maybe?" I squirm in my seat, tugging the seat belt away from my neck. "His day is as big as mine. You don't see me texting him."

My mom fights a knowing smile. The smile wins.

"You're right," she says. "I don't. But there are other ways to say good luck."

I purse my lips and stare out the window at the suburban streets with their old houses and big yards. Okay, so I asked Olivia to slip a note inside Theo's tabard, a note that lets him know I believe in him, too. I *might* have written it on fancy parchment, in a hackneyed attempt at medieval verse and calligraphic lettering. I also might've singed my fingers attempting to use sealing wax, but if I was going to send a good-luck note into another kingdom, I wanted to get it right. Still, it's only a note.

"We agreed to leave each other alone," I remind my mom.

"I know what you agreed to." My mom eyes me sideways as she drives. Her look speaks volumes, setting my mind humming with questions I don't want to ask or answer. "If he gave me something to give to you, would you want it now or after the test?"

I stop fidgeting with the seat belt. A rush of curiosity almost overwhelms me, swiftly tempered by a jolt of caution. I'm dying to know what he gave me, but I can't allow myself to get distracted. The last thing I need right now is a catalyst for obsessing about meanings and subtext, not that his gift would come with any, but I'm so messed up about him, I'd find a way to read into even the simplest gesture.

"After," I say.

"You sure?"

"Yes. No. Of course not." I turn on my phone and stare at his texts. "We agreed. No mixed messages. They're too confusing." I shut off my phone and flip it upside down. Then I turn it over and open it again. "Why is he giving me a gift? Or texting? Why is he doing anything other than leaving me alone until I can obey his 'just friends' rules? One night he practically runs away from me. The next, he's inventing reasons to be close again. Now he's doing everything he said he wouldn't do. What's up with that?"

My mom gives me one of those looks that says I'm missing the obvious.

"Maybe he's confused, too," she says.

"But he said—" I stop there. My mom's still giving me The Look.

"You're not the easiest person to read, Harper. Theo probably has his own questions, and everyone's been known to change their mind at least once in their life."

A rebuttal presses at my lips, but I hold it inside. Her points are well taken. I'm hardly a model of clarity and consistency. Theo probably has no idea how I really feel, despite all the texts I sent him shortly after he left town. I might've tempered those more than I realized at the time, afraid to say too much. Like usual.

"You really think he might give me another chance?" I ask.

"I think neither of you wants to be avoiding the other. I'll leave it there."

A sliver of hope forces its way past all of my defense mechanisms. My mom's the last person to encourage me to pursue a relationship with a guy who isn't interested. If she's opening up room for doubt—or for whatever words Theo used for doubt—she's doing it because she truly believes that room exists. I want to rejoice in the thought. It also terrifies me. The higher I hope, the farther I'll fall. This summer has been hard enough already. I don't need to make it harder. Also, I believe in taking people at their word. Theo said *friends*. Many times. Pushing that boundary wouldn't be fair to him.

My mom pulls into the parking lot a few minutes later. She wraps me in a big hug by the side of the car and gives me an earnest pep talk. It does little to quell my nerves, but we both know I studied my ass off. The rest is out of my control.

"How big is Theo's gift?" I ask before I head inside. "Will it fit in a pocket?"

"It will. You want to hang on to it?"

I shuffle, shift, and practically shoot anxiety out my fingertips.

"Yeah. I can wait until after I take the test. But *only* until then."

My mom ducks into the car and gets a box from the glove compartment. It's white, about the size of a matchbox car, and tied in a red ribbon with no tag or card. I slip it into my backpack where I will now attempt to ignore it for several hours. Thank god I'm good at math so at least one of today's objectives feels within reach.

Half an hour later, I'm sitting in a big lecture classroom with about fifty other students my age, filling in an answer sheet. My eyes glaze over at the columns of dots that will dictate my entire future. The pressure's way too high, so I pretend I'm taking a practice test. The math section of the SAT is straightforward, as before. I complete the problems in the allotted time and even check back through the more complicated ones, fixing a few mistakes. The vocabulary gets me thinking though, and not only about the synonyms and definitions I match as I go. *Palliative: easing sorrow or pain to make it more bearable.* Keeping away from Theo is a palliative measure for combating my heartbreak. *Tantalizing: arousing desire for the unattainable.* Theo's tantalizing athletic displays make thinking of him as only a friend uniquely challenging. *Gustatory: relating to the sense of taste.* Theo's kisses excite gustatory delight.

Despite the implications of this test, words don't have a set meaning. I bring meaning to them. Treating words the same way I treat numbers is an exercise in futility. Three months ago I might've considered aspirin palliative. A Snickers bar would've been both tantalizing and gustatory. Now these words have new context. Tomorrow their context could change again. Words are malleable. Whether or not I know how to define them, the real challenge lies in knowing how to use them, and in being aware of how they're felt, how they're expressed, and how they're received. I don't know how Theo will feel about the note I wrote him. Maybe I used the wrong words. Maybe only one word really counts, the one I've never said to him, though I feel it deeply in my heart.

♥

After the test, while waiting for Pippa in the parking lot, I tug on the red ribbon and lift the lid on Theo's box. Inside lies a fun-size Snickers bar, my Halloween favorite. I can't help but smile. The gift is perfect. It's thoughtful and personal without being a grand gesture I don't know how to process. A token of our lasting friendship.

I remove the candy bar and unwrap it, lacking the sentimentality to put it under my pillow as a talisman to wish on. It's only a candy bar. I'm ravenous. Snickers are awesome. As I shove the wadded-up wrapper into the box, a flash of gold catches my eye. The Snickers bar wasn't the only thing in the box. Still lying on a little pad of white batting is a thin gold chain holding a charm that reads **Official Word Nerd**.

Okay, now *that* I can get sentimental about.

Damn Theo! He seriously needs to lower his game if he expects me to hang out in the treehouse again, listening to him cry about other girls. I can't even be mad about the mixed messages. I know him. He didn't give me the necklace to dredge up my feelings or confuse matters. He did it because he's proud of me. That's all. It's also everything.

I'm still staring at the charm, battling the questions it raises in my mind, when Pippa pulls up to the curb in her bright yellow Mini.

"How'd it go?" she asks as I climb into the shotgun seat.

"Good. Great. Way better than last time." My grip tightens on the box I'm still clutching. "I have Theo to thank. He got me started, even if I took over midway."

Pippa purses her lips and glares out her windshield.

"I'm glad he helped you," she says. "But I still think we should pie him."

I laugh, but not for long, turning the box over in my hands.

"My mom thinks he's just confused," I say.

"It's possible."

"And that I don't help matters by being so hard to read."

"That's probably true."

"And I've never actually told him I'm in love with him."

Pippa slowly turns to face me, her eyes widening as she pivots my way.

"You know," she says, "your mom can do without us for a couple of hours."

A spike of anxiety shoots through me, even though I had the same exact thought.

"It's a risk," I say.

"He brought you, like, a million flowers even though he knew you liked another guy. If he's willing to risk that level of rejection . . ."

I tip my head back against the headrest and blow a sigh toward the ceiling.

I know, I think. *I know, I know, I know.*

After a long pause, Pippa gives a nudge. "Which direction am I driving?"

I close my eyes and picture Theo shuffling and shifting on my front patio, plunging his épée into a scarecrow, sobbing over his accordion, marching into battle, tickling me in my living room, jamming a sparkler into a pot pie, staring out over the Delaware River, reaching for my hand, always reaching, never afraid.

"North," I say. "To a faraway kingdom. It's time I clear up some confusion."

THIRTY

THE PARKING LOT'S PACKED. WE HAVE TO PARK IN the third overflow area, half a mile from the trail entrance. The ground is muddy from a recent rain. My canvas sneakers and thin socks are soaked through by the time Pippa and I near the valley. I also have mud splatters up to my knees and my braid's unraveling. Pippa's in better shape. As if in anticipation of our excursion, she wore combat boots and a jumpsuit today. She jogs several paces ahead of me, giddy about our mission. I try to keep up, but anxiety slows my pace. What exactly am I supposed to say? How do I lead up to something so big? What do I do if he just stares at me? Or if he's with someone else? Also, why can't I have a sword and a suit of armor, even if the demons I'm fighting are in my head?

Pippa spins around to wave me onward. "What time's the fencing match?"

"I don't know. He didn't say."

"Then let's hurry!" She jogs on.

I chase after her, swiftly winded thanks to my lack of exercise. I can't believe I've spent the better part of this year lusting after athletes when I can barely jog a city block. It's seriously hypocritical on my part, but I'll worry about a fitness plan *after* I talk to Theo. For now, I lay a hand against the little charm that's nestled below my collarbone, pressing it to my skin as I puff and pant my way into the valley.

The crowd is three or four times bigger than it was the last time I was here. Tents dot the landscape, as do clusters of chairs, coolers, and other gear. People in assorted costumes and costume pieces mix and mingle, as before. Jugglers toss batons back and forth. Vendors sell flower crowns, henna tattoos, and silver jewelry. A dozen or so kids sit in a semicircle, eagerly watching a puppet show. Most of the villagers are gathered over by the tournament field, lining all sides so I can't see what's happening within.

A roar rises from the crowd as fists pump into the air. Pippa scurries over to grab my elbow and drag me onward. I stumble along beside her until we're able to wedge our way into the crowd, peering over shoulders and between heads. Six people in full armor fight with swords, staffs, and daggers on the muddy field. To our right, on a small stage, a quartet sits in a set of thrones. They're dressed in rich brocades and jeweled crowns with a row of crested banners behind them. I squint at the players on the field, searching for signs that Theo's among them. Three have their faces obscured by helmets, but no one has his wiry build, his dancer-like movement, or his windmill-crested tabard.

A beefy guy in a full helmet swings a sword at a woman in leather armor. She somersaults away and regains her stance.

"Holy crap!" Pippa grips my arm. "They fight with real weapons?"

A cheerful-looking woman in a low-cut wench outfit turns around in front of us.

"It's a demonstration," she says. "The fight's choreographed. The players are total pros. Pretty remarkable though, aren't they?"

Pippa lets out a relieved sigh. "I thought someone was about to lose their head."

The wench laughs. "As far as I know, no one's ever lost a body part here, though if you misbehave, you could get put in the stocks." She nods at something behind us.

Pippa and I spin around to see a skinny guy on his knees with his neck and wrists wedged between two boards. A trio of little kids stands by taunting him. I find the sight disturbing until one calls him Daddy and they all laugh.

I turn to the woman in front of us. "Has the fencing match happened yet?"

"It's up next. It'll be a good one this year. We have four serious contenders."

"We're rooting for Theo," Pippa says.

"Sir Theodoro de Montiel," I amend with pride. "How long until they start?"

"An hour, maybe?" the wench says. "We don't operate on clocks and watches here. Those are for the steampunk crowd. We obey the herald." She points out a guy in a quartered tunic with fancy sleeves, a piled-up headdress, and a trumpet tucked under his arm. "Don't worry. You'll know. That bugle really carries."

Thankful we haven't missed Theo's event, I search the crowd for his windmill tabard or his black waves, though I doubt he's watching the fight right now. Knowing him, he's off prepping on his own somewhere. This will suit us both. He won't be busy sizing up opponents. I'll be able to tell him how I feel without a crowd of wenches and bards hovering nearby. Even if he reiterates that he just wants to be friends, he'll know I'm here for him. He's important to me. Nothing about him will ever be meaningless.

"I'm going to go check his campsite," I tell Pippa. "You cool to wait here so I can find you if I need a getaway car? Or a getaway carriage?"

Pippa gives me a hug. "You can count on Dame Pennington of the Green Locks."

I return her embrace, noting that she may need to be reassigned to the Maroon Locks, thanks to today's wig, but no matter her hair color, she'll always be my secret lover. We part with plans to meet back by the field in time for the fencing match. I jog through the campgrounds until I near Theo's tent. It's in the same spot as last time, not far from the river, inside the circle of trees. Two girls with black twist-outs and chubby cheeks halt me several yards away. They look like they're about six or seven years old, twins maybe, both dressed in Disney princess outfits and plastic tiaras.

"You shall not pass!" Elsa from *Frozen* says with unexpected ferocity.

Belle from *Beauty and the Beast* folds her arms and gives me a death glare.

"Is Sir Theodore in his tent?" I ask.

"He's keeping Virgil," Belle asserts.

"Vigil," Elsa corrects. "We're not allowed to let anyone interrupt him."

"We're his pages." Belle squares her shoulders. Elsa follows suit, twinning Belle's obvious pride in her assigned role.

I step forward but the girls close ranks, forcing me to step back again.

"These are special circumstances. I have a message from a neighboring kingdom in great peril." I try to dodge around the girls, but they counter my movement, their expressions determined. "Can you at least tell him I'm here? Please?"

The girls whisper to each other, casting me furtive glances.

"Name?" Elsa asks after extensive consultation.

"Maid Harper." I make a faltering attempt at a curtsy, holding out the hem of my dress. "From the Land Beneath the Veils."

Belle scurries off and peeks into Theo's tent while Elsa keeps a watchful eye on me, her arms folded and her feet planted. My feet do not remain planted. I pace and fidget while playing out entire conversations in my head, ones that all end badly, no matter how carefully I imagine treading. I know I need to tell Theo the full truth, but being open and vulnerable about my feelings still scares the crap out of me.

After a minute or so, Belle returns.

"He says he's not interested," she announces with her chin held high and a distinct air of authority. "I should thank you for stopping by and ask you to leave."

My hand flies to my necklace as her words hit hard. That's all he has to say to me? *I'm not interested. Go away?* I'll give him credit for being clear, but the dismissal hurts. A lot. I thought he'd at least come say hi. If the mood felt weird, I could wish him good luck and wait until after the tournament to make my big confession, but now . . .

I glance back and forth between the girls and the tent, wondering if I should make a run for it, tear aside the tent flaps, and say what I came to say. With a little misdirection, I'd probably make it, but these girls are taking their job so seriously, I don't have the heart to thwart them. Besides, if Theo doesn't want to see me, I have no right to force myself on him. No right at all.

I trudge back to the field, utterly gutted. Pippa's flirting with a bare-chested guy in shaggy fur pants and clog-like shoes molded to look like hoofs. He resembles Mr. Tumnus from the Narnia books Theo made me read when we were kids. Actually, Theo only pushed the first one on me. I read the others because I loved the first one so much. I don't think I ever told him that. Wow. I seriously need to work on my communication skills. Guess I'll address those after I've improved my coping with rejection skills.

Pippa's smile drops away when she spots me. "That was quick."

"His bodyguards sent me away. He didn't want to see me."

"Ouch." Pippa pushes out her bottom lip. "You want to head home?"

I consider the idea as I toy with my necklace, replaying the words *not interested* until they're etched in my brain. I'd love to forget we ever came here, and yet . . .

"No," I say. "Let's stay for his big match. I want to see Theo win."

"Good. Also, I'm totally getting that dude's number before we leave."

With an hour or so to kill, Pippa and I wander the valley. She takes in the atmosphere while I try to sort out why Theo was so sweet this morning and so dismissive this afternoon. I keep Ping-Ponging between two convictions that hold equal weight. Theo didn't want to see me because he needed to focus, just like I did with my test. Theo didn't want to see me because he didn't want to see me. I have a hundred theories for the latter, all of which make the thought of confessing my feelings seem like the worst idea, ever.

When the herald blows his bugle and announces the start of the fencing match, Pippa and I find a spot on the sidelines across from the royal party, tucked behind a row of sparkly princesses. The king and queen praise the combatants in the previous event and offer blessings on their country folk. Sixteen fencers soon take the field and line up with their backs to us. They wear a motley assortment of modern fencing attire and medieval costume pieces. Fortunately no one's wearing a fencing helmet so I pick out Theo right away. He's fifth from the left, with his stance confident and his shaggy black waves fluttering in the breeze. I beam with pride. I can't help it. Even if Theo will never be my boyfriend, he's still my friend and I love seeing him in his element. He's shorter and less beefy than many of his foes, but I bet he'll kick some serious ass today.

"Is this choreographed, too?" Pippa asks.

"Not according to Theo." I peer around a shifting princess. "It's a real competition."

"Then shouldn't they be in those padded suits? And those weird space helmets?"

"Apparently the rules are less stringent here. But Theo swears everyone's careful. They're all here to have a good time and enjoy the atmosphere. Not to poke out someone's eye."

The fencers pair off. The first round is fast. Theo bests his opponent within a few minutes, landing a perfect lunge at the girl's chest. Sixteen shifts to eight. Eight soon shifts to four. Then the matches get serious. The less experienced fencers have been defeated. Those remaining are swift and watchful. They wait for the perfect moment before they strike. They dodge and parry with incredible reflexes. They circle each other like wary cats, knees bent, leaping forward and back, spinning away and returning to gain another point. I don't know the scorekeeping rules, but I keep a close eye on a rack to the left of the stage, where a peasant girl flips wooden plaques to display each new point.

By the time Theo wins his semifinal round against a stocky guy dressed entirely in black, I'm white-knuckling my grip on Pippa's wrist.

"That was close," she says as she pries my fingers free.

"Too close. He has to win this. He wants it so badly and he's worked so hard."

The king steps up to the front of the stage and praises all of the entrants while Theo and his final opponent rest between rounds. Theo will fence a tall Asian girl with high cheekbones and a thick mane of umber hair. She swishes her blade in the far corner of the field, looking brave and determined, as if she belongs on the cover of a YA fantasy novel. Over near the stage, Theo . . .

I grab Pippa's wrist again, my eyes locked on Theo. He's talking with the girls I met earlier in the summer. They're giggling and eyelash batting. The one who was hoping his broken heart would be healed by now tucks a flower behind his ear. He smiles and kisses her hand. Nearby observers let out a collective *aww.*

"He's working the crowd," Pippa murmurs beside me. "Don't read into it."

"Was I—?" I catch Pippa's look. "Okay. I totally was. I didn't know this about myself until recently, but apparently I have a few issues with jealousy."

Pippa talks me down until the final match starts. It's intense and it seems to go on forever. Both fencers are really good. Forward and back they go. Strike, parry, dodge, repeat. At least fifteen minutes in, they're both breathing hard, covered in mud, edging away to wipe a brow or tighten a grip on their blade. The girl corners Theo, but he rolls away, gaining a point with the tip of his blade tapping her back. He drives her toward the opposite side of the field, but he misjudges the arc of her blade as it meets his shoulder. The crowd is silent for long moments, as if I'm not the only one holding my breath. They also cheer and gasp with each clear hit. The points are even. It's anyone's match.

The girl strikes hard. Right, left, right, driving Theo backwards. He dances aside and takes the offensive. Now she backs up, but with a swift flick of her wrist, she catches his blade with her own, wresting it out of his grip. It flies sideways, leaving Theo defenseless. The opponents pause, panting at each other as the girl's eyes fill with triumph. With a showy flourish, she lunges, her blade perfectly poised to meet his chest. He rolls away, grabs his blade, and thrusts it toward her, landing the tip against her waist. I don't even realize what's happened until the crowd goes wild.

I turn a frantic look on Pippa. "Did he win?"

"Looks like it."

"Thank god!" I release a breath I feel like I've been holding on to for an hour now. By the time I check the field again, Theo's shaking hands with his opponent as two little kids toss handfuls of flower petals onto the field. Theo's opponent steps aside as Theo kneels before the stage and the king stands. He declares Theo champion and invites him to choose a lady who will honor him with a favor. My ears perk up. I'm finally going to find out what this favor thing's all about.

Theo rises and approaches a cluster of girls near the stage. They vie for his attention with coy looks and fluttery waves. He passes on, scanning faces until he stops in front of the girl who tucked the flower behind her ear. The flower's long gone, but the girl holds out another. Theo reaches forward.

"Noooooo!" I holler before I can think better of it.

Faces all around the field turn toward me.

"Harper?" Pippa sets a hand on my shoulder, cringing with embarrassment. "This might not be the best time and place to—"

I march onto the field before she can finish. Now that I've halted the proceedings and drawn everyone's attention my way, I have to do *something*. I don't know what that something is yet, but by the time I reach Theo, hopefully I will have figured it out. If not, I'll pretend to faint and sort out the repercussions later.

The king shoots me a fierce look that makes me suspect the stocks are in my future. Or the dungeon, if they have one here. He claps his hands twice in sharp succession. A pair of burly knights steps onto the field, marching my way. Theo spots me and waves them back. He jogs over, meeting me in the middle of the field. He's a muddy mess up close. I can barely read his expression.

"What are you doing here?" he asks.

I need to tell you I love you, I think but I can't make myself say the words.

"It's your big day," I say instead. "I didn't want to miss it."

Theo smiles a little, maybe. It's hard to tell with all the mud. He might be confused, pleased, or thoroughly and understandably annoyed. While he blinks at me through mud-encrusted lashes and I battle my tenacious cowardice, the crowd around us grows restless, murmuring among themselves or calling out to finish the ceremony.

"I'm kind of in the middle of something." Theo points over his shoulder toward the royal party. Or toward the girls. The one with the flowers shoots me a look of pure hatred behind Theo's back. "I'll catch up with you later, okay?"

"Okay. Sorry to interrupt. I just . . . sorry." I bite my lip as he backs up. I try to walk away or at least revisit that faux-fainting idea, but my body won't budge. I stand there, panicked and paralyzed, flashing through a hundred other retreats: mine, Theo's, both of ours. They only created distance between us, distance I hate and never want to feel again. "Wait! No. It's not okay."

He stops, midstep. The crowd noise dims as I plant myself in front of him. I take a deep breath and force my shoulders to relax as I anchor my twitchy hands to my sides.

"I didn't come here to watch. I came to say something, and I need to say it, even if I have to say it in front of an entire kingdom." I glance around at the curious faces, collecting nods from the king and queen before I turn back to Theo. "You once told me you wanted to be the kind of guy who didn't need to know if his feelings were returned before he acted on those feelings. You wanted to love boldly and bravely or not at all. I told you to protect yourself, to withhold, to doubt, to question, to fear, but I was wrong about that. I was wrong about everything. While I was teaching you how not to fall in love, you were teaching me the opposite." I attempt a smile. It feels forced so I let it fade. "I don't care if you're not interested, or if you wear someone else's favor today, or if you're dating the girl in the bikini, or if you never want to kiss me again." I grimace as I shift my stance. "Actually, I care about all of that, but none of it changes how I feel. Since I've never told you how I feel, I figure it's about goddamned time." I suck in a breath as I meet his eyes, glinting beneath muddied lashes. "I love you. I'm in love with you, not like a friend, but, well, the other way."

He gapes at me, unmoving. The crowd barely makes a peep. I wrap a hand around my *word nerd* charm, suddenly aware of how big our audience is. My shoes squelch in the mud. I can't stand still. My anxiety mounts. A weird quiet has fallen over the field. It makes me even more anxious, so I fill it.

"You don't need to do or say anything," I tell Theo, wishing to god he'd do or say something. "I just needed to be clear for once. So, um, okay, I'll let you get back to—"

He sweeps an arm around me and draws me against him. His lips meet mine, and the crowd bursts into cheers. For a moment I don't fully register what's happening. Then the noise blurs as I melt against Theo's body and kiss him back, flooded with a rush of pure euphoria. Theo's lips taste like dirt, but his breath is warm, bringing with it a familiar hint of chocolate and caramel. I loop my arms around his shoulders. He holds me close. We kiss, and kiss, and kiss, until I'm so on fire with wanting him, I almost forget where we are and why we're standing in a muddy field, surrounded by people in costume.

Theo pulls away first, looking as breathless and awestruck as I feel. For a few seconds we simply stare at each other, locked in an embrace.

"I tried to think of you as only a friend," I say once I can form words.

"I know. Me too."

"I couldn't do it."

"Yeah. Me neither." Theo grins, drawing out his dimple.

I touch his face, his hair, his neck, stunned that we've reached this new, uncertain, terrifying, but glorious place together.

"I want to be that person whose eye you catch across a crowded room," I tell him. "The hand you reach for. The person who's as excited to see you as you are to see her. Every day. The one you fight for, knowing she'll fight for you, too."

"Even though I have a windmill, a sword, and an accordion?"

"Especially because you have those things."

He laughs and gives me a bonus kiss, sweet, quick, and wonderful.

"Good," he says. "I want to be that person for you, too."

We do that thing where we just stare at each other again. It's weird, but I love it.

"Wow." I set a hand to my tingling lips. "Are we finally doing this? For real?"

"Looks like it." He makes a scan of the crowd as they hoot, holler, and whistle. "Which means I'm going to need a favor."

"Like, more sewing repairs?"

"No. Like, something of yours I can wear. A scarf or ribbon or handkerchief."

I stifle a laugh. "*That's* what a favor is?"

He shrugs and backs up to assess me. We swiftly conclude that the only garment I can part with and still retain any sense of modesty is a sock. So, with much fanfare from the bugle, and much cheering from the crowd, Theo kneels at my feet. He removes a soggy shoe and sock, letting me tie the sock around his wrist. It's the most ridiculous thing I've ever done in my entire life, but I couldn't be happier.

I wait by the stage as the queen puts a garland around Theo's shoulders and the kids throw more rose petals. Goblets are raised. Proclamations are made. I search the crowd for Pippa, worried I've abandoned her. My worries prove unfounded. She's chatting with the satyr and doesn't appear to be in a hurry to regain my company. I catch her eye long enough for her to sneak me an enthusiastic thumbs-up. I reply with a lift of my brows and a nod toward the satyr. She slyly fans her face and turns her contagious smile on the satyr. He's a lucky guy. That smile is magical. As her secret lover in this realm, I feel well qualified in saying that.

When all the dubbing, bowing, praising, and *buzzah*ing ends, Theo wraps an arm around my shoulders, I wrap an arm around his waist, and we head toward his tent.

"Strong choice with the timing," he teases.

"I stopped by your tent earlier, but—"

He slaps a palm against his forehead. "The harpist from the kingdom in purple?"

I let out a breathy laugh as a lingering knot in my gut finally loosens.

"Harper. Kingdom in peril," I say. "Yeah. That was me."

He stops and faces me. "I'm so sorry. I had no idea." He cups the side of my face with a warm hand. His thumb shifts against my cheekbone, the thumb that's always moving, always caressing and exploring, though I never fully realized it until now.

"You might want to reconsider your staffing choices," I suggest.

"No way. But I'll introduce you so the girls know you get a free pass." He kisses me again, drawing me into his arms where I'd willingly stay forever. This time he pulls back after only a moment, brushing what I assume is mud off my chin. "Three things. First, I really want to keep kissing you, but I should clean up. Second, I love you, too, like, crazy a lot. Third, who's the girl in the bikini?"

"Never mind." I pull him closer. "Go back to that second point."

My favorite twinkle tints his eyes. "I love you, harpist in purple."

I smile so hard I think my face could break. "I love you, word nerd idol."

Theo nuzzles my nose with his. "You aced it, didn't you?"

"I won't know for sure until mid-September, but I did a lot better than last time, thanks to you."

"Then I suggest we go ahead and celebrate."

THIRTY-ONE

THEO AND I LIE FACING EACH OTHER IN HIS TENT
as the last rays of evening light seep through the canvas. Thankfully, his idea of celebrating was the same as mine. He's also
impressively expedient at washing off mud in a river. He's been
humming one of his favorite old songs for the last few minutes,
something about dreaming an impossible dream. The habit is so
Theo: a constant transmission of emotion, accompanied with an
enviable absence of self-consciousness. I circle his dimple with an
outstretched finger. His dimple's been especially persistent since
we climbed into the tent together. While I smile at that thought,
Theo combs a hand through my hair. The waves fall over my
shoulders, having been released from their braid while I was far
too distracted to care.

"Do you still like it?" I ask.

Theo's forehead wrinkles. "What, your hair?"

I shake my head. His eyes shift between mine until they register my meaning.

"Um, yeah." He presses his naked body against mine. "I still
like it."

"Me too." I snuggle into him, wiping off a bit of dirt he missed on his collarbone. "I'm sorry it took me so long to realize, well, everything."

"Whatever. It was only seventeen and a half years of pure torture."

I poke him in the side. He retaliates by targeting the ticklish spot at the base of my ribs. I writhe against his touch, laughing, until he rolls on top of me, pinning me in place. I push back against his hold but not very hard. I'm perfectly happy where I am, as I am. Above me, Theo's eyes light up with mischief and joy. God, I've missed that look, and it's even more striking than usual when it's the only thing Theo's wearing.

"Think we're still going to fight all the time?" I ask.

"Totally, but making up will be way more fun now." He leans down and places a row of deliciously slow kisses on my neck.

My toes curl and my breath hitches. "I'm really sorry about the dating lessons."

"Spoiler alert. I wasn't really in it for the lessons. I just wanted to spend time with you. Though I basically dared you to fall in love with some other guy. Not a super-genius move on my part." He trails a hand from my cheek to my neck to my breast to my belly, drawing little spirals on my skin. He watches me respond with an open fascination that slows his movement and makes me shiver with anticipation. "Our other deal was better. We can keep doing vocab if you like. I kinda owe you after bolting last month."

"I think I have enough words in my brain now."

"Oh, yeah? Show off what you've learned."

I think for a moment, not because I can't come up with any vocabulary words, but because I'm way too distracted. Every touch of Theo's lips or fingertips awakens another inch of skin, making my muscles tense and release in the best possible way. I don't know how he learned to be so seductive with his perfectly planted kisses and electric caresses, but I suspect he's just being himself, sensitive and hyper-alert to those around him.

"Obfuscate," I eventually manage. "To render unclear. What you're doing right now obfuscates the central purpose of this conversation."

"So hot." His spirals inch past my belly button. "Tell me more."

"Anfractuous. Winding or circuitous." I arch into his touch. "Your anfractuous caresses are rendering this conversation impossible."

"Not impossible. One more."

"I can't." I push against him, encouraging his hand to travel lower still.

He leans closer. "Did we cover cataglottism?"

"I don't think so."

"Then let me demonstrate." He kisses me hard, pressing his tongue against mine until I gather that cataglottism has something to do with kissing or tongues. What that something is, I don't really care. Judging by Theo's little moans of pleasure, he doesn't care, either. I lace my hands through his hair and hold his face close to mine. He supports his weight on his forearms as his legs slip between my thighs and I no longer have to guess if he's mirroring my thoughts. I let myself want, knowing I'm wanted, too. It's a powerful feeling and one I'm grateful I don't have to hide, even from myself. Theo tugs on my lower lip as he pulls away, his breath quick and his eyes glassy. "How in the hell did I tell you I only wanted to be friends? And how did we both believe it?"

"I don't know."

"You're never going to believe another word I say."

"Keep kissing me and I'll believe pretty much anything."

"I like the sound of that."

We stop talking as other forms of communication take over. For several hours, we explore each other's bodies with a beautiful blend of sweet affection, raw desire, and simple curiosity. During a rare moment of quiet and stillness, I send a silent thank-you to the guy at the leg-of-mutton stand who also stocks the not-so-medieval condoms. I send another thank-you to Pippa, who agreed to explain the situation to my mom so I could stick around for the weekend. My third thank-you goes to my mom, for teaching me to be intentional about sex instead of afraid of it or careless about it. My fourth thank-you goes to Felix and Liam, both of whom taught me what I wanted from a relationship so I could enter this one with the full certainty that it's perfect for me. My final and most heartfelt thanks go out to the universe for letting me fall in love with this amazing boy, and for somehow making him love me back.

Somewhere in the middle of the night, when Theo and I have fully exhausted ourselves, we lie beside each other again, eyelids heavy, swallowing yawns. Somewhere outside the tent, voices drift our way. A balladeer with a lute. A bit of chatter around a campfire. Otherwise the world is quiet, at least until my stomach lets out a low rumble.

Theo chuckles beside me. "Guess it's well past dinnertime."

"Don't suppose you brought snacks?" I scoot up and glance around in the dim glow from the flashlight that's nestled in the corner. My eyes land on Theo's backpack near our feet. "Trail mix? Granola bars? Medieval gummies?"

"Not exactly. But something you might like is in there."

I rummage through his bag while he watches me, propped up on his elbows. Beneath a fantasy paperback and a rumpled T-shirt, I find a half-empty bag of Snickers bars. I reach in and hold up a fistful of empty wrappers, displaying it like evidence.

"I knew it," I say. "You love them, too."

Theo flinches as if genuinely confused. "Do I?"

"Your breath always smells like chocolate and caramel, and while I love that you ceded your Snickers bars to me every Halloween, now that new information about our friendship has come to light, I suspect that action was nobler than you claimed at the time. Admit it. You're as addicted as I am."

"I'm not, actually." He shrugs, all cute and bashful. "I buy them because they make me think of you."

I open my mouth to tell him that's precisely the sort of

information he should keep to himself if he doesn't want to scare off a girl, but since I don't feel the least bit scared and I have no intention of going anywhere at all, I say something else instead, forgoing all the fancy words for the ones that are most important.

"I love you, Theo Turner. Like, crazy a lot."

THIRTY-TWO

THE LAST WEEK OF SUMMER PASSES IN A BLUR OF passionate kisses, long walks, lazy hours spent reading with Theo in the windmill, and *so* much laughter. I eat at Theo's house most nights, greatly improving my diet. Sometimes my mom even quits work early so we can all sit around Shay and Olivia's picnic table like one big, happy family. Theo teaches me basic fingering on his accordion, but I'm not that invested in the lessons. I'd rather listen to him play, though I can't believe I'm saying that. We also watch rom-coms at my place, where I force myself to restrain my sarcasm, even when Theo cries at the cheesy bits. He even joins me at Denise's end-of-summer party, where I don't hesitate to introduce him as my boyfriend.

In the middle of September, shortly after starting our senior year, Theo and I attend the Connor-Armstrong wedding along with half the population of New Hope. Despite my many rants about weddings, the ceremony is beautiful, totally lacking in the obsessive details that so often overshadow the event's core meaning. The old boathouse is decked out with garlands of local wildflowers that run a full gamut of colors. Attendees cram onto row after row of borrowed benches and chairs. One of Ms. Connor's music students plays a violin near the sunlit windows that open out to the river. Ms. Connor and Mr. Armstrong walk up the aisle together, eschewing the creepy handoff from father to husband I once complained about to Felix. A local pastor officiates, welcoming everyone without pomp or formality. The pair exchanges vows they wrote themselves, ones that omit the word *obey* and the mention of death doing them apart. Instead, they describe what they love and admire about each other, making promises to be kind and patient.

Best of all, there's no ostentatious row of matching bridesmaids and groomsmen, all carefully attired to look less attractive than the bride and groom while tacitly proving the couple's popularity. Instead, their kids act as best man and maid of honor, so the foursome stands together forging both a partnership and a new family.

My mom sits to my left, staring out the windows with a wistful look in her eyes. Maybe she's thinking about What's-His-Name. More likely she's picturing a perfect princess seam on her next gown. I used to think it was weird that she didn't date. I worried that some basic desire for human connection was missing, passed down genetically and making me messed up about my own relationships. Now I know her choice was never that complicated. We can't force things to make us happy. We want what we want. We don't want what we don't want. From there, all we can do is reach.

Olivia and Shay sit to Theo's right. Olivia tears up during

the vows. Shay hands her a tissue, responding with an efficiency that suggests this is a common pattern for the two of them. Theo manages to hold himself together, barely. I find his little sniffles sweet now. I'm also dying to make a joke. I'm deeply, madly in love with him, so everything he does these days is adorable, but we haven't become different people overnight. We still tease each other mercilessly. We also attend to any hurt feelings swiftly, clearly, and with a whole new range of ways to make each other feel good.

Felix and his family sit across the aisle and up a few rows. Mrs. Royce works at Mr. Armstrong's company, as do a lot of other people in this room. Felix glances over his shoulder and offers me a subtle, conflicted smile. I respond in kind. We're not getting fish and chips together yet, but he walked me to the coffee shop last Saturday when I bumped into him after his workout. By the time we reached my destination, our pauses were less stilted and we weren't completely avoiding each other's eyes. I joked about getting running tips so I could alter my sedentary lifestyle. He agreed to help, as long as I paid him back in tap-dance lessons. I don't know if either of us will follow through with the idea or if we were being polite, but we're in a few classes together this year, so who knows? The me that resented my ex for an entire year is skeptical we'll ease into a comfortable friendship. The me that finally forgave that ex feels otherwise.

Pippa didn't make it to the wedding. She's out at the LARP-ing location with a ten-step plan to seduce the satyr. Considering the sexy fairy outfit I helped her put together this week, I bet she only needs two or three of those steps. Actually, she's Dame Pippa Pennington of the Green Locks. She's fabulous. She doesn't need any steps at all.

I tip my head onto Theo's shoulder. He squeezes my hand where our laced fingers rest on his thigh. Together we watch Mr. and Mrs. Armstrong retrace their steps up the aisle and pause in the boathouse doorway, inviting us all to join the party. The room empties onto the lawn where a massive buffet awaits, along with games, music, and dancing. There are no annoying seating charts, agonizingly selected multi-course menus, or arguments erupting over centerpieces. There's only food and fun. And of course, love.

Theo and I grab some chocolate cake and join our moms under a big shady tree.

"Anything you want to criticize?" my mom asks through a teasing smirk.

"Actually, I've been thinking." I lower my fork and scan the crowd, stopping when I spot the newlyweds, laughing with a group of friends, bursting with joy. "What if, after I get my degree, I don't head off to run some other business? Instead, I come back and help you run yours? I know the industry. I'll have the right skills. We can get that branding plan going, expand your visibility, target the right clientele. We make a good team, the two of us. Good teams are worth holding on to."

My question is followed by an awkward pause. I worry everyone's about to laugh. I've spent so long pointing out everything I hate about the wedding industry, they all probably think I'm kidding. But after a moment, my mom sets a hand to her heart. As her eyes go glassy, Shay whips a tissue from her purse and holds it out. My mom takes it and dabs at the corners of her eyes.

"I'd like nothing better," she says.

We fall into an awkward hug, plates in hand. Then I hug Shay and Olivia and Theo, who looks like he's fighting back a few tears of his own because, of course. We all chat about the possibilities while we finish our cake or sip champagne, but as the conversation shifts to other topics, I lose focus on what everyone's saying. Instead I gaze longingly into Theo's dark brown eyes, tracking reflections from the dappled sunlight. He looks soooo good today. He's wearing a gray linen suit with a bright yellow tulip in his buttonhole. His dress shirt has been carefully pressed, his silk tie perfectly knotted, but his disco llama socks peek out beneath his trouser cuffs, letting me know he's still Theo. I'm wearing a green cotton sundress I made to match my avatar in the treehouse. Mine's sleeveless and it only goes to my knees, but the neckline, bodice shape, and decorations all match. After much debate, I blew out my hair. I'd go to a lot of lengths to surprise or impress Theo, or to elicit his upturned smile, but I have my limits.

As we glance around at the well-dressed people standing in clusters with their trimmed-out sun hats, little plates of food, and flutes of champagne, we decide it's not really either of our scene, so I take Theo's offered elbow and we wander off, meandering our way to the bridge that crosses the Delaware River. We stop in the middle where Theo once swore off love, a promise I'm elated he didn't keep. Cars speed by behind us while a few scattered pedestrians wander past or snap selfies. It's a beautiful afternoon, tempered by a light breeze that tells us fall is on its way. Senior year will bring new challenges, as will the years beyond. Hopefully I'll be heading to Bryn Mawr. I don't know where Theo will be, but I won't let my anxiety about that ruin my joy that he's here with me now. Not all relationships last. That doesn't mean they aren't worth having.

Theo rests his forearms on the railing and gazes off at the sparkling water.

"So?" he asks. "What're you going to teach me next?"

I copy his pose. "How to do your taxes?"

He laughs as he rotates to face me. "You have officially out-weirded me."

"I take that as a compliment." I brush his hair off his forehead, but to little avail. The medieval knight still stands before me, even though he's wearing a suit. "Actually, Sir Theodoro, I'm not going to teach you anything at all. I'm simply going to love you."

A smile tugs at his lips. He slips an arm around my waist, and we turn to face the river together. I tip my head onto his shoulder. He rests his cheek against my forehead.

"Good plan," he says. "I think I'll do the same."

Acknowledgments

One day I hope books will get printed with a list of collaborators, as happens with my work in the theatre. So many people are involved in seeing a project like this toward completion, and I can only skim the surface with the names I know. Let me start by thanking the three editors whose hearts and minds are so deeply embedded in these pages. Emilia Rhodes, who nurtured the seed of an idea toward a first draft. Nicole Sclama, who knew precisely what that draft needed in order to focus the story and the scenes, sending me the kinds of notes that inspired and energized, turning the editorial process into a consistently joyful task. Amy Cloud, who took the final draft and steered it through the detailed work of copyediting, production, and marketing. I'm deeply fortunate to have all of your input, and the work is stronger for your voices and insights. Thanks also to the copyeditors who added more commas than I can count and caught a multitude of blunders before this went to print. And thanks to the marketing and publicity teams who will help get this book into the hands of readers.

Thanks to my agent, Laura Bradford, who guided me from one idea, to twelve, to five, and back to one again.

Thanks to my first readers, Rona Bird and Jodi Jacyk, whose input and support have been invaluable.

Thanks to Kaitlin Yang for her book design and to artist Naya Ismael for bringing Harper to life.

Thanks to all the brides who inspired the scenes in these pages. I've made a lot of wedding dresses and I share some of Harper's cynicism about the industry, but I've also witnessed some truly beautiful unions that celebrate love and community. So thank you in particular to Peter and RJ, and to Heather and Dirk, whose respective weddings filled my heart with such joy, I carry that sense of celebration with me many years later. Hints of your weddings are in this story. As the four of you already know, color schemes and seating arrangements have their place, but so do big ol' barns, potluck meals, scavenged theatre equipment, and the willingness to let your friends wear whatever the heck they want to your wedding.

Thanks to the LARPing communities who let me frolic around in homemade costumes long after it was socially acceptable to do so. Maybe I'll dig up some photos for social media, but probably not.

Thanks to my dogs, Ffiona and Stella, who've taught me more about how to fall in love than anyone I know.

Thanks most of all to Miguel de Cervantes, whose novel *Don Quixote* affected me so deeply in high school, I wrote my college entrance essays on how if I could be anyone, I'd be Cervantes' off-kilter knight, tilting at windmills, smiling through adversity, and seeing beauty in the most unlikely places. I hope this novel honors your hero, because he's my hero, too.

Fall in love
with a great book!